Here's what (Jennifer

"It grabbed me by the han(until the very last page. Hi̟ ......ended."
—*Melody's Bookshelf*, on "Unbreakable Bond"

"Weaves mystery with laughs (and a few tears). This delightful tale is a definite read! I would read it again as well as the rest of the series."
—*Should You Read This Book?* Review Blog, on "Secret Bond"

"The characters are always so well written. They feel like they could pop off the page. I can't wait for the next book in the series!"
—*Wakela's World*, on "Secret Bond"

"I approached this book with the idea that it would be the light reading many of us look forward to enjoying in the summer. It turned out to be more than that and I couldn't put it down."
—*The Birch Bark*, on "Secret Bond"

BOOKS BY JENNIFER FISCHETTO

Gianna Mancini Mysteries:
Lipstick, Lies & Dead Guys
Christmas, Spies & Dead Guys (holiday short story)
Miniskirts, Mai Tais & Dead Guys

Jamie Bond Mysteries:
Unbreakable Bond
Secret Bond
Lethal Bond
Dangerous Bond

Danger Cove Bakery Mysteries
Death by Scones

Disturbia Diaries:
I Spy Dead People

MINISKIRTS, MAI TAIS & DEAD GUYS

a Gianna Mancini mystery

Jennifer Fischetto

Miniskirts, Mai Tais & Dead Guys
Copyright © 2015 by Jennifer Fischetto
Cover design by Designer

Published by Gemma Halliday Publishing
All Rights Reserved. Except for use in any review, the reproduction or utilization of this work in whole or in part in any form by any electronic, mechanical, or other means, now known or hereafter invented, including xerography, photocopying and recording, or in any information storage and retrieval system is forbidden without the written permission of the publisher, Gemma Halliday.

This is a work of fiction. Names, characters, places, and incidents are either the product of the author's imagination or are used fictitiously, and any resemblance to actual persons, living or dead, business establishments, or events or locales is entirely coincidental.

MINISKIRTS, MAI TAIS & DEAD GUYS

CHAPTER ONE

The tip of my right index finger tingles, as if it's my very own voodoo doll, and pins are being jabbed into it. I raise my arm higher and turn in all directions, playing a weird game of hot and cold. My finger is a beacon to Freezer Dude, the creepy, old ghost that crossed from the other side back into the world of the living a week ago. Truth be told, I feel like ET.

"Phone home," I say in a creaky voice as a woman walks past me on the sidewalk. She stares at me with a frown and picks up her pace like I'm about to eat her young. Not that she has any kids with her.

There you go again, Gianna. Scaring the locals.

The tingling is sharpest when I turn east, so I jump back into my car, which I haphazardly parked in the grocery store's lot, and drive in that direction. Very slowly. So I don't miss him or run into an unsuspecting *Return Shopping Carts Here* sign. Ghosts are notorious for turning invisible in a blink, and shopping cart holders have a nasty habit of appearing out of nowhere, despite their ginormous-y. Just ask Pop's old car when I ran into one many years ago. Okay, so maybe I have the minor flaw of not always looking where I'm going. I'm working on it.

The first time I met Freezer Dude, aka the ghost with shocking white hair and electric blue eyes, I was eight. Well, "met" isn't accurate. It was more like he reached out to me after I died. It was just a small death. Only one minute and thirty-two seconds, according to the paramedics who lifted my unconscious and partly frozen body off the floor of the walk-in freezer of my family's deli.

It was after this freezer-slash-death incident that I could see and talk to ghosts. Normally it wasn't a big deal. They'd die and pass over through the freezer. I still haven't figured out why the freezer is the portal to the other side, but it is. Sometimes the ghosts would linger because they're not ready to leave, and sometimes it's because they need help. So far, one ghost has needed my help in solving her murder before she crossed. Considering my sister, Izzie, was being framed for the ghost's death, it was the least I could do. Then the ghost passed over, and I thought all was good.

Until Freezer Dude, the same white-haired, blue-eyed, grabby ghost from when I was eight, crossed through the freezer into the deli. That disturbing sight left me with nightmares for the past seven days and told me two things. One, what the heck else could possibly come back from the beyond? And two, I wonder if he knows where my pink yo-yo is. I swear I lost it in the freezer fifteen years ago.

I take a left on Jefferson Street and hope my finger doesn't explode when we're face-to-face. The tingling's turned into a throbbing, and it pulsates faster the farther I drive. The first time I felt the tingling was a little over a week ago when I went into the freezer to get a tray of eggplant parm for Ma. After I found the tinfoil-covered pan, I saw a swirling tunnel at the back wall. I reached my finger out, because I'm obviously very curious and have little sense for my safety, and the tip of my finger turned icy cold, almost numb. A bony hand poked through and tried to reach for me, but I pulled back quickly. That was when I saw Freezer Dude's face. I immediately recognized him from the near-death experience. He didn't enter the world of the living then. That took a bit more time.

The numbing pain went away later that day and then reappeared yesterday when I was slicing turkey for an order. I work at the deli part-time. I thought I nicked my finger on the slicer, but there was no blood. Thank goodness, 'cause customers get miffed when you bleed on their gobble-gobble.

I didn't see Freezer Dude in the deli yesterday, but I didn't search either. I had no clue what the tingling meant. Until today. I drove to the grocery store to get dinner for my brother, Enzo, and me. I have twenty-five bucks in my wallet, and I promised dinner if he'd hang with me. It's a shame when you have to bribe your full-time employed, cop sibling to spend time with you, but I've been bored. Okay, maybe even lonely. And I'm tired of sitting in my apartment alone channel surfing.

My sister, Izzie, is preggo, and she's in her first trimester, which means there's a lot of crankiness and vomiting going on. My is-he-or-isn't-he boyfriend, Julian, is...well, I'm not sure, but we're taking things slow, so we don't see each other every night. And my parents are my parents. I love them to death, but Pop listens to the TV at decibels that make my ears wanna bleed, and Ma has been on this kick of telling me I should get married and give her more grandkids soon. 'Cause my niece, Alice—the one Izzie's already given her—and the one Izzie will be giving her next spring aren't enough. So that leaves me in my apartment above the family deli with the remote in one hand and a bacon, tomato, avocado grilled cheese in the other. I make mean sandwiches.

Anyway, I pulled into the parking lot, and my finger started doing its weirdness. I looked up and saw Freezer Dude. He was standing smack-dab in the middle of the automatic doors, and some beefy guy in a Yankees sweatshirt walked through him. Beefy Guy shivered, 'cause walking around a ghost is cold as heck. Walking through one is probably like pouring a bucket of ice water over your head.

Beefy Guy went to his car, and Freezer Dude walked into the store, turned around, came back out, and vanished. He didn't see me, but I definitely saw him. He's hard to miss. Then the throbbing eased up, and that's when I realized it's a beacon for his whereabouts. Instead of a shoulder or joint that aches when it's going to rain, my finger starts jonesing for one particular ghost. Lucky me. Aside from the whole "how the heck does someone cross *back* over," I have a feeling this dude is going to be a lot of trouble.

I drive to the corner, and the throbbing lessens. I brake at the stop sign and look all ways, just in case he shows himself. On a hunch, I put my silver Kia Rio into reverse and head back. Sure enough, my finger feels like it has a pulse of its own. He's somewhere on this block. I pull up in front of a small white house with a blue front door and put the car in neutral. I take a quick glance at the gas gauge. I have half a tank. I can wait for a bit, but I don't want to waste too much. Working at the deli hasn't allowed me to change my name to Rockefeller yet.

It takes longer than I think, so I end up shutting off the engine and waiting. My finger still feels like it's about to explode, so I must be in the right spot. Either Freezer Dude is around here, or I need emergency care. Stat!

Just then, I see the old buzzard. A house up, he floats out of another white house, but this one has a red front door. He hangs on the porch for a second. Then the door opens, and a woman steps out. She's wearing a camel-colored, long, wool coat, brown boots, and a matching pair of gloves. It's the beginning of November, chilly, and it rains a lot, but it's not that cold. Of course, I think this while I shove my frigid hands into my fleece jacket.

The woman steps onto her sidewalk, and Freezer Dude follows really close. Does he know her? Does he want to know her? Do ghosts get horny?

She walks down the street, in the opposite direction of me, and he continues acting like a puppy dog. In another minute, she'll either cross the intersection or turn the corner, and I'll lose them. But if I start my car and drive really slow behind them, they'll notice. I'm more concerned about her calling the cops on the weirdo with dark, gorgeous, curly hair in the silver Kia than I am about him. What's he going to do? Boo me to death?

The only choice is to hoof it. I quietly open my door, step out, and push it shut softly. There's enough traffic on the surrounding streets so they probably don't hear me distinctively, but I still feel like my movements are deafening. I run onto the sidewalk and stay three houses behind them.

When they get to the corner, she stops and looks like she's going to turn around. I pull my cell from my jacket pocket, almost dropping it in my haste, and pretend to be on it. But she doesn't fully turn. She does, however, round the corner.

I take a deep breath and run to the end of the block. I peek around an annoying bush that almost takes out my eye. Daylight faded several hours ago, so I have to squint against the darkness and streetlamps to make them out.

The woman stops in front of a brick house and puts her hand on the owner's wrought iron gate. Freezer Dude is so close to her face he's either whispering in her ear or licking her cheek. Both options are incredibly gross, and my stomach churns.

Just then my phone buzzes, and a loud, mechanical voice sings, "It's your brother calling. Yes, he is annoying, but he is calling, so pick up the phone. It's your brother call..."

Shoot! I poke the face of my phone until the ringtone shuts up. I keep the volume way up because it's hard to hear when it's in my pocket. But now I wonder who else may have heard. I bite my lower lip and glance up.

The woman is already at the front door of the house. She knocks and doesn't seem to have noticed me. Freezer Dude, on the other hand, is staring straight at me.

Crap!

Before I get a chance to turn and flee, he flies at me. Actually lifts off the ground and soars, minus the arm flapping. I expect him to stop just before me and say something annoying, but he doesn't stop at all. And before I realize what's happening, he's inside me.

Immediately a sensation of deep, bone-chilling cold overtakes me. Yep, just like a bucket of ice water. It intensifies rapidly, and I wonder if it looks like I'm having a seizure from all the trembling. Then my vision clouds, and my hearing tunnels. Pressure fills my body, presses on my chest. Everything around me slips away, and it feels like I'm floating. A low growling sounds inside my body, like a couple of dogs getting ready to battle. My gut tells me to fight, but I'm not sure how. For some reason, I think of Ma's favorite song and start singing.

"The sun will come out tomorrow." Normally I'm a bit shy about public singing, but since it feels like I'm being crushed from the inside, I think I can tolerate the possible embarrassment. Suddenly the pressure lifts, and the air gets warmer. Not warm enough to stop shaking, but it's definitely on the rise.

And just as fast as Freezer Dude entered me, he leaps back out.

I stagger, and my breath comes out jagged. What just happened? I glance around to see if there are dogs in the area. I don't see any, and the sound is gone. I look to Freezer Dude. He's floating a couple of feet in front of me. His expression is a mixture of surprise and confusion too. Then something changes in his eye. He cocks a brow as if he just had an epiphany, and a slow, creepy smile takes over his face. He looks like he has a whopper of a secret.

"What?" I shout. I'm still freaked out, and I really hate secrets unless I'm the owner of them.

"You've been such an inspiration, Gianna."

He knows my name? Even though he's been a part of my life in some way for eighteen years, it didn't dawn on me that he knew me. Maybe he asked one of the many people who crossed over. Maybe he heard Ma and Pop call me over the years. It feels pretty stupid to not realize this now that I think about it.

I open my mouth to give a witty retort, but my brain is still in slo-mo, and I come up blank.

He lets out a maniacal chuckle and then vanishes. The echo of his crazy laugh lingers behind like the stench of a backed-up sewer.

* * *

I show up at Enzo's house forty-five minutes later. It took me a while to stop trembling. I couldn't shake the chills, even with my heat on full blast. I kept looking over my shoulder too, waiting for Freezer Dude to show back up and try to possess me again. But luckily he didn't.

Then I went back to the grocery store. But by time I got there, they were closing up, so I grabbed the first thing I saw that I know Enzo likes.

Now here, I park in front of my brother's ranch-style home. He bought it several months ago. He's a twenty-eight-year-old homeowner, who has his life together. Career, house, savings. He's probably already started a retirement fund and all of that responsible stuff. Our parents are super proud of him. I am too. But considering how Izzie and I don't have half of what he does, sometimes I just want to kick him for being such a good person. Show some flaws. Make us not look so immature. The only thing he needs is a wife and some kids. Hey, why isn't Ma on his back for more grandkids? He's next in line. He's the middle child. I'm the youngest and only twenty-six.

I sprint up the walkway, painfully aware of how late I am, and knock on his front door.

When he opens it, I put on a Cheshire cat smile and hold up two bags of Crunchy Cheddar Jalapeño Cheetos.

"That's dinner?" he asks with a yawn. His brown hair is tousled on top, and he looks like he's been asleep. He probably dozed off on the couch. He has on an olive green T-shirt and navy sweats. White socks cover his feet, and he's guarding the door like a Doberman.

"It's all they had. Are you going to let me in?"

He shakes his head and stifles another yawn. "No. I have to be up at the crack of dawn. It's too late to hang, Gi."

I roll my eyes because this means another night of channel surfing. Who knew moving back home would be so boring? I spent three years living in Connecticut with my cousin and Julian—not at the same time. I just moved back to South Shore Beach a few weeks ago, and while it was fun at first, now it's snoozeville. Maybe I need to make some friends who aren't family.

"Another night," Enzo says.

"Seriously? You're actually going to turn your baby sister away?" Yes, I'm aware I woke him, and he has to work in the morning, and my idea of dinner is only impressive to a twelve-year-old boy, but I really don't want to be alone. Especially not after the event with Freezer Dude.

But even if Enzo lets me in, I won't talk about my very own unfriendly Casper. The family knows I can see and talk to ghosts, but this guy is not the average, run-of-the-mill deadie. This dude means business. If I can only figure out what kind of business. Why come back to the land of the living if you're dead? Unless he has unfinished business. Maybe he wants revenge for however he became dead. Or he wants to see someone. Was that woman a part of his family?

These questions lead to so many more, like who did he used to be? How long has he been dead?

"Come by tomorrow," Enzo says, interrupting my thoughts. "Dinner's on me."

That perks me up. I even smile. "It's a deal."

I turn, ready to head back to my car when he says, "Wait."

My heart does a momentary jig, assuming he's changed his mind. But instead of opening his door wider and allowing me in, he reaches forward and snatches one of the bags of Cheetos out of my grasp. "Thanks."

Then he shuts the door as I'm left there holding the bag. Okay, so my puns aren't too great when I've been robbed.

"Fine," I shout. "Be like that. May your intestines hate you in the morning." Then I head back to my car, feeling even more immature than normal.

* * *

Once I'm in my apartment, I toss my jacket onto the corner of the couch, flop beside it, pull off my boots, and grab the remote. It's Wednesday. I can either catch the ending of *Nashville* or that new cop show. Hmm, sassy soap opera set around country music or police hunting down killers. Both sound equally stimulating, but after my experience with Freezer Dude, I pick *Nashville*.

I turn it on in the middle of a commercial for Jared the Galleria of Jewelry with some handsome guy giving some gorgeous woman an open-heart diamond necklace. I reach into my jacket pocket and pull out my phone. I bring up my contacts and scroll to Julian's face. He's squinting because the sun is nearly blinding him. I took that picture over the summer, back when I thought he was perfect for me. Now, I still want to believe that, but I'm just not sure.

My finger hovers over his name. I want to call him to see how he's doing. It's almost 11:00. If he's not working, he may be asleep. I don't want to disturb him. I sigh heavily and place the phone on the coffee table.

The show comes back on and Scarlett, the quiet blonde who gave up a singing career because she couldn't handle the attention and being on tour, is sulking about something. I know the feeling, girl.

Julian's job is the reason we're taking things slow. Not only did he recently learn I communicate with the dead, but I learned that he's a fixer. He works for a lawyer whose clients are bigwigs. Whenever a client is in trouble of some sort, Julian intervenes and makes things right. Sounds noble, but it's not. That murder Izzie was framed for...if Julian hadn't moved the dead body and *fixed* it, Izzie probably wouldn't have been accused. He made things better, but I was the one who saved my sister in the end.

Hence, this is why we're taking things slow. I'm not sure I can be with a person who doesn't firmly stand on the white side of the law.

The show soon ends, and I immediately look for anything to watch that isn't the news. I can't stomach all the negativity. I get to AMC, and the guide says *The Terminator* is coming up. This'll do.

The commercial break is of Hellmann's Mayonnaise, and while I'm now hungry for a BLT, I don't feel like cooking. So I reach for the bag of Crunchy Cheddar Jalapeño Cheetos and pull it open. What can I say? I'm easily influenced.

I may regret this tomorrow, but what the heck. I pop several long, orange-red, crunchy nuggets into my mouth. Being mature is overrated.

CHAPTER TWO

A loud banging seeps itself into the corners of my dream, where I'm on a Ferris wheel, and Freezer Dude is in control of the ride. It's choppy and not smooth, and he's laughing the entire time. I'm not afraid of reaching the top, but I'm terrified of landing at the bottom where he floats an inch above the concrete. Right before I reach his wide, toothy grin, I open my eyes and stare at the coffee table.

My mouth is partly open, and I'm drooling on the couch cushion. Gross. I pull myself up into a sitting position and must look like a zombie rising. My head is groggy, and my stomach is rumbling. I fell asleep on the couch. There's a kink in my neck, and I need a nice long, scalding soak. But I don't have a tub. Unless I want to lay a washcloth over the drain in the shower stall and sit with my knees up to my chin, it ain't happening. I'll settle for scalding coffee though.

I push my cover-like jacket off me. I must've reached for it while sleeping. I swing my feet to the floor, and that banging noise sounds again. It wasn't a part of my dream. Something is clanking, and it's coming from the deli downstairs.

I grab my phone. It's barely 6:30, and the deli doesn't open until seven. What's going on?

I jump up and run down, imagining a really loud burglar, and here I am with only my phone as a weapon. Or *The Terminator* movie has become a reality and machines have taken over. I really should put my vivid imagination to good use and write a book someday.

The back staircase to my apartment leads to the small, gravel-infused parking lot behind the deli. It's for employees only, and beside my car is Pop's, Ma's, and a van with a side panel that says, *You Clog it, We Drain it, Frontier Plumbing*. It's kinda catchy mixed with a lot of eww.

I pull open the back door to the deli and step into the kitchen. The three vehicle owners are huddled around the freezer, like they're discussing a football strategy. I step forward and catch a glimpse of my bed hair in the reflection of the fridge and remember I must have jalapeño breath.

Ma turns and glares at me. Surely she can't smell it from all the way over there. Her arms are crossed over her chest, and she looks like she wants to chew glass and spit it out at someone's jugular.

"What?" I suddenly feel like I'm in the doghouse. I already have sleeping on the couch down pat, so maybe it won't be so bad.

"The freezer's leaking again," she spits out.

Oh, so this isn't about me. Whew! I hate getting on Ma's bad side. It doesn't last too long with her kids. She's a big softie with us, but her old threats of Santa knowing when we're naughty or nice still rattle me.

"It just started last week," Pop says as if the three of us don't know. This is the second time I've seen the plumber who knows how to wear his pants correctly here. And I'm all too aware that the leak started after Freezer Dude crossed over. But I don't want to tell Ma and Pop—partly because I feel like it's my fault and partly because I don't want to creep them out. I could try to put a positive spin on it, but after last night, I'm not sure if even I can lie that well.

"I don't think there's anything else I can do," says the plumber.

Pop gets that look in his eye that says maybe duct tape will work, but Ma starts tapping her foot, and his inspiration vanishes. He knows Ma won't put up with taping it. He did that to their last washing machine, and Ma moaned and grumbled every time she did a load, fearful it would burst and leave her with a basement full of water. I doubt one load would fill the basement like the Titanic, but all of Ma's collectibles are on shelves down there, so she understandably won't take any chances.

"Maybe if we..." Pop starts.

But Ma cuts him off. "No, Lorenzo. No crazy schemes, no duct tape. We'll have to order a new one." She huffs and takes several steps back.

Pop glances at her but doesn't respond.

I love watching how they interact. Sometimes, like now, they know each other's limits and don't push. I know Pop wants to argue. He did the first time they found it leaking. He didn't want to spend money on a plumber, so he tightened some bolts, and it stopped. For a day or two. Then Ma called the plumber. Pop must've known it was more than he could handle, or he didn't want to argue with Ma, so he conceded. But there are times those two bump heads and seem to deliberately push one another's buttons.

The mechanic picks up his box of tools. "Sorry I couldn't help." He gives me a curt nod as he walks out.

"What does this mean?" I ask.

"It means we have to spend money we don't have on a new freezer," Ma says.

My stomach churns, and it's not because of the Crunchy Cheddar Jalapeño Cheetos. I didn't ask Freezer Dude to come through. Far from it. But I still feel partly responsible. If I had the money to give them, or even the credit, I would.

"We have the anonymous money," Pop says.

Ma looks momentarily relieved. "I thought we weren't going to spend that in case the owner wanted it back."

After my sister, Izzie, was arrested for murder last month, Ma and Pop had to put up a significant portion of their savings to the bail bondsman. Since that was Julian's doing, what with moving the body, he made an anonymous donation to the deli to compensate my parents. It was really sweet of him, and he scored major points in my book. But no one other than me knows where the money really came from. I can't tell because his job is confidential. Even I'm not supposed to know what he actually does for a living. Everyone thinks he's a simple private investigator.

Pop bugs out his eyes. "I think this situation warrants us using it. Besides, people don't usually give a gift anonymously and then ask for it back."

"Yeah, he doesn't want it back." I don't realize what I said until they're both staring at me with frowns. Shoot, Gianna, shut up.

I fumble over my words. "I-I just mean, uh, if it was me, I wouldn't expect it back."

Ma nods, accepting my lie. "Fine. We don't have much of a choice. But we need to get everything out of there so nothing defrosts. Gianna, we'll pack your freezer and bring the rest home." She points her finger at me. "Don't eat any of it."

I scoff. "Like I need to be told not to dive into the family profit. Am I a glutton? Don't answer that."

Pop smirks. "We should close up until the new one arrives. I'll put a rush order on it."

Ma rolls her eyes and steps into the freezer.

"I know a guy," Pop says.

Ma emerges with several frozen lasagnas in her arms. She shoves them at me. "As long as it doesn't arrive duct taped, fine."

* * *

After a million trips up and down the stairs, with achy thigh muscles to prove it, I get under the hot spray of the shower and wish I could stay there all day. But I promised my sister I'd go with her to the obstetrician. Her husband, Paulie, has been pulling doubles as a paramedic to make a little extra money for the baby. It's sweet. And I'm pretty sure Izzie is fine with him not being home more often, since their marriage isn't exactly solid.

The murder she was accused of was a woman Paulie had an oral thing with. If Izzie hadn't found out she was pregnant shortly after, I'm not sure if they'd be in counseling trying to salvage their relationship now.

When I honk in front of Izzie's two-story, Colonial-style home, the front door immediately opens. She's not one for being late. She steps out wearing jeans, a red sweater, a denim jacket, and three-inch heels. She has this thing about her height. She's five-four, two inches taller than me, and refuses to ever be under five-five. Even her slippers have a wedge. I don't know why she's so obsessed with it. She can't even put the reason into coherent words.

She sits in my passenger seat and fastens the seat belt around her. Her short, brown hair frames her face. "Morning." It doesn't come out as perky as it used to. Not that Izzie's ever been a perky person, but she usually loves mornings. That is, until she got pregnant. Morning, afternoon, and night sickness has hit her hard. She was the same way when she was pregnant with my niece, Alice, too.

"Morning," I say and emphasize some perk. "How much longer are you going to keep wearing heels? Won't you have to stop when you start showing?"

I assume that having gravity against you twice isn't a good move, but what do I know? I've never been pregnant, and I hate heels. I prefer feeling the solid ground beneath my feet, which is why I have a somewhat unhealthy obsession with chucky-heeled boots. I didn't mind a good platform heel back in the day when they were in style or now a wedge on a sandal. It's not like I can wear boots in the heat anyway, but I can't do the pointy stiletto types. As for my sister, she wasn't always like this. When she was having Alice, she was a senior in high school. Ma and the school didn't allow her to wear heels every day then.

She scoffs. "I will be in heels in the delivery room. Now let's go. I don't want to be late."

I pull into the tiny strip mall parking lot and park close by the Subway. I'm starved, but I won't eat their sandwiches. Not when I make the best ones in the whole wide world. I'm not conceited. I just truly make awesomeness between bread. Everyone says so.

"You're not supposed to park here for the medical building," Izzie says while climbing out of my car.

The beige stone structure is right next door. On a busy weekday morning, who's going to know?

"Then maybe they shouldn't charge for parking. Besides, on the way out I'll stop and get..." I glance at the surrounding stores—a manicure place, CVS, a psychic, and a used bookstore. "A book."

Izzie gives a half smile. "Yeah, sure. Come on."

The OB/GYN's office is ultra modern with sleek, curved blue and green, armless chairs and love seats. The walls are painted in a pastel blue, several shades lighter than the furniture, and several framed photos of pretty purple, white, and orange flowers are hung up. One wall is all glass, where the receptionists sit. I need to come here for my next exam. Not that I'm rushing to get into stirrups.

Izzie walks over to the glass, and I sit in one of the chairs, facing a woman with a belly so big it looks like she'll give birth any second. We do that polite smile thing, and she goes back to reading a *People* magazine. Izzie speaks softly to a receptionist with a very high ponytail. Then my sister sits beside me.

She lets out a shaky breath and stares straight ahead. There's nothing directly in front of her, so she must be in deep thought.

"You okay?" I whisper.

She nods.

My stomach moans. Loud. I glance up at the woman, who offers a sly smile. Sometimes my body loves to embarrass me.

Izzie looks at me from the corner of her eye. "Are you okay?"

"I haven't eaten yet today. The freezer in the deli is kaput, and I've been carrying around casseroles all morning. On the plus side, I'm building tone." I flex the muscle in my arm.

Izzie snickers. "I ate, but it didn't stay down."

I grimace and start to call her Pukey Izzie, but if I do, she'll slug me. She has the weakest gag reflex in the universe, and after an incident of her vomiting all over a classmate on the bus during a school trip many, many moons ago, she inherited that nickname. It stayed with her for years.

A side door opens, and a nurse calls in the other woman. She struggles out of her seat, and instead of standing and offering a hand, like a good Samaritan, I just stare at her. I don't mean to. It's just so mesmerizing.

"That's going to be me some day," Izzie says with a tone full of regret or fear.

"I thought you liked being pregnant," I say in my normal voice.

"I was seventeen. What did I know?" She pats her mostly flat belly. "I'll be fine once I get past the first trimester. Just another month."

I glance at the magazines, but they all look old. "How is my niece?"

"Surly." That time there was no mistaking the disgust in her tone.

I chuckle. "So she's still the same?"

Izzie laughs. "Yes, thirteen and believing she's smarter than me."

Sounds about right. "Don't we still think we're smarter than Ma and Pop? I don't think that'll ever change."

She sighs. "Not true. When I was pregnant with Alice I went to Ma with all my questions."

The left side of my mouth creeps up. "So you'll be good when you're a grandma?"

This time she groans, and I snort. Hopefully it'll be a long time before that happens. Last I knew, Alice wasn't sexually active, and she better keep it that way. Or at least never leave the house without a suitcase full of condoms.

The telephone on the other side of the glass rings.

"Have you and she had the talk yet? Not the birds and bees one but the protection one," I asked.

Izzie turns her head and stares at me. Her top lip is curled into a snarl, and her eyes are huge. Too bad I don't have the camera on my phone ready. That would an awesome photo to post to my Facebook wall. "She's thirteen."

It's my time to be shocked. "Seriously, sis? You were seventeen when you got pregnant. That's only four years. What are you waiting for?"

She turns back to her very rigid position, staring straight ahead. "When hell freezes over."

My thoughts immediately spring to Freezer Dude and last night's version of hell. I want to share it with someone, especially Izzie. I tell her everything. But I don't want to worry her. Enzo and I even swore to her that we won't do any Mancini scares while she's in her *delicate condition*.

One of my family's favorite pastimes is jumping out and scaring the crap out of each other. It's fun, a hoot, and really gets the adrenaline going. We all do it, but it's mostly just us kids nowadays. Mostly. I'll still get Ma or Pop if the timing is right. But the big scares, like sneaking into each other's homes and waiting in the dark, we keep between us three. I do not want to be responsible for heart attacks or the sudden death of the people who raised me. Nope. I couldn't live with that.

But now that Izzie's off limits and I've been hanging with Enzo more, it's gotten pretty boring. He and I are always suspecting the other of being up to no good, so we're super vigilant about not taking our eyes off each other. It makes it hard for sneak attacks. I'm not sure if I can wait another seven months before I scare someone though. I need to meet some new people.

My stomach grumbles louder than before.

"How are you and Paulie doing?" I bite the bullet and ask. If she doesn't want to talk about it, the worst she can do is growl or tell me to shut up.

Surprisingly, she doesn't do either. She shrugs. "Better but not great. We have our moments."

That's good. Right? As much as I think Paulie is scum for cheating on my sister, he's also a good guy and really loves her and Alice. He screwed up, and I believe he'll never do anything like that again. He's not that stupid.

I'm about to ask how therapy is going when the door opens, and the nurse reappears. "Isabel Donato."

We both stand, but Izzie puts a hand on my arm. "Why don't you go get something to eat? I can do the next part alone."

My stomach cheers, but I don't want to leave her since she asked me to come to begin with. "Are you sure?"

She nods. "Absolutely. Besides, your noises keep making me think of my breakfast, which makes me queasy."

I hold back a laugh. "Okay. I'll be right back, and if you want me to come in have the nurse get me."

She nods and kisses my cheek.

I stand in that spot until she's through the door, turns down the corridor, and I can't see her anymore. Then I hightail it out of there and over to the strip mall. I pass Subway and hold my breath. There's something about the smell of their bread that makes me queasy. There aren't many choices left though, so I go into CVS and purchase a pack of trail mix. Not exactly breakfast, but it'll do until I drop Izzie off. Maybe I'll head to Ma's and raid her fridge. Mine, minus the deli inventory, is getting a bit bare.

I lean against the brick part of the building and tear open the slender packet. I hold it up to my mouth and tilt it back. A peanut slides into my throat, and I choke. I cough and end up spitting a mouthful of nuts, raisins, and mini chocolate pieces onto the sidewalk. Oh no, not the chocolate pieces.

"You should be more careful," says a deep, feminine voice close by.

I cough and gag a couple more times and turn to the woman. She walks over and hands me an unopened bottle of water.

"Thank you," I say and cough some more, just in case the nut thinks it's going to win and kill me. Not today. I twist the cap, take a slug of water, and swallow hard.

The woman wears a blue-and-white floral maxi skirt, flats, a denim jacket, and has a royal blue top on beneath. She returns to her spot in front of the psychic's shop, whips out a lighter, and lights a cigarette.

"You should be careful too." I jut my chin to the cigarette in her hand.

She smiles and nods. "Yes, but I can foresee my future."

So she's the medium. "Did you come out here because you knew someone would need water?"

She blows a ring of smoke out of her mouth and chuckles. "No. Unfortunately, I don't get visions. I do read cards and auras though, and you have a lot on your mind."

Doesn't everyone? I hold up my pack of trail mix. "Just hungry."

"Hmm," she says and takes another drag of her cigarette.

I don't disbelieve her abilities. Ma is friends with one psychic who really knows his stuff. But every other one she's been to didn't know or foresee anything. Most of them are scams.

"You don't believe?" she asks.

"No, I very much believe that there are things in this world that we cannot see."

She raises a brow. "You are right."

Maybe she's a fake, maybe not. There's one way to find out, and I do have questions.

I take a step closer but try not to get in the way of her smoke. I'm not a fan of the smell. "What do you know about getting rid of ghosts?"

This time she raises both brows. "You think your home is haunted."

Ha! Ain't that the truth. "No, not my home. I don't want a cleansing. I want to banish a ghost to the other side." There, I said it. She can call the men in white coats, but really, who's going to believe the psychic?

She stares at me, which makes me wonder if I accidentally got a peanut lodged in my nose. Then she points to the window of her shop and the black lettering:

Mystic Aurora – Tarot Card Readings, Tea Leaves, Chakra Cleansing & more

She wants me to pay. I scoff. I know she has bills to pay too, but if she's legit, she'd want to help. A total scam. "Never mind."

I step off the sidewalk and walk across the parking lot, back to the medical building. As I turn the corner, I glance back. She's still standing there. Watching me.

CHAPTER THREE

I let myself into Ma and Pop's and listen to a quiet house. Ma's car is in the driveway. Pop's is gone. I assume Pop is with his guy buying a new freezer, and Ma is in the basement, singing and dusting her collection. I walk into the kitchen, and sure enough, the basement door is open.

"Lorenzo, why are you back so soon?" she shouts up.

"It's me, Ma. Can I find something for lunch?" I open the fridge and admire her fully stocked assortment.

"Of course, honey. There's leftover lasagna in there. Make a plate, and then come down to see my new piece."

Oooh, lasagna.

I pull it out and want to sink my entire face into it but figure that's rude, so I open a cabinet, grab a plate, and stick a healthy-sized portion into the microwave. Ma makes the best sausage and spinach lasagna. I've tried to duplicate it, but it's never quite right. Either too bland if I use fresh spinach and too watery if I use frozen. Plus, the seasonings seem to be off. I think she has a secret ingredient she isn't sharing. Call me cynical, but I don't believe her when she says it's her love.

I sit at the table and chow down while listening to her rendition of "Memory" from *Cats*. Ma loves her musicals. She told me she auditioned for an Off-Broadway production before she had us and before she and Pop married. I sometimes wonder if I'd be sitting here stuffing my face if she'd gotten the part.

When I'm done, I wash my plate, set it in the dish drainer, and head down the creaky basement steps. It's not that the basement is spooky. I'd love it if it was. It's just that the stairs are so narrow I have to walk down sideways. It kinda makes the descent awkward and a bit dangerous. Ma doesn't have this problem, but her feet are a size six while mine are an eight.

I don't see her instantly, but I hear her humming. Then she moves, and I realize she's at the far end of shelves staring at something.

There are rows and rows of shelving down here. They hold up precious items Ma's collected over the years. Not porcelain angels or spoons from every state. No, nothing quite so mainstream. Ma collects what I call murderabilia. If it once belonged to a murder victim, she wants it.

It all started when Ma's sister, Aunt Stella, died. What turned out to be an accident looked like foul play at first. After the police finally realized she'd simply slipped in the tub and hit her head, Ma's obsession with collecting murder objects increased. Now, she has friends all over the country who send her things as well. She goes by the name Clarice in her online groups.

She sees me, and her eyes light up. "Look at this. Isn't it lovely?" She holds out a plain, ordinary blue lighter.

"What's it from?" I ask. It has to be important. Ma wouldn't own it if it simply came from the 7-Eleven, and she surely wouldn't be showing it to me.

"That man who was killed in Arkansas, Mike Brady."

I quirk a brow.

Ma smirks, knowing my exact thoughts. "Not from the Brady Bunch. He was a recent college graduate who worked as a salesman and had just proposed to his girlfriend."

I have no idea where this story is going. I haven t heard of this man. I'm too busy dealing with Freezer Dude to learn about deaths in other states. "So, what happened?"

"He disappeared for three weeks. No one saw or heard from him. His family was frantic."

Suspicion creeps into me. "And the fiancée?"

Ma's smirk widens. "That's the thing. People say she was acting normal. Going to work, hanging with friends. She acted as if nothing was wrong."

"Which made everyone notice and suspect her."

Ma points her feather duster at me. "Exactly. They found his body in her bed. He died from cyanide poisoning."

Eww. "No one noticed the smell of his remains?"

She shrugs. "The fiancée lived alone. I guess she didn't invite anyone back to her place. She told police she was tired of him leaving her when he went to work, so she made him stay. His job made him go on a lot of out-of-town trips."

"The woman's obviously insane."

Ma doesn't disagree. "She also told the police that she slept beside him every night."

"Ma, that's sick."

"That's life, dear." She puts the item back on the shelf and continues humming. "Are you eating and leaving?"

Ugh, the attack of guilt is unbearable. "Is that terrible?"

Ma smirks. "Maybe if my daughter appreciated all I do more."

"Ma! I do appreciate you. You're awesome and kind, and I love you."

She smiles and takes the feather duster and dusts my face. "I'm only messing with you. Go on. Go live your life. I plan on staying down here a little longer."

I sneeze as the dust makes its way up my nose. "You're a cruel mother."

She giggles. "Ah, the joy of parenting."

I roll my eyes and kiss her cheek good-bye.

I walk into my apartment and stare at the tiny space. Now what? At least if I was working I wouldn't be so bored. Ma said to go live, but what does that mean when you're broke and don't have any friends?

I plop down onto the couch and reach for the remote when a loud boom blasts. Everything in my place trembles slightly. Oh my God, what was that? Do we have earthquakes on Long Island?

I jump up and race downstairs. The stench of smoke fills the air outside, and I hear people yelling. I run to the road and see people running down the street. Maybe because I'm bored or because I'm nosy, I follow.

I spot a billow of thick black smoke rising toward the sky. It's coming from two blocks down. Now with a purpose, I take off and sprint toward it. That has to be more than a fire. It felt like an explosion. Not that I know what one feels like exactly. The closest I've ever come to one is in the movies.

I hit the corner of Pacific Avenue, and not only does the crowd get thicker but so does the air. It smells rancid, and the smoke burns my throat. I cough and step around a woman and man. I walk across the street, to get a better angle.

The smoke and a small fire comes from the property three houses down from the corner. What once was a two-story house similar to the ones around it now looks like a soot-covered dollhouse. Other than the wall around the intact front door, the rest of the front wall is gone, and you can see inside. There may be some furniture left in the front room, but it's hard to make out. There's so much smoke and blackness. Sirens are far off but getting closer. In minutes, the street will be filled with emergency vehicles. I'm not so sure I still want to be here.

I take a last look around and spot a black SUV parked a few feet away. I stare at the driver, who's watching me.

Julian.

What is he doing here?

I sprint to his car, open the passenger door, and step up. I slam the door shut and realize my stomach is in knots. I'm just not sure if it's because I fear he's involved in this or that he looks scrumptious. He's wearing faded jeans, black boots, his leather jacket, and a tan sweater. He should've worn the soft gray one. It compliments his eyes so well.

"What are you doing here?" I ask and cough. The smoke is starting to dry out my throat, and I doubt I'll get its odor from my clothes anytime soon.

"Hello to you too," he says with a half smile.

I softly sigh. "Did this happen because of you? Did you cause this?" I wave my hand toward the burning house.

He frowns at me, and the look of hurt in his eyes is undeniable. "No. This has nothing to do with me. I was on the way to the deli and heard the explosion."

My stomach calms down, and I instantly smile. "Why were you going to the deli?"

He glances at me from the corner of his eye. "To buy some prosciutto."

Oh.

"And to see the pretty woman who works behind the counter," he adds.

Oh!

"Did you run out when you heard the explosion?" he asks.

"Yes, but I wasn't working. The deli's closed today. My folks have to buy a new freezer." I consider telling him about Freezer Dude. He may not freak out, and this would be an awesome test to make sure he's really okay with my ghostly abilities. He only learned about them a week ago.

"Losing business has to hurt," he says, watching the house.

The sirens are much closer now.

"Yeah. Listen..." My finger starts to tingle. No. Not now.

I search the crowd, looking for the old buzzard.

"Listen what?" Julian asks.

Then I spot him. Freezer Dude is up ahead in the crowd of people across from the house. He jumps into a man standing beside him, just like he did to me. The man's body trembles, but it doesn't look as powerful as it had felt. I expect the man to drop onto the ground and have a seizure, but he doesn't. Then Freezer Dude stumbles out. It looks as if he's thrown out. It wasn't voluntary. I'm going to assume that two souls can't occupy the same body, so one pushes the invading one out.

"Gianna?" Julian asks. "What are you staring at?"

Freezer Dude seems to shake himself for a second, as if the experience leaves him as loopy as it does us. Then he looks up, and we lock stares.

Julian touches my arm, but I continue ignoring him. I can't take my gaze away. Not even for a moment.

Freezer Dude gives me one of his slow, creepy grins and poof. He's gone.

I seriously need to do something about this guy.

* * *

Julian pulls up behind the deli and stops beside my car. "You sure you're okay? You seemed to be in a trance back there."

"I'm fine." After Freezer Dude disappeared, I asked Julian to take me home. A fire truck was pulling onto the street anyway. Soon, the police would ask all vehicles to leave and people to get back. There'd be plenty of time to tell Julian about the new apparition in my life. Right now though, I need to find out more about him.

I push open the car door. "Thanks for the ride home. I'll talk to you later."

He stares at me. His eyes drift to my mouth and back up. "Will you?"

I half chuckle, trying to lighten the mood. "Of course."

He puts his hand on my arm. "You seem more distant than usual."

Really? He wants to talk about our feelings now? As much as I want to, I also want answers from the dead. I look into Julian's chameleon gray eyes, which look smoky right now, and give in. He's more important than Freezer Dude.

"It's only been a week since we said we'd take things slow," I remind him. But I totally get where he's coming from. It has felt like an eternity.

"I'm not trying to push you into coming back. I would just like to see you more."

"What do you mean coming back?" Did he think I'd move back to Connecticut, where he and I met? "I'm not leaving Long Island."

He shakes his head. "No, I don't mean that. I just hope that we'll go back to the way we were when we lived together in Connecticut."

He wants me to move in with him. I like my apartment way too much for that to happen. I guess he could move here... Wait, what am I thinking? The whole reason we're taking it slow is because I hate his job. I hate that disrupting a murder scene was just another day for him. Take Izzie out of the equation, and being a fixer still sucks. What happens the next time his job interferes with the law, someone's freedom, my life?

"Haven't you been working a lot?" I ask.

"It's been mostly days."

I start to ask what he's been doing, but I know he can't or shouldn't tell me, and I'm not sure I want the details. In fact, I'm not a hundred percent what I want, although I know I still love him. This isn't the time to contemplate it all though.

"Well, I'll call you, or you can call me."

Before he stops me again, I say, "Bye," and hop out of his truck. I run up to my apartment, grab my purse, and head back down. I peek through the back door, making sure Julian's gone, then go out to my car. The only lead I have on this demented ghost is the woman. Hopefully there's a connection to him through her.

I pull up in front of the house I saw her walk out of and park. I glance at the time on my cell. I have plenty of time to sit here before heading to Enzo's for dinner. This street looks like every other. Nothing unusual stands out to me. It's pretty quiet. No movement. Not even a barking dog. There are no cars parked anywhere on this side of the road. There's a red sports car across from the corner house, but that's it. There isn't a car in her driveway, and it hits me that I'm not sure if this is her house or the one she went to around the corner.

I lean my head back and think of Julian. I want to get more serious. I want to spend nights in his arms. I want to know he's there for me no matter what. But I'm not sure he'd put me before his stupid job. And how can I trust someone like that? More importantly, his work is just plain wrong. Just because someone rich can pay for cleanup doesn't mean it should happen. Whatever. I don't want to think about this anymore.

I concentrate on the house.

Two hours later, my neck has a kink, and no movement has happened anywhere on the block. It's like a well-manicured ghost town. I grab a pen from my purse and a napkin from the glove compartment and jot down the address. Then I start the car and head to dinner. Sitting around doing nothing makes a person hungry.

* * *

When I pull up to Enzo's, I'm a bit early. He leaves the station by four, but he still has to drive home. I wiggle in my seat, starting to feel cramped. I don't know how private investigators and cops do stakeouts. This would drive me crazy on a full-time basis. Not to mention that I stopped and picked up fried chicken, and while my car smells amazing, my stomach is making unhappy sounds. It wants me to tear into the succulent, moist meat and its crunchy shell.

Ten minutes later on the nose, Enzo pulls up in front of his house. He steps out and frowns at me.

I grab my bucket o' chicken and purse and follow him inside.

He eyes my bucket. "I thought I was cooking?"

"Yeah, since when do you cook? I'm ravished and wanted to make sure there was something edible." I set the bucket on his coffee table and kick off my sneakers.

"Funny." He heads into his room, and I run into his bathroom in desperate need to relieve my bladder.

When I'm done, I hear him in the kitchen. I go to the living room and take my new favorite spot—the right corner of the couch. I grab the remote and turn on his television. Yes, this is my same routine at home, but here there's someone to talk to when the commercials come on.

Enzo walks into the room with a bowl of salad on top of some paper plates, a bottle of French dressing is wedged into the crook of one arm, a couple of beers in the other, and two forks in his hand.

I help him lower it all to the table carefully and see that he's no longer in uniform and is now wearing jeans and a red tee. Thank goodness. It's not easy digesting while staring at all that blue. I don't have a problem with cops. Well, not most of them. I've never been arrested or even had a speeding ticket. The closest I got to feeling like I might be fitted with handcuffs was when Izzie was arrested. And even though my own brother is one of them, I feel a bit uneasy in their company. Maybe it has something to do with that asshat, Detective Burton. The cop who has a vendetta against me because I rebuffed his advances when

I was in college. Our animosity has become so much more than that, but that's when it started.

"Why are you here?" Enzo asks.

"For dinner. Duh." I peel back the lid to the bucket and grab a succulent breast. Yum!

"I mean why have you been coming by so much?" He puts both drumsticks on his plate and sits on the opposite end of the couch.

"Can't a sister spend time with her big brother?" I peel a piece of the breading-slash-skin off and set it on the side of my plate. I'm saving that sucker for last.

"No." He bites into a drumstick and continues staring at me, waiting for an answer.

I tell him how Izzie's pukey, and I'm bored. "Besides, what do you have to do that's so important?"

"I have plans."

"Tonight?" Man, I hope I'm not about to get booted out.

"No. Tomorrow." He grabs a beer and pops it open.

"Oooh, is it a hot date? Enzo and some lucky lady sitting in a tree. K-I-S-S-I-N-G." I can't help teasing him. When you talk about sex in any way, his face gets all red. Like right now.

He throws a piece of chicken crust at me. Is he crazy? Dude, that's the best part. The only reason to eat it.

I maneuver my neck and jut out my head. It lands right in my mouth. Score!

He smirks and shakes his head. "No. I'm going to see a game with a friend." His voice dips when he says the last word, and I immediately think of Kevin, aka Detective Burton, aka the man who wants to ruin my life.

"Who are you going with?" My stomach knots. If these two made up and became actual friends, I may upchuck the good bits of chicken.

"Does it matter?"

I put my plate into my lap. "Since you're acting all mysterious, it does."

"Fine. I'm going with Julian." He takes a swig of beer.

Wait. What? "My Julian?"

He arches a brow. "I didn't know he belonged to you but yes."

While the nausea and fear fades, confusion takes its place. "Since when have you two become so close?"

Enzo shrugs. "It just kinda happened. We got to talking about sports at Sunday dinners."

Every Sunday, Ma insists the whole family gets together for dinner. It's been a tradition forever. Ever since Julian's moved to town, she invites him too. I always end up being surprised he's there. I guess I should get used to it. And yeah, I've seen him and Enzo chatting, but it never dawned on me that they were scheduling playdates.

"Is this going to be a problem?" Enzo asks.

I sulk for half a second. I have one sibling left to hang with, and he has a date with my...what is Julian to me? "No, it's fine. I hope you guys have fun."

"What's with you two, by the way? First you're pissed he moved here, and then you seemed close and now... What?"

I can't tell Enzo about Julian's job and how much it pains me, but I hate lying to him too, so I say, "It's complicated." That's exactly the status I chose on my Facebook profile too.

I unscrew the top off the bottle of French, drizzle some on my lettuce, and change the subject. "So, that explosion. Do you know what it was?"

Enzo reaches for a thigh. It works out great because he likes the dark pieces of chicken while I prefer the white. "Yeah, it was a homemade bomb in a box of flowers."

Whoa. "Seriously?"

"And they can't find out who delivered them. It wasn't any of the local shops."

The hairs on the back of my neck rise. That's even more interesting than Ma's crazy cyanide giving fiancée. "Who lived there?"

"A woman named Serena Tate. Why? Did you know her?"

I shake my head. "Just curious. It was so close to the deli, everything in my apartment shook. When I got there it was so unreal."

"You went to the explosion? Doesn't a loud bang, smoke, and fire suggest you stay away?"

I roll my eyes. "Everyone was running there."

He widens his brown eyes. "So if everyone jumps off a bridge..."

I hold up a hand. "Okay, I get it. I was just curious. Geesh. What's the big deal?"

"The big deal is that you almost died last week when confronting a killer. I kinda don't want to be the youngest."

My heart swells with feelings. "Aww, you worry about me."

"Yeah, 'cause you don't think and do some crazy stuff."

Well that mushiness ended quickly.

"I am not involved with the explosion or anyone who lived there. So, was this Serena woman home?"

"No, but her fiancé was."

Oh crap. That's awful.

He sucks down the rest of his beer and gets up. "Need another?" he asks before looking at the table. I hadn't even opened mine yet. He wanders off.

When he gets back, I ask, "So can you find out who lives at an address for me?"

He cocks his head. "This is why you're really here, huh?"

I laugh. "Why are you so suspicious?"

"Well, I would think you're here to scare me, but since you haven't moved from that spot, there must be another reason."

I shake my head. Brothers are so silly. Oh, I have every intention of scaring him but when he least suspects it. "No. I wanted dinner with you because I owe you for last night and because I hate sitting at my place alone."

"You need friends."

Tell me about it.

"But I'm also curious about this woman who lives at six-oh-nine Ventura Avenue."

"Why?"

"Do I need to tell you that?"

He stops chewing and stares at me. "This is one of those ghost things, huh?"

When I don't respond, he asks, "Does it have to do with someone who recently died? An open case?"
"No." I love when I don't have to lie.
He nods. "Fine. I'll look into it."
I squeal and get back to my chicken. Sometimes brothers are cool.

CHAPTER FOUR

I leave Enzo's, and instead of going home, I head back to the woman's house. Yes, I am a dog with a bone. But a fabulously accessorized one with a diamond collar and a pretty pink bow. Hopefully Enzo will have concrete answers for me as to who the woman is soon. I don't bother parking in front of her house because it's still dark inside. I have a feeling no one's been home since I last visited. There's no sense in staying and waiting.

Next, I drive to the explosion house in hopes of spotting Freezer Dude. I don't know what I'll do when I find him though. Tea and scones are out of the question. Plus, I'm more of a coffee girl.

I park across from the waterlogged, ashy, burnt shell and can't believe this used to be someone's home. It doesn't look much different than earlier, except it's dark out, and everything that's still standing inside looks blacker. It's hard to make out the details, and the entire property is roped off with yellow crime scene tape. Not that that could stop me from walking under it, but I don't have a lot of desire to trample around in the dark.

I sit there for a while, just staring at the debris and thinking about the day. What does Freezer Dude want? Why was he here earlier? That's the question that baffles me the most. I get coming back to the land of living because...well, who wouldn't? There have to be several reasons, like leaving behind loved ones or maybe wanting revenge for why you're dead. But showing up at an explosion? He couldn't have had something to do with it. He can't pick up a daisy, let alone assemble a bomb. Was he simply in the area and heard the ruckus, or is he following me?

A trio of chills, one after the other, slither down my back and cause me to shiver. I don't mind helping deadies. I do mind the creepy ones though.

Just as I'm about to start the car and go home, I notice movement in the rubble. I stare hard in the area that used to be the living room, but I don't see anything. What was that?

I squint to try to zoom in.

There it is again. Something moves, but I can't make out what it is. In my attempt to turn and get a better angle, I lean on the horn and blast my heart into overdrive. Shoot!

The thing across the street moves again and again, until it glides out of the rubble and onto the front yard. The streetlamp illuminates its shape. Its figure. Its face.

Oh my god, it's a man. No. I can see part of the front door through him. He's a ghost.

I fling open my door and run over to him. "Hey."

Up close, it's obvious he was a part of the explosion. Soot and ash is caked onto his skin and what's left of his clothes. They look like they used to be pants and a jacket. Perhaps a suit. His hair is brown or burnt. I can't tell.

"Are you okay?" Stupid alert, Gi. Try again. "Who are you?"

He sways and frowns at me, edging closer to where I'm standing on the sidewalk. "What happened?" He shouts so loud, I flinch. Is he hard of hearing? Or is it a residual effect from the bomb? But he's a ghost, so how much residual can there be? Deadies don't have the same abilities as when they were living. No need to eat, sleep, or use the bathroom.

"Do you remember anything that happened to you?" I step as close as I can without ducking under the crime scene tape.

He looks back at the house. "I-I came to see her. We're getting married."

Poor guy. He seems so disoriented. I never dealt with a deadie who didn't know they were dead. This just sucks!

He stares at me, wide-eyed. "Do you know Serena? I have to find her, to save her."

"She's okay." I think. I hope. "But you're not."

Might as well yank off the Band-Aid fast, right? So I go in for the kill. No pun intended.

"You're dead."

* * *

I finally manage to convince him that he is in fact a ghost and that he should come home with me. At least long enough for us to chat. I don't want anyone to drive by or look out their window and see me standing there talking to the burnt house.

I toss my keys on the breakfast bar and sit on the couch to take off my sneakers. The ghost hovers near the front door. My apartment isn't very big. One stretch of the neck takes you from the three front windows to the funky teal tile backsplash above the sink. A bedroom large enough for a full-sized bed, two small end tables, a half dresser, and a bathroom without a tub completes the apartment. It's a good thing I'm not a woman who can afford more clothes, because I'd have to hang hooks from the ceiling in addition to the little closet space there is. It's bad enough that I have shoeboxes lined beneath my bed and stacked between my closet and bathroom doors. And not the normal sized ones that dainty heels come in, but the ones for boots. I'm not complaining though. I love this place. It's my first time living alone.

"You can enter." I get back up and toss my sneakers into my room. One smacks against the wall. I go to the cabinet beside the fridge and take down a glass then grab the bottle of white wine from beside the toaster oven. Yes, I am the woman who keeps her liquor out on the counter. But only because the kitchenette lacks adequate cabinetry.

"I'd offer you a drink. I'm sure you could use one." When I turn around, he's hovering by the breakfast bar. That's a start.

"I'm Gianna Mancini. What's your name?"

It takes him a few seconds, but he finally looks me in the eye and stands a bit taller. "Thomas Sterling."

"Nice to meet you Thomas..." My mind does a double take. "Wait, Sterling like the automotive Sterlings?"

He nods. "Yes, that is my family."

Whoa! I take a step back and bump into the sink. They're loaded. I'm talking Daddy Warbucks style. And one of them is dead in my living room. If I was a less scrupulous person, I'd consider holding his ghost for ransom and seeing how much they'd pay for the family secrets. But that thought would never enter my mind.

"So Thomas, can you tell me what you remember?" I walk around the breakfast bar and pull out a stool.

He's just inches away, and I get a whiff of charred flesh. That's odd. I've never been able to smell a ghost before.

"Wait, can you change?" I point at him and twirl my finger in front of him.

His brows pucker. "I don't think so."

Silly me for not explaining fully. I forget that while this isn't my first rodeo, this is his first time being dead.

"No, you can. Other ghosts have. I'm just asking you to."

His eyes widen, and then he turns his head and looks around the room. "You've seen other ghosts?"

"Yes, but they aren't here now. They've crossed over. To the other side. Where you'll go."

His reaction goes from surprised to horrified the longer I speak, so I guess I should shut up for a minute and give him time to process.

"I have to see Serena before I leave."

Well, at least he's not trying to hang around. That's a good sign. I nod. "Sure. But first." I twirl my finger again.

"Oh, right. How?"

Hmm, I never asked my last set of ghosts. "Not exactly sure, but I believe you just think of yourself during another day, like how you look when you're just hanging out at home."

He shuts his eyes. His face is serene. He doesn't look like he's straining. But suddenly the soot and charred bits are gone, and he looks like he took a very long shower. His hair is brown and side parted. He has a pale complexion, and when he opens his eyes, they are blue-green. There's a baby chubbiness to his cheeks, something he should've outgrown years ago but never did. My guess is that he's in his mid thirties.

I gaze down at his clothes and push up a brow. This is his idea of relaxing at home casual?

He's wearing a white button down and white tie beneath a black tuxedo complete with tails.

I cock my head to the side. "What exactly do you do for relaxation?"

He glances down and smiles. "I don't have a lot of down time. I wore this the night I proposed to Serena."

Aww, sweet.

"So tell me what you last remember." I sip my wine.

He glances to the door. "I really think we should find Serena. I want to make sure she's fine."

"I'm sure she is."

"But how do you know that?"

"My brother's a cop. He told me how she lived there, but her fiancé was the one who was in the explosion."

He grimaces.

"If she'd been hurt, he would've mentioned it."

He widens his eyes until they look as round as his cheeks. "That's it? You don't know for certain."

"Well, no, but—"

He turns and heads for the door. "I will find her myself."

"Wait," I shout and jump off the stool, sloshing wine on my hand. "You probably haven't heard yet, but the freezer downstairs is the portal to the other side." Although technically there is no freezer at the moment.

His frown is deep. "That's absurd."

Tell me about it.

"I'm not going anywhere until I make sure Serena is okay and until I tell her how much I love her." He steps forward and walks through my door.

"How will you do that? You're dead."

He pushes his head back through and only his head. It seems to just float right smack dab in the middle there. Oh boy, and I thought the nightmares about Freezer Dude were bad. Add in this, and I'll look like the Bride of Frankenstein in the morning.

"You have a point," he says.

I set my glass down and sigh. "I can help but..."

He pushes his whole body through, and my brain stops screaming. "What do you want in return?"

I smile. "We find her. I somehow tell her you love her. And then you move on to the other side. You get peace."

He thinks for three seconds and says, "Agree."

That wasn't too difficult.

* * *

Thomas points out the passenger window. "There. That's where her friend Zoe lives."

Coincidentally, the apartment complex is only a few blocks away from Julian's. It has the same setup too. A set of stone steps lead to a veranda of sorts with four doors that separate the building into four sections. They're called garden-style apartments although there isn't a garden anywhere in sight. It's across the street from the boardwalk. And in between the two is a wide, two-way street with parking spaces as a median.

"I really don't want to knock on a stranger's door unless we know Serena is there. Do you see her car?" I drive slowly past the cars, then turn around and come the other way.

"No, Serena drives a brown hatchback. It isn't here, and neither is Zoe's."

Great. I was hoping this would be a quick excursion. I pull into an empty space while we figure out where else to look. "Maybe they're someplace together."

"Where?" He sounds frustrated already. He's obviously never been on a stakeout.

"I don't know either of them, so I can't say. But you do. Where does Serena go when she's upset?" I already called Enzo to make sure she hadn't been injured and wasn't at the hospital. He said no. The detectives had questioned her briefly, but Enzo wasn't sure where, and he couldn't find out until tomorrow. *If* he found out. He was a bit miffed that I disturbed his beauty sleep to grill him. I didn't bother mentioning Thomas the Tuxedo Ghost was beside me in my car. I planned to have him outta here by time Enzo woke tomorrow.

"She'd visit Zoe. She doesn't have any other friends."

"What about family?" I'm certainly not going to knock a girl for only having one friend. I have none if you don't include my siblings, although in my defense, I did just move back to town less than a month ago.

"There's a sister, but they aren't close, and she lives upstate," Thomas says. "Serena's a private person. She doesn't let many people in."

I understand that. I can be a blabbermouth, but when it comes to the deadies, I'm pretty tight-lipped. Most people don't want to know that there are ghosts wandering about, standing beside them while they check out the melons in the produce section or sitting next to them while eating their Frosted Flakes.

"Then perhaps she's on the boardwalk or the beach," I say. That's where I'd go if I was grieving and didn't want to be around people.

"Maybe," he whispers but doesn't sound convinced.

"Is she a drinker? Maybe she's at a bar drowning her sorrows."

He seems to contemplate this. "She doesn't drink. She works in a nightclub-slash-restaurant though. Sparks. That may be where Zoe is now. She works there too."

I put my car in reverse. "Okay, so where is this club?"

He shakes his head. "I doubt she's grieving there. Her boss isn't happy with her."

My internal radar begins beeping. Maybe the boss is responsible for the bomb. "Why?"

He's staring out his side window and finally faces me. "She was quitting. She gave her two-week notice, and her boss wasn't pleased. Serena was her favorite server, so I don't think she'd go there."

Yeah, that doesn't sound right. I think harder. "What about your family?"

His eyes widen, and panic leaps onto his face. "Oh, no."

I want to ask why, simply because of how funny his expression is, but I figure it's not my business, and he has enough on his plate right now. Yes, I have compassion. I'm not always nosy. "Okay, and you're sure there isn't anyone else she's close to? Maybe someone from work she's only mentioned in passing."

"There isn't anyone else. Just me and Zoe."

I blow a raspberry with my mouth. Think, Gianna. If something horrible happened to Julian, and I was in a world of pain, what would I do? I'd get drunk on the beach with Izzie. But if that wasn't possible or after I sobered, I'd go... I'd want to stay close to Julian.

Duh. I slap the steering wheel. "What about your place? Does she have a key?"

He smiles big. His top teeth are straggly, one shorter than the other, and I'm surprised an orthodontist wasn't a part of his past considering all the money his family has. "Yes, of course. I live over on Mediterranean Avenue."

Of course he does.

Mediterranean is over in the East End, the ritzy part of town. When the streets were named, someone with a sense of humor named the richest part of town with the cheapest *Monopoly* property names. Baltic Avenue isn't far from him.

I pull up in front of a modern, square structure that's all glass and wooden. It reminds me of a contemporary log cabin. It sits at the curve of the road, so it only has one neighbor, and their minimansion is a good 'nother house length away.

That may not sound like much, but in the rest of South Shore Beach, the homes are so close. Some are just a person width apart. Not in the East End though. Here, there's more space, and they have the best view. The boardwalk doesn't extend into this part of town. Homeowners do not want tourists hanging out in their backyards.

I stop in front of Thomas's house. A brown hatchback is parked in the driveway. Behind it is a silver Benz.

"Oh no," Thomas mutters.

I put my car into park. "What is it?"

"My mother."

I swear I hear dun-dun-dun-dun shark music.

"I'm assuming that's not a good thing?" I open my car door and wait for his answer.

"Brenda Katherine Sterling doesn't approve of Serena. She says she's backwater swamp, not fit to be a Sterling."

Ouch!

"But you're still marrying her." Or were.

"Yeah, I love her. She's great. You'll see. You have to save Serena. Mother is a shark. She'll eat her alive if I'm not there to intervene." He floats out of the car.

I knew I had the right music in my head. I jump out and slam the door. I have to run to catch up with him. "Wait. Who am I? Why am I here?"

He stops before floating through his front glass-and-wood door and looks back at me. He opens his mouth, and there's a crash inside. Without a sound, he turns and passes through the door, leaving me to fend for myself.

Crap.

I raise my hand to knock but decide to try the knob. It twists, so I let myself in and hurry toward the loud voices.

"Look what you've done," shouts a woman.

"I'm sorry." Another one sobs her words.

Laying bets they are Mother and Serena, in that order, I step down two steps to a sunken living room with a dark, hardwood floor and a thick, beige center rug. The furniture is beige too. A stiff-looking, rectangular couch and love seat face a wood and rock fireplace. Several dark wood tables, some accessories, and a couple of potted plants complete the room.

A lamp is on its side, on the rug, the glass base has a huge chunk missing. Its several large shards lie beside it. The bulb still shines though. If this was my family, we'd superglue it back together. I have a feeling the Sterlings will buy a complete new set. Maybe even hire an interior designer to remodel the whole room.

Thomas hovers by Serena, who is slightly bent at the waist, crying into her hand. She has on black jeans and a pink sweater with a plunging neckline.

Mrs. Sterling wears an ivory-colored linen skirt suit with nude pumps. Her brown, shoulder-length hair is coiffed in waves around her head and looks like it doesn't move in the wind. Her back is to me, and neither of them notice me.

Thomas tries to rub Serena's back, but his hand goes through her. She shudders and hugs herself.

I clear my throat, and both women look to me.

Mrs. Sterling flinches and gasps. "Who are you?" Her eyes dart around as if she's looking for a weapon.

Before she thinks to grab a shard and thrust it into my heart, I hold out my hand. "Hi, I'm Gianna Mancini."

When your family owns a business with your last name, you hope not everyone has heard of it in times like this. Ma would be appalled at my thinking. She expects every interaction her children have should result in new deli business.

"Do you always walk into strangers' homes, Ms. Mancini?"

"I-I." I stare at Thomas and widen my eyes, hoping he understands my nonverbal plea for help.

"Why are you here?" Mrs. Sterling asks.

If only I could blurt out the truth.

"Tell them you're my new assistant," Thomas says.

"I worked for Thomas Sterling. I was his assistant." I add a half smile to my face, not too happy and not too threatening. I hope.

Serena starts crying again.

Mrs. Sterling rolls her eyes. "Stop sniveling, child." To me she says, "I wasn't aware my son hired you. When did this happen?"

I glance at Thomas.

"Last week," he says, keeping his gaze on Serena. "Serena's been on me to hire help for some time. I just didn't think I needed it."

"A week ago," I say to Mother. "He finally caved, he said." Hopefully she won't ask me for details because I don't even know what Thomas does for work. I assume it's something in the family business, but he could be CEO or sort the mail for all I know.

Mrs. Sterling's gaze starts at the roots of my curls and slowly travels down until she's at my worn sneakers. She scoffs and turns to Serena. "You have no business being in my son's home."

Serena looks up, and her eyes are puffy and bloodshot. "This was going to be our home."

"Was. Not any longer."

Wow, harsh much?

Thomas's face scrunches up into a deep frown. "Mother, stop being so mean. She's welcome to be here as long as she wants."

Too bad Mother can't hear him.

"You have no right to be here. Give me back your key." Mrs. Sterling holds out her hand.

Serena pulls back and seems to turn into herself more.

"Mother!" Thomas shouts. When she doesn't respond, he looks to me. "Do something."

"Thomas would want Serena to stay here until she's ready to leave," I say and hold my breath, waiting for the verbal smackdown I'm about to get.

"Who the heck... You've worked for him for a week, and you think you know his wishes?"

I don't know this woman, and I kinda get that she's uptight and in as much grief as Serena. Instead of crying though, she's lashing out and trying to hold on to her son. Serena, the woman she doesn't like, is in his space and tarnishing Mother's memories. At least that's my five-second armchair psychoanalysis.

But she's also a bully, and I can't stand anyone using their size, power, or authority to threaten another. So I do what I've been getting really great at. I lie.

"Because he told me." Well, that part isn't a lie. "We were going over some business, and he said that everything he owned was Serena's, even if they weren't married yet."

Instead of screaming at me, Mother turns to Serena. "You only have a few days, and then I want you gone. Regardless of what my son wanted, you have no legal say. Make sure you clean this up, and when I return, I better not find anything missing."

She turns on her heel and storms past me with a huff.

The front door slams shut, and I flinch. I release a deep breath. For a moment, I thought she'd slug me, but I imagine someone of Brenda Katherine Sterling's upbringing doesn't resort to violence. At least not with her own hands.

Thomas looks into my eyes. "Thank you."

I nod and step closer to the grieving fiancée. "I'm so sorry for what you're going through, Serena. Thomas loved you so much."

She sniffles and looks at me.

Wow, despite the bloodshot eyes and red nose, she's stunning. High cheekbones, almond-shaped, light-brown eyes, a pixie nose, and full bow lips on a heart-shaped face. Her rich, dark hair is pulled back into a low ponytail and is shiny and slick looking.

"Thank you," she says.

"Are you sure you want to stay here?"

"She's stronger than she looks," Thomas says.

"I have no place else to go. Besides, it helps to be close to him. This never should've happened."

I take her arm and lead her to the uncomfortable looking sofa. "Sit down. Do you need anything? A glass of water?"

"The kitchen is around the corner." She starts crying again.

I look to Thomas, and with my head, I motion for him to follow me. I round the corner and step into a kitchen-slash-dining area that would make Ma drool. Stainless steel appliances nestled among wooden cabinets and granite tops. I'm getting a bit excited myself.

I open the fridge, find a bottle of water, and ask, "Do you want me to tell her something more specific than how much you love her?"

He looks off into the distance. "That I'll miss her tremendously." His voice cracks.

That goes without saying, but I nod and head back to Serena. I uncap the bottle, hand it to her, and sit beside her.

"I don't know what I'm going to do. The police acted as if they blame me for the bomb."

Thomas flies to her feet and kneels before her. 'That's crazy. You'd never hurt me."

"The police can be clueless at times," I say. Especially Detective Kevin Burton.

"Tell her to call my lawyer, just in case. Mr. Hamilton."

I stare at Thomas in disbelief, and panic climbs into my chest. You have to be kidding me. Thomas's attorney is Julian's boss? Of course he is. Does this mean Julian lied to me again?

I relay the message and know exactly who I'm visiting when I'm done here. Suddenly in a rush, I tell her that Thomas loved her, and he'll miss her.

She gives a small smile. "I'll love him for the rest of my life."

Thomas grins, but it looks pained. Then he disappears.

That's it? He's moving on now? Well, that was easy.

I reach into my purse and pull out a brochure for the deli. Ma and Pop have recently added catering to their already ridiculously long days. I find a pen at the bottom of my bag, amongst some Oreo crumbs, and scribble my cell number onto the corner.

"Here. If you need someone to talk to, or if I can help you in any way, just give me a call." I feel bad leaving her here all alone, but it's getting late, and I'm on a mission. I still want her to feel she has someone though. "Will you be okay?"

She nods. "I'm going to crawl into his bed and cry myself to sleep."

My throat tightens. Fun night.

CHAPTER FIVE

I park in front of Julian's apartment building and call his cell.

"Gianna, what's wrong?" His tone is groggy and full of concern.

Don't listen to his sexiness, Gi. You're here for a reason, and it doesn't involve getting naked.

"I need to talk. Can you come outside? I'm parked out front."

His hesitation is slight. "I'll be right there."

I hang up and toss my cell onto my passenger seat. This can't be true. He can't be lying to me again. If he is... My stomach has tied itself in sailor knots. I wring my fingers until they almost pop off. And I bounce my heel up and down so fast I knee the steering wheel twice.

A minute later, I see him emerge from the back of his building in jeans, a gray hoodie, and sneakers. My pulse rises. Even in clothes he probably grabbed off the floor he looks amazing. He jogs across the street and starts heading to my passenger side.

No, no, no. I can't do that. If he gets in the car, just like if I go up to his apartment, we may end up horizontal. Not that I don't have self-control, but he's highly irresistible.

I roll down my window and stick my head out. "Hey."

He stops at my right headlight and walks to the driver door.

Thank goodness.

He leans on the door, on the open window, and stares into my eyes. "What's going on? Why didn't you come up and knock?"

"It's late, and I can't stay long. I just have to know something."

But I notice the smirk lifting the corner of his gorgeously stupid mouth. He knows exactly how much I can't usually resist him.

"What is it?" he asks.

"Are you involved with the explosion in any way?"

He scratches the side of his head. "You already asked me that."

"Yes, and you answered, but I know you can't really confide in me, so maybe you..."

"Lied?" he asks.

"Yeah." Guilt builds up.

He takes a step back, still with his arms on my window, and bows his head in the space his body makes with my door. Then I hear a long sigh. When he looks up, a small frown accentuates his expression. "I'm not lying. I had nothing to do with anyone associated with the explosion that I am aware of."

I nod over and over and stare out the windshield.

"You still don't believe me?" His tone sounds incredulous, and I'd like to point out that if he hadn't lied in the past maybe I wouldn't have trust issues now, but he's not the only one who lied. The only difference is that his lie almost cost my sister her freedom, and my lie about seeing dead people didn't even disturb his sleep. Well, not until we broke up.

"I swear on my grandmother that I have no knowledge of any ties to the explosion," he says.

Whoa, it's as if he can read my mind. His grandmother was incredibly important to him and part of the reason we broke up, and I left Connecticut to return home. When his grandmother's ghost became our houseguest, only I could see her, but he wasn't aware I could see the dearly departed yet. Up until this point, I hadn't seen another deadie in the months he and I lived together, so it hadn't come up yet. I had to relay her message of how much she loved him. It wasn't as easy as with Serena just now. Grandma had specific words she wanted me to use.

So I figured the best way to do it was to write him a letter from her and make it look like she wrote it before she died. I stuck it in one of his books, but when he found it, he knew it wasn't from her. I didn't realize he'd read that very book the week before. I lied, we fought, a lot, and he ultimately wanted space. I overreacted a bit, or a lot, and moved in with my cousin. After a week of not hearing from him, I decided to move back home. Less than a week later, he was here in town with his new job.

When I look back on it all, I definitely believe fate had a hand in all of this. If I hadn't walked out and he hadn't followed me, I wouldn't have told him about my ability.

"I didn't say that. I do believe you," I say.

"Now," he adds.

It's like he plucked the word straight from my mind.

"Why are you asking again? Does it involve you somehow?" Now he sounds concerned.

I look at him. "You can say that. I just spent the last few hours with the guy who died in the explosion."

Julian looks to the back and passenger seats. "Is he here now?"

I shake my nod. "Nope. He's moving on. He just wanted me to tell his fiancée how much he loves her."

"And this involves me how?"

"He mentioned that his lawyer is Mr. Hamilton, your boss."

Apprehension hits Julian's eyes. "I see. I've been on a stakeout most of the day and haven't seen my boss. I had no idea."

"A regular stakeout?"

He raises his brows. "As opposed to what?"

I shrug. "I don't know. A fixer's stakeout."

"I am a regular private investigator as well as a fixer. People, luckily, don't need fixing every day. I still need to make a living."

I never thought of it that way. I just assumed he was moving dead bodies and covering for Hamilton's clients daily. Tension fills the space between us.

"So I hear you and my brother have plans Saturday." Changing the subject seems like a good idea.

He grins. "Yeah, it should be fun."

The breeze picks up and blows the hair off my neck. I shiver.

"Are you sure you don't want to come up?"

I stare into his eyes for a moment and then down to his lips. The last time I was in his apartment, I threw myself at him and ended up spending the night. That was before I learned about his job.

I turn the key in the ignition. "No, I gotta go. Thanks for the info."

He takes a step back as I shift the car into reverse and pull out of the spot. "I'll talk to you soon," he shouts.

I watch him in my rearview as I drive off. I believe him, but I wonder if we'll ever be the same again. How do you learn to trust someone who lied to you?

* * *

The next morning, I wake up to clanking. Again. At least this time I'm in my bed. I shower, dress, and gulp down a mug of coffee before I head downstairs. Pop stands in the kitchen surveying a couple of men—older than me but slightly younger than Pop—install the brand new, superduper, shiny freezer. The old one sits in the middle of the kitchen causing a major holdup to traffic. Good thing the deli isn't open yet.

I wish I was here last night when Thomas crossed over. I would've liked to see it, what with the freezer not working and all. Did he just pass through the outside wall? I doubt the condition of the freezer changes how a ghost moves on, but being that the freezer is...well, freezing, it made the whole departure more fitting in the past. One day I'm going to find out why that thing is the portal. I'm pretty certain it's something to do with the land this building sits on and not the specific freezer. I mean, all freezers everywhere can't lead to the other side. That's ludicrous, right?

I try to sneak back out of the kitchen before Pop sees me and puts me to work. If the deli was open today, my shift wouldn't start until the afternoon, but I've been pulling some doubles with Izzie being all pukey. As I step out the back door, Ma pulls in and parks beside Pop's car. Crap. I have no time to make it upstairs without her seeing me. So I do the only thing a child does when trying to get away with something. I become a statue and freeze. I really need to work on my reflexes.

Ma doesn't seem to notice the stricken expression that I feel on my face. "How's it going in there?"

"Fine."

"Great. Since the freezer is new, I figure we can spend the day tearing the place apart cleaning. Come on." She opens the deli door.

"But I don't work now." My voice comes out weak and whiny.

She raises one brow and gives me her best *I birthed you, raised you, and give you half rent on your apartment* guilt. Mothers do that so well, but Italian moms add an extra special kick to it.

I sigh and follow her back inside. I start to tell myself that it shouldn't take too long. Ma is a neat freak, so how much can there be to clean? But I lived with this woman most of my life, and with her, clean takes on a new meaning. It won't matter that you can see your reflection in the stainless steel. She'll still have you polish it until you're tired of looking at yourself.

When I finally make it back to my apartment, my arms are so sore I can't condition my hair without groaning, and my back feels like I've slept on the floor for forty-eight straight hours. I manage to scrub all the sweat and grossness off my skin, dress in black leggings, boots, and a purple tunic. The entire day cleaning the deli. I don't want to see another sponge again in my life.

I leave and head over to Enzo's. I pull up behind his car and park. The journey to his front door is torture. I should be home on the couch with a pint of ice cream and a pizza, but I'm so sick of the people on my television. I curl my fist and knock, but it's light and wimpy, and I doubt Enzo heard it. I try again, but even my joints hurt from that darn sponge, so I just lean my head against the door and send telepathic waves.

My body decides it's time to allow gravity to win and slump against the door. I grab the doorknob to right myself, and as I stand back upright fully, the knob twists under my weight. It's unlocked? How very foolish of not only the cop in my brother but the brother in my brother. If this isn't the time for a scare, I don't know when is. Achy joints be damned.

I turn the knob slowly and use my shoulder to push open the door. Of course, if he's standing on the other side waiting, this will all be for nothing. But if he's not...

The door opens, and I step inside an empty foyer. Yes. The living room is to the right and the dining area, which is rarely used, to the left. Both are dark and empty. There's a light coming from the kitchen, but it's dim. It may be the one above the stove. It's definitely not the overhead. Is he in his room?

I tiptoe toward the back of the house and hear it. The shower is running. The bathroom door is open just a smidgen, and light peeks through. That means I can slip into the bathroom without him hearing the click from opening the door.

Suddenly my muscles no longer feel like they're atrophying, and my mind steps into scare mode. I bite my tongue to keep from giggling and set my purse on the floor beside the door. Scare rule number one: you don't want any distractions or anything that can make noise. I'm grateful my soles are rubber and not hard.

I place my hand on the door and gently push it forward. Steam greets me, which is extra delicious. It means he won't see me approaching either. I make it to the center of the room—his bathroom is three times the size of mine, so there is a center—and decide the best scare would be to throw back the curtain. He'll scream at me being here and him being naked. I definitely don't want to see his junk, but it'll freak him out even more. I debate going back into the hall to get my cell to record this. I won't actually upload it anywhere, but just knowing I have it will drive him crazy.

It's all in love.

Yes, filming it would be ideal, so I turn and spot Enzo standing in the doorway.

My heart skips a thousand beats, and I scream.

A scream echoes behind my head from the shower, and I scream again.

Enzo just stands there with his arms crossed over his chest and a smile on his face. "Hey, sis. Whatcha doing?"

I turn to the shower. Who the...? Oh my God, he has a girl in there? I'm about to fly out, when the curtain parts and a soapy, squinty, familiar face emerges. "Enzo," she says. "What's wrong?"

"Nothing. My sister just thinks she's smart."

"Carly Walton?" I say with a chuckle. I haven't seen her in almost eleven years.

She wipes the soap or shampoo from her eyes. "Gianna? Oh, my God, you look so good."

Carly was Enzo's high school sweetheart. They dated from freshman through senior year. Everyone thought they'd get married and have kids. But one day Enzo said it was over. It was a month before they graduated. I never got the nitty-gritty of it all, but I got the sense that they broke it off because she was going away to school, and neither wanted a long-distance relationship.

"Why don't we let her finish?" Enzo says.

"Oh, yeah. Sorry." I rush out, shut the door behind me, and grab my purse. I walk back to the front door, knowing I should probably leave so they can do whatever they were going to do, but I want to see her too. My fondest memories of Carly are the times she brought over some of her dolls for me to play with. Yes, I was in junior high, but she had the most expansive and coolest collection of dolls, from porcelain to baby and everything in between.

"It's not what you think," Enzo says.

I face him. He's changed into jeans and a tee, his usual off-work attire. "What do you mean?"

"Carly in the shower. I wasn't about to join her."

Wow, he'd make a great detective.

"Then why is she in there? And since when have you kept in touch with her?"

He runs a hand through his short, brown hair. "I haven't seen her since we broke up. Then today I'm about to leave the precinct, and I see her talking to a cop. Turns out she was mugged and filing a report."

Oh my gosh, that's horrible and so scary. "Is she okay?"

"Yeah, just shaken up and a bit dirty. She didn't let go of her purse right away, and the mugger yanked on it, knocking her into some mud. I didn't want to just leave her at the station."

"So you offered to take her home and give her a bath." Yeah, that makes perfect sense. I snort.

He rolls his eyes.

The bathroom door opens, and Carly steps out in one of Enzo's tees and a loose pair of sweats. She's rubbing her shoulder-length, dark blonde hair dry with a towel. "How long until my clothes are ready?" she asks my brother.

"They're in the dryer now." He looks to me. "I washed them."

Of course you did. I nod and smile. "So, Carly, how have you been?"

"Good. What about you? I didn't know you were back in town."

I raise a brow to Enzo. Didn't he just say he hadn't seen her since high school? "I didn't know you knew I wasn't."

"Yeah, a few years ago I ran into that old friend of yours. Hilary something. She told me you moved to Massachusetts."

Oh, gag. Hilary Porter, now Burton, was my best friend growing up. Then she one day confided in my crush about my ghostly abilities, and he stayed far away from me. It wasn't so much about him but that she squealed simply because she wanted him and didn't want him to want me. Then in college she started dating my archnemesis, Kevin Burton, and I just found out they got married the day I moved back to town.

"It was Connecticut, and I wouldn't believe anything Hilary has to say about me. We no longer speak."

Carly's brows pucker. "Oh, sorry."

I wave my hand like I'm pushing her words away. "It's nothing." Except it's still very much something.

"Well, this has been great," Enzo says, obviously anxious for me to leave so he can get back to...washing her clothes.

I can take a hint. "It's great seeing you. I'd love to catch up some time." Of all the girls Enzo's dated, and there have been only a handful, Carly was always my favorite.

She smiles wide. "That would be great. Enzo has my number."

I bet he does. Bow chicka bow wow. I jab a finger into my brother's shoulder. "Walk me to my car?"

Outside, I turn on him and squeal. "So you and she...?"

He shakes his head, but a smile teases the corner of his mouth. "We're just friends."

"Okay." I won't push it. For now. "So before I go spend the night alone, did you find out anything about that woman?"

His expression becomes gravely serious. "Yes. Stay away from there."

Goose bumps break out onto my arms. Oooh, this has to be good. "Why?"

"She's Deborah Young."

I frown. "Is that supposed to impress me? I'm clueless."

"Her father was Mitchell Young."

Still feeling unwowed.

"He was a criminal. He robbed a string of banks back in the seventies. He died in prison years ago."

Now that's interesting.

* * *

As soon as I step inside my apartment, I drop my purse on the floor and reach for my laptop. I make coffee while the slow piece of crap loads, and the coffeemaker drips its last drop when Google finally opens. I key in *Mitchell Young* and grab a beloved cup of joe.

Settling on the sofa, I click the first link, and Freezer Dude's face pops up. Holy creepiness!

The picture is much younger than I know him, but those piercing blue eyes are unmistakable.

Mitchell Young had quite the career. Similar to Clyde, just without a Bonnie. He was arrested for eight counts of armed robbery and the murder of a security guard at his last bank heist. He got sentenced for life without parole. When he went to prison, he had a wife and infant daughter. Deborah. He was in prison for ten years when a cellmate killed him.

He'd been shanked to death? No wonder he's so pissy and desperate to get out.

So what's his plan? To catch up with his daughter? He had to know she can't see or hear him.

I stare at his face on my screen. Even as a young man, he was scary looking.

CHAPTER SIX

Next day I get up early, shower, dress in a lime-green sweater, jeans, and combat boots with laces and buckles, and head over to Izzie's. Ma and Pop opened the deli today, and I have just enough time for a quick breakfast with my sister before I have to go in and slave away over the oil and vinegar salads and the never ending aroma of cured meats.

Izzie opens her door on my second knock. She's dressed in her thick pink bathrobe. It's untied at the waist. The belt long gone, probably in the same space as all the missing socks. Beneath it she has on a pair of blue-and-gray plaid pajama pants and a dingy white tee with a torn hem by the collar. Her hair is in a low, side ponytail. Or was. Most of it is loose and frames her face in a crazy halo effect.

"What are you doing here?" she asks.

"Good morning to you too, Sis. Can I come in?"

As soon as I step over the threshold, my niece Alice charges toward the door. Her light-brown hair whips around her face when she stops short. "Hi, Aunt Gianna. Bye, Aunt Gianna. Bye, Mom." Then she's out the door.

"She's running late," Izzie says and walks to the kitchen.

The bus stop is three blocks north. The junior high is in the East End, not far from the high school. Izzie's house is more in the center of town.

I follow Izzie through the living room and into the kitchen, where I stop short and mouth "whoa." It looks like a food bomb went off. The counters are littered with bread, mayo, a head of lettuce, deli meat packages, butter knives, a cereal bowl, mug, a couple of plates, and various other breakfast-slash-lunch making items. Izzie is usually immaculate, just like Ma.

Which totally drove me crazy growing up. So I'm a bit surprised, but I won't say anything. Maybe it's a pregnancy symptom.

She grabs the dishes and places them in the sink. "We woke up late. It's been a last-minute morning."

I sit at their round, oak table and pull a banana off its bunch. I peel the top half and bite off a chunk. "How are you feeling?"

Izzie grimaces at me. "Like I shouldn't watch you talk with mushed banana in your mouth."

I swallow hard. "Oops, sorry."

She puts away the lunch items. "And why are you here?" She directs a raised eyebrow my way. "Don't you normally sleep until about now? Is something going on?"

I wait until I fully chew and swallow my next bite before speaking. "With you feeling queasy, I've been a bit bored."

She smirks. "You need more than me as a friend."

Tell me about it.

She picks up a dishrag and wipes down the counter. "Do you want coffee? I'm on decaf, so that's all I can offer."

Oh, it suddenly makes perfect sense. I thought the morning sickness was the only reason for her extra grumpiness, but it's also the lack of caffeine. I totally understand too. I once tried kicking the habit. I lasted fifty-two hours before I ran to Dunkin' Donuts. Uphill. In the snow. It wasn't pretty. I'm pretty sure the guy behind the counter thought I was a junkie looking for a fix—in which case, I was—or about to hold up the store. Maybe both.

"Yeah, sure, I'll take a cup." And if the shakes start later, I'll grab some espresso to make up for this.

She grabs two clean mugs, pours coffee into each, and carries them over with milk, sugar, and a couple of spoons.

I dump two teaspoons into my cup, a dollop of milk, and stir. "So, guess who I saw last night?"

She takes a sip and sets her cup down with a shrug. "Julian. Pop. Lady Gaga."

"Ha, you're funny. No. Carly."

Izzie gets up, grabs the dishrag, and returns to the table. She scrubs at a reddish stain. "Who's that?"

I scoff. "Come on. Carly Walton. Dark blonde, green eyes, about yay tall." I hold my arm up as far as it'll go in my seated position. "A certain brother's ex."

Izzie stopped scrubbing when I said Walton. "Where did you see her?"

"At Enzo's. She was in his shower." I wiggle my brows as best as I can, but it's not as easy to do as one might think.

She turns and flings the rag across the room. Whoa. It whips through the air and whacks the wall above the sink, falling an inch shy of its spot. "They're back together?"

Dang. Why is she so angry? I'm now scared to answer. "Um, well, no, I don't think so. I don't know."

She puts her hands on her hips and narrows her eyes. "What do you know?"

Wow. She impersonates Ma perfectly with the arched brows, the cock of her head, and that tone.

I fill her in on what I saw and what Enzo told me last night. "So, it could all be innocent."

Izzie takes a deep breath and lets it out slowly. Then she sits back in her chair and sips her coffee. "Okay. That's good. Enzo's too smart to get involved again. I hope."

It takes me almost a full minute to get up the nerve to ask why my sister went all El Diablo on me a second ago.

She cocks her head toward me, and I grip the edge of my chair. "Don't you remember how much she hurt him when she dumped him?"

No. I shake my head. "I thought it was a mutual breakup."

"Oh, no." She gets up, goes to the cabinet beside the fridge, and takes down a box of Entenmann's chocolate-frosted donuts. Yum.

I pull a napkin from the pile in the center of the table.

"I guess you were too young to remember. Carly wanted more." She sets the box between us and lifts a donut out.

I grab one and set it on my napkin. As much as I want to sink my teeth into the chocolaty-vanilla goodness, this conversation is way more delicious. "More? They were high schoolers."

"That was the problem. Enzo planned on going to college and then joining the police academy, and Carly wanted something more exciting. She wanted them to get married and travel around Europe or some such fantasy." Izzie rips off a third of the donut in one bite.

"But Enzo wanted to be a cop since he was a kid. She had to know this."

She nods and swallows. "Exactly, so it shouldn't have been a surprise. But she acted like a brat. He suggested he get through college, and then he'd be willing to put the academy on hold for a few months for them to gallivant around Europe, but that wasn't good enough for her. She wanted it all right after graduation. And when he refused to change his life plans to accommodate her dreams—'cause really, how could a couple of barely adults afford her lavish trip—she dumped him. He was beside himself. He tried to not let it show, but you could see it all over his face and demeanor. And I once heard him crying in the bathroom."

Oh, poor Enzo. How dare she.

I stare at my donut and finally take a bite. Part of me instantly wants to kick Carly for how she treated my brother. But they were kids, and kids do stupid things. So do adults. I have not grown above stupidity yet, and I have a sneaking feeling I may never.

"Well, Enzo can take care of himself," I say not wanting to dump all over Carly either. My memories of her are fun and full of laughter. She didn't treat me like a kid sibling.

"I hope so, but I don't like it."

I raise one corner of my mouth. "Right now you don't like anything."

"True. But in my opinion, he needs to stay far away from her."

* * *

I leave Izzie's, go home, grab a bowl of sugary Cap'n Crunch's Peanut Butter Crunch to go with the sugary donut and coffee so they can all be sweet friends in my belly, and then head downstairs to my shift at the deli. The morning is especially busy. Maybe because we were closed yesterday, but I don't mind. It makes the time go by faster, which means I don't notice how bad my feet hurt from hours and hours of standing. Not until I go home and sit down.

In the middle of my day, shortly before Ma goes home and after Pop arrives, there's a small line in the store. A woman stares at the menu on the wall behind us, a young man in a suit waits for roast beef and Swiss on rye, and there's an older man who comes in every other day for a cup of tortellini salad. You'd think he'd buy a pound and come in less frequently. I think he has a crush on Ma.

Pop is slicing the roast beef, and I'm spooning the salad into a cup, when Ma goes into the kitchen to grab a tray of sausage, onions, and peppers. She returns and is humming "Do-Re-Mi" from *The Sound of Music*.

It immediately gets stuck in my head, and I start singing the words. "Doe, a deer, a female..."

Before long, Ma has joined in, and Pop is humming it. Roast beef guy belts out a couple of lines, and soon everyone in the joint is singing the chorus loudly and clearly.

Ma bumps hips with me. Pop grabs her hand and spins her before getting back to the sandwich. After our final note, which we hold extra long, we stare at one another and start laughing.

Pop hands over the man's sandwich.

"Thanks," the man says. "This is a great place. I'll be back."

Ma nudges me with her elbow. "Maybe we should add a karaoke machine for business."

I chuckle, assuming she's kidding, but when she doesn't laugh with me, I'm concerned. "I don't think that's a good idea. This isn't a bar, Ma. We don't want people lingering. Plus, there's no room." Not to mention it's completely bizarre.

She nods. "That's true."

The older man walks out with his tortellini and doesn't pay Ma any extra attention. I guess he isn't in lust. The woman orders a pound of the sausage, onions, and peppers. Ah, the persuasion of scent. If TV cooking shows had the ability to transmit scent, I firmly believe most people wouldn't leave their couches.

Ma pulls off her apron. "How is my son?" she asks me.

I eye a large shrimp in the tortellini salad that's calling my name. If I reach in and pop it into my mouth though, Ma will slap my hand, lecture me for the rest of my life, and keep an eye on me forever. Totally not worth it. "What do you mean?"

"You've been spending a lot of time with him," she says.

I nod, but I'm confused. I had two dinner dates with him this week, but our other hangouts were later in the evening, well after dinner, which Enzo usually has at Ma and Pop's. "Yeah, but you're acting like you don't see him. Doesn't he still eat over every night?"

"Not lately. He didn't show up for spaghetti last night."

I open my mouth to make some sexual comment about him and Carly, but I remember these are my parents. I can discuss anything with them except sex. I don't know what it is. My folks are awesome, but put a bird and a bee in the conversation, and I'm outta here. I had no problem when Ma told me about periods and lady parts, but I wouldn't listen to how babies were made or how to save myself for marriage.

Obviously none of the Mancini children have listened to the last part of that, although I'm pretty sure Pop still thinks I'm a virgin. Izzie had to tell me about sex, and by time she sat me down, I already knew. The internet has information on virtually everything.

"Well?" Ma asks with impatience in her tone.

I also think of what Izzie said about Carly. I don't know how my parents feel about her, and I don't want them worrying. "Um, he's fine. Works hard. Looks healthy. Too darn suspicious for me to scare."

She smiles, obviously pleased with my answer. She kisses my cheek. "Have a good day, dear."

After she gives Pop a peck on the mouth and leaves through the kitchen, Pop looks to me and says, "You'll find the opportunity to get him. He can't be on guard all the time."

Pop's wisdom is the best.

* * *

I get off work, go upstairs, shower, and have another few moments with the Cap'n. With a belly full of peanut-butter-nugget goodness, I head out and drive several blocks over to the police station. It's situated behind Town Hall and on the back side of the seedy part of town. The visitor parking area is small and not too far from the main doors. I park at the back of the lot, by a street lamp, and wait. Enzo should be off soon, and I want to catch him before his big date with my boyfriend.

I grab my cell to pass the time with a riveting game of Word Whomp. I love those little gophers. But my charge is down to thirty-eight percent, and I'd rather not kill my battery. So I toss it back into my bag and look at the radio. I don't have that much gas, and since money is low, I shouldn't waste it jamming to tunes. I also don't want to strain that battery either. My Kia isn't as young as she used to be, and I can't afford car parts.

I blow a raspberry in the air. How else can I pass the time? I open my glove compartment, but other than making art on napkins with packets of ketchup, I just have to sit here and entertain myself.

A line from "Do Re Mi" plays in my mind. My windows are up, so this is as good a time for singing at the top of my lungs as ever there has been. After two rounds of a needle pulling thread, I decide to switch the song. "Do You Want to Build a Snowman" comes to mind, but while young Anna is utterly adorable, the song is sad and makes me want to throat punch the *Frozen* parents. When I have kids, if my daughter can freeze things with one touch, I won't lock her up in her room. I'll get her help. And move to Antarctica. Or whatever parts of the world are still cold despite global warming.

Another fifteen minutes go by, and my throat is getting hoarse, and my toes are forming into icicles. I always thought global warming meant it would get warmer, not that Mother Nature was on crack. Whatever. I prefer the cold over the heat anyway. But I'm not ready for this quick of a shift from fall to winter. My cell says it's two minutes after five. What's taking my brother so long?

I open my door and step outside. Yeah, there's a slight breeze out here, but at least I can stomp around and try to keep warm. And I do just that. I stomp in a circle, as if I'm doing a rain dance.

A white sedan pulls in and parks up front. A woman and little boy get out. She stares at me while pulling open the door. It's a good thing I don't mind looking foolish. I'd fail miserably if I did.

I step on a rock bigger than a pebble but smaller than a breadbox and wince. Guess these boots aren't that great after all if I felt it through the sole. That's what I get for thinking I could save some by going to Payless. I know better. I kick the rock and watch it roll several inches away, into a small pile of foil wrappers. The kind from sticks of gum. A quick glance around to many other wrappers tells me that someone has an oral fixation and loves their Juicy Fruit or Wrigley's. I sometimes wonder if I have an oral fixation too. But I don't think pizza and Good Humor Strawberry Shortcake Dessert Bars qualify. And let's not forget sandwiches.

A dark blue pickup truck pulls in but parks over near a patrol car. The door opens, and Detective Kevin Burton gets out. Ugh, of all people I have to see today. He walks to the station and spots me about midway.

I stop my dance and consider jumping back into my car, but I don't want to look like a coward. I never want to give this jerkwad the impression he can rattle me. Once I do, he'll believe he's won our little war.

Last time he and I were face-to-face, he shoved me against the wall in my apartment and wrapped a hand around my throat. Then my super, mega-awesome ghostly friends scared the crap out of him. He ran out of my place with a scream I wish I had recorded for posterity.

He stops walking and just stands there for a second.

Please, don't come over here. Don't come over here.

Just then Enzo, my brother, my bro, my knight in shining armor, exists the station and notices both of us. He passes Kevin. They don't speak. Their dislike for one another is almost as thick as the hatred I have for Kevin.

Enzo crosses the parking lot to me, and Kevin finally goes inside.

I wrap my arms around myself and smile. "Thank you for coming out before he came over."

"I don't think he would have. Ever since that night at your place, he hasn't been as cocky as before. Not just with me but the other detectives too. I heard a couple of them talking about it. They think there are problems at home with his wife."

I roll my eyes. "You had to bring her up, huh?" Hilary is the second person I dislike most.

"Sorry. Why are you here? You know I have plans tonight."

I smirk. "I'm aware of your date. Are you meeting up, or is he picking you up?"

"Ha-ha, very funny. So what's going on? It's cold out here."

"Tell me about it. Okay, so first, Ma misses you. She wants you to continue stopping at her house every night and mooching dinner." I chuckle.

He stands there unaffected, obviously not finding me nearly as hilarious as I do.

"Second, have you heard anything else about the explosion?"

He shrugs. "Nothing more than I already mentioned. Why?"

"I met the fiancée the other night. She was rightfully inconsolable. I just thought some information might help her get through this."

He raises a brow. "Are you a grief counselor now?"

Hmm, counselor or a therapist. Would I be good at those jobs?

Ever since I returned home last month, I've been extremely aware of how lacking I am in the career department. Not that I need one, I guess. Izzie doesn't have one. She never wanted one. Her dreams were to get married and raise a family. She's doing that. Enzo loves being a cop. Ma and Pop run their own business, and even Julian is happy breaking the law and recreating crime scenes. Okay, in all fairness, helping his boss's clients sounds like a nice gig, if you forget about the illegal stuff.

So, will I be content just working at the deli? Probably not. But I'm also not in a rush to find something else.

"Is that all?" Enzo impatiently asks, sounding a bit like Ma.

Geesh, where's the fire? Does he need time to go home and beautify himself? I start to ask but figure I've made enough jabs at him tonight.

"That's it. But someone should clean up around here. It's a pigsty." I point to the gum wrappers.

"Have a good night, sis," he says before walking off to his Jeep.

You mean, have a boring night.

I get back into my car, turn it on, and crank up the heat. On my way home, I drive to Deborah's house. I don't know why. I doubt I'll see anything worth seeing, but it feels right. I park in front of the house before hers but don't turn the car off. I won't be here long.

A light is on in the front room to the right. Does she live alone? How does she feel about her father? Uh, Gianna, you're talking to yourself again. If I don't make a friend soon, I need to find a hobby.

I put the car in drive and start to take my foot off the brake.

"Why are you here?" asks a deep voice behind me.

I jump and nearly drive onto the sidewalk. I glance in my rearview mirror, and seated in my backseat is Freezer Dude.

CHAPTER SEVEN

———

I turn at Deborah's corner and drive. I have no idea where I'm going. I'm barely paying attention to the stop signs and lights, let alone my location. I'm way too busy keeping my gaze between the road and the master of creepiness in my backseat. I just couldn't stay by his daughter's house, in the middle of a strange, dark street. I want to be near people and light, even if no one can see my passenger.

Goose bumps have taken permanent residence on my arms and along the back of my neck. I've never been afraid of ghosts in the past, but this one definitely knows how to chill a person through and through. Problem is, most ghosts don't have beefs with me. They are either confused and don't know they're dead, or maybe they do but haven't gotten around to moving on yet. Then there are the ones that need some help before passing. Like Thomas Sterling.

The common denominator with all of them is that I'm just a mediator. With Freezer...uh, Mitchell Young, though, we have a past relationship. That makes this a bit more personal. Plus, those eyes are just terrifying.

"What do you want?" I ask him.

"I want to know why you were at that house." He suddenly disappears.

Oh my God, is he gone?

He reappears beside me, in my passenger seat.

Darn.

"Well?" he asks. "Do you know the woman who lives there?"

"You mean your daughter, Deborah?" There's no sense in playing coy. "No, I don't know her."

He narrows his gaze. "Then how do you know her name?"

"Google." I turn onto States Avenue and then realize he's frowning. "Oh yeah, you don't know about the internet, huh? Well, I'd explain it all, but I'd rather hear about why you're here. And no, I don't mean in my car. Why did you come back over from the other side?"

He smirks. "I wasn't ready to die. Why shouldn't I come back?"

That makes sense, but most people don't have the choice. What makes him so special?

"When you died but didn't cross over, I knew I would find a way home," he says.

He's been waiting and scheming all of this time? That's so determined and creepy. A healthy dose of fear settles in my chest. I spot lit-up stores a couple of blocks ahead and drive toward them.

"That was eighteen years ago." My voice shakes, and I pray he doesn't notice. I don't want him to know I'm scared. The tough girl act usually keeps people on their toes.

"I didn't know that much time had gone by until I was on this side." His tone sounds sullen.

"Were you hoping to find your daughter still as a child, to reconnect with her?"

He doesn't respond.

That must mean I'm right. And it's such a sweet move, or it would be if he wasn't dead.

"So now what? She can't see you. You can't do much. Why not just move on?"

His face scrunches up into an angry scowl. "Because I'm not done. My life was stolen from me, and that's not fair."

I stop at a traffic light. "Life isn't fair, buddy. Do you think I want to be able to see ghosts? That talking to the dead is fun for me? I would love to be normal."

Okay, so that's a lie, but no one ever said the rules include telling ghosts the truth. Sure, normal is great. It's normal. And seeing ghosts has its drawbacks, especially when they're ex-cons. But I like being able to help some of them move on.

Maybe I *should* consider being a counselor. Then I'd get paid for helping people. And maybe I could afford boots from a slightly more expensive store, like Marshall's, instead.

The light changes, and I drive down the next block.

"What's your plan now?"

"Does it matter? You have no say in what I do or if I stay."

A car darts out of the shopping center, and I almost have to slam on my brakes.

"Watch where you're going, buddy," I shout.

Mitchell snickers. Ugh, calling him by an actual name is weird, and it makes him feel human. Not only is that no longer the case, technically, he's too creepy. Freezer Dude suits him better.

"At least I know I can't die if you crash. Women drivers still suck no matter what decade," he says.

I scoff. "Screw you. At least I can eat hot dogs and...and have sex."

I immediately hear the connection of the two and realize my mind's in the gutter. I shake the thoughts away and focus on what he could possibly want. What all ghosts want. "Would you like me to give a message to your daughter?"

"Is that what you think? That I'll peacefully cross over as soon as you tell Debbie I love her? Do you think I'm that pathetic?"

Well, since he's asking.

I make a right turn into the strip mall and realize it's the one next to Izzie's doctor. I must've driven here on subconscious autopilot. I pull into a spot, put the car in park, and turn off the engine. Enough of the stores are still open that if I need, I can run inside and get help. That doesn't make complete sense. How can a regular person help me with a ghost? But the thought makes me feel safer.

"Then what? You're just going to hang around her place until she grows old and dies?" I don't like being crude with the dearly and nearly departed. It makes me sad to know they'll never hug their loved ones or eat Fettuccini Alfredo again. But this guy is neither dear nor near, so I don't mind adjusting my attitude.

He looks out the windshield and seems to be lost in thought.

There is a dozen or so cars in the parking lot. A car pulls in beside mine, and a woman with a teen boy get out. They head to CVS. As they reach the door, a man opens it from the inside and lets them enter before he walks out. He holds a small bag, the size that only a greeting card fits in. It must be someone's birthday or anniversary.

I'm so lost in watching the Card Guy that I don't notice Freezer Dude has turned toward me until Card Guy walks past my car. I flinch when I notice Freezer Dude's creepy, wide smile. He's a pro at that bone-chilling expression. I bet he was an excellent convict—great at keeping other prisoners in line.

"Don't worry about my plans. They have nothing to do with you. And stay out of my way." He shouts the last sentences so loud I lean back against my door.

Then he shimmies out of my Kia through the passenger door and stands on the pavement. In a split second he rises and dives into Card Guy.

"Crap!"

Card Guy shudders and shakes, and he looks like he's going to crumble to the ground. I want to run out and help him. I remember all too clearly how scary the experience is, but what can I do? Hold his card for him?

Then Freezer Dude jumps or is thrown out and manically laughs as he glides past my car.

I turn in my seat and watch him go, hoping he'll stay away from me for the rest of tonight. Maybe I should help all ghosts except him. But with all of his body hopping, I'm afraid he may hurt someone. What if the next time he body jumps, it's in a person crossing a busy street or driving a car? He can kill someone. Is it possible that's what he wants? Some sort of revenge on those who are still living? I certainly believe he's capable of pettiness and bitterness.

Card Guy gets into his car and peels out of the parking lot. He may have nightmares tonight.

I turn my key in the ignition and see movement from the corner of my eye. Up ahead, standing in the doorway to Mystic Aurora's is Mystic Aurora. Her mouth is open, her jaw practically lying on her chest, and her eyes are wide like she saw a ghost.

Oh, shoot. She saw the ghost.

* * *

I try to get Mystic Aurora to unlock her door and talk to me, but she backs away and hides in the store. I pull a deli brochure out of my purse, add my cell to the back, and stick it in the door as far as it will go. These brochures are sure coming in handy.

I go back to my car and sit there for a minute, hoping she'll take the brochure, and it doesn't blow away. If I start getting crank calls I'll know she didn't get it. She doesn't come forward, so I decide to leave. This has been a crazy evening, and now I don't mind being friendless. Spending the rest of the night in front of the TV sounds like an awesome plan.

When I pull into the small parking lot behind the deli, though, there is Julian's black SUV. What's he doing here? I park and step out of my car. Julian is by my side immediately.

I shut my door and lock it. "What are you doing here? Aren't you supposed to be with Enzo?"

"He canceled. Said something came up."

More like he rose up around his ex. Ha-ha, I'm so goofy. "So you thought you'd come here?"

"I wanted to make sure you believe that I had nothing to do with that explosion or the people associated with it."

He's been worried I don't believe him? How sweet. "I believe you. Do you want some coffee?"

"Sure." His lecherous smile makes me slightly regret my offer. Things were much easier before I knew what he did for a living.

I lead the way up and go straight to the coffeemaker. He makes himself at home by removing his jacket and stretching out on the sofa.

"Are you hungry?" I ask and open my fridge, not sure what I'll make if he says yes. Packets of cold cuts and a couple of pounds of salads sit on the top second shelf between the eggs and fresh broccoli. None of that was in there this morning.

Ma likes to sneak up here, although she'd probably say it isn't sneaking since she owns the place, and stock my kitchen like a food fairy. She's awesome. She loves to feed people, and I love to eat. We're a fantastic pair.

"I could eat. Do you plan on making a sandwich?"

The desire in his tone makes me turn and study him. His brows are raised, and he looks very hopeful. I laugh and turn back to the fridge. "Sure. Turkey or pastrami?"

"Pastrami."

That's my choice too. I grab the Swiss cheese, an onion, mayo, and hot sauce, 'cause I like things spicy. Too bad I wasn't downstairs. I could use the panini press. I could run down. Nah, I'm too lazy.

As I slice and then sauté the onions, we're quiet. I hum "Let it Go" because I now have the soundtrack of the movie *Frozen* stuck in my head, and when I look up, Julian is smiling at me.

I wag my wooden spoon at him. "Don't look at me like that."

"Like what?" he asks and stands up.

I stop shaking and point the spoon at him. "Stay where you are."

He chuckles and keeps putting one foot in front of the other. "Why?"

"You know why." My voice cracks.

He's right in front of me. Dang, this apartment is too small. I take a step back, but it does no good. I'm up against the counter between the fridge and stove with nowhere to go but forward. And that's where he is in his dark jeans and black tee, with bulges in all the right places. Those damn bulges.

"God, I hate you."

His smile deepens. "Do you?"

I know what's coming. My body knows what's coming. I like to pretend I don't want him this close, but deep down and even not so deep down, it's not true. I want him near me, on me, inside me all the time. But once we cross that line, I know everything will get more muddled in my head. And while I love him like he's a piece of me, I still haven't come to terms with his job.

He leans down. His breath tickles my ear. His lips graze my neck. "Do you still hate me now?"

I giggle and push at his chest.

Julian stands upright and glances to my right. "The onions are burning."

I turn quickly and sure enough they're blackening at the edges. I didn't put enough extra-virgin olive oil in the skillet. I move the pan off the burner and push the onions around to see if I can use them.

"Look at what you did," I say playfully.

"I am not responsible for your horniness."

"Mine?" I wag my spoon at him again. When I look back to the stove, there's a man standing between me and the burnt onions.

I flinch and yelp. It's Thomas.

"Did you burn yourself?" Julian asks, suddenly serious.

"What are you doing here?" I ask Thomas. "I thought you moved on."

"Who are you talking to?" Julian asks. "Oh. Your new friend."

Thomas's eyes are bugged out. "You have to help her."

"Help who?" I ask.

"Serena. Please. She's thinking of taking pills. Hurry."

* * *

Julian insists we take his car. I have no complaints. He's much better, calmer, under pressure. My hands immediately start trembling, and I feel like I'm floating out of my body. Maybe counseling isn't the best choice. What if a patient has a breakdown? Will I freak out alongside him?

Thomas is in the backseat looking as spacey as I feel. He's trying to tell me what happened, but it's not making a lot of sense.

Julian rolls down my window, and a gust of cold wind attacks my face. "It helps clear the mind," he says.

Yes, he knows me well.

"Okay, Thomas, start again. From the beginning," I say.

"I've been with Serena since you left my place."

I repeat Thomas's words to Julian as he speeds to the East End.

"But I thought you said you were going to move on."

"I couldn't. She was distraught, and I love her."

I glance at Julian's profile. I don't think I could do it either. "Okay, so what about the pills?"

"She went into the bathroom, opened the medicine cabinet, and took out an old bottle of ibuprofen. She stared at them weirdly, like her gaze was out of focus and she was trying to figure out what they were. She went into the bedroom and put them on the nightstand. Then she sat on the edge and said, 'I love you, Thomas. I'll be with you soon.' I came to get you. Can he drive any faster?"

"Not if you want us to live long enough to help Serena."

Julian almost passes Thomas's street and has to make a hard right. I brace myself with a hand on the roof of the car and the other on the side of Julian's seat.

"Sorry about that," Julian says.

"Shouldn't we just call the ambulance?" I ask. "They'd be quicker and are prepared for this sort of thing."

Julian gives me a quick glance. "If she hasn't taken the pills, though, what are you going to say? A ghost told you she was planning on it?"

He has a point.

"I can go ahead and see if she has," Thomas says.

"No," I shout before he tries to disappear. "I don't remember how to get there, and we don't want to waste time keying the address into the GPS."

Thomas nods, then points ahead. "It's right there. I'm going in."

I tell Julian which house belongs to Thomas and hold on as he comes to a stop. I open my door, jump down, and run to the front door. What if it's locked? How the heck are we going to get in?

Julian's right by my side, and sure enough the door is locked. I lay my hand flat on the glass and bang. If I can't get Serena's attention, I can at least get Thomas to tell me what's going on.

"I'll look out back," Julian says and runs around the house.

I continue banging and hope the neighbors don't call the cops. Actually, that won't be a bad thing.

Finally, Thomas appears by my side. "She took them. Do something." His voice sounds tinny, and if ghosts could cry I have no doubt he'd be balling.

I pull out my phone and dial 9-1-1. I give the address and mine and Serena's names. When I hang up, Julian rejoins me.

"I found an opening. Come on."

I follow him around back to a kitchen window. It's a small one and kinda high. Without words, Julian cups his hands beneath it.

I look from his hands to the window and to his face. "You want me to squeeze through there? I won't make it."

"Sure you will. Try."

I guess I shouldn't debate whether or not I'm too thick to fit through a window in order to save a woman. I place one booted foot in Julian's hands and then bounce up on the other. The last time I broke into a house through the window, Izzie was with me. We were sneaking into Enzo's to scare him. Izzie pushed me up and smacked my head on the window frame. Julian's touch is gentler.

A counter with a juicer is beneath the window. I manage to make it in without knocking it onto the floor. Success. I hurry to the back door and unlock it, and then I unlock the front for the paramedics. Julian and I race upstairs and find Serena in the master bedroom lying on top of Thomas's red comforter.

Julian picks up her arm and presses two fingers to her pulse. Does he know CPR and first aid too? I have no idea. He may know me, but how much do I know him? I push the sad thought away and sit beside Serena.

Thomas floats behind me. "Is she still alive?"

Her eyelids flutter. "She's still awake."

Thomas breathes a sigh of relief. "Now just stay that way," he whispers.

Sirens sound and get closer with each second.

Julian walks to the door. "I'll go down and meet the paramedics."

I nod and lean close to Serena. "Can you hear me? Stay with us. Thomas wants you alive. He loves you and can't lose you like this."

She stirs but doesn't say anything. I have no idea if she can hear me.

"You fight this, and I promise I'll do what I can to help you."

Footsteps thunder upstairs. Julian enters the room first. Behind him is my brother-in-law, Paulie, and his partner, Harry. Oh my, Harry. I met him when I first moved into my apartment. We shamelessly flirted. That was back when Julian and I were broken up, before I knew he moved to town.

I get up and step back, out of the way.

Paulie hurries around the bed and picks up the empty pill bottle. "Gianna, what happened?"

"I'm not really sure. I stopped by to check in on her, and we found her like this." I glance at Julian in my peripheral.

Harry smiles at me and gives me a very quick body check. His smile is lecherous. "Nice to see you again, Sally."

Oh gosh, this isn't really the time or place.

"Sally?" Julian whispers.

"Not now," I say and pray he'll forget to ask me again later. I don't want to explain how I introduced myself to Harry as Sally, the whole time thinking of the fake orgasm scene in the movie *When Harry Met Sally*. Julian and I were over, but it's not something I want to admit.

When they have Serena in the ambulance, Thomas corners me by the front door. "Did you mean it?" he asks.

"Mean what?"

"That you'll help her."

I sigh, not wanting to get involved with another homicide. It's murder on the stress level. No pun intended. But after tonight, I don't have much of a choice. I can't just let this go. Plus, I always follow through on a promise.

"Yeah, I'll help find your killer."

His expression turns to one of confusion. "I thought you were going to watch her, keep an eye on her, become her friend. You know, so she doesn't take any more pills. So she realizes she has people who care."

Is he serious? I'm not a shrink.

"Serena may need professional help for that. I'm not promising to babysit her, but I do promise to get to the bottom of this all."

Here I go again.

CHAPTER EIGHT

Here's the thing about solving a murder. Since this is my second, and the first almost concluded with a permanent shovel indent in my skull, sleeping is futile. Yep, I've learned that tossing and turning is the way to spend those seven to eight hours per night because my head is too full of what-ifs.

What if helping Serena causes her more harm? What if I uncover some deep secret that destroys lives? What if I screw it all up? What if I die this time?

That last one should keep me huddled under my pink paisley comforter for a week, but my bladder needs to be relieved, so while I'm up I may as well stay that way.

I do the usual morning routine: washing up, applying winged eyeliner, mascara, blush, and a nude-tone matte lipstick, dressing in the most comfortable, clean clothes I can find, adding silver hoop earrings and a charm bracelet, and drinking a fishbowl-size mug of coffee. The matte lipstick comes in handy here. No stain on my favorite mug, and no reapplying the color. Today I decide to grab some food too since I need to go play sleuth and then head to work later, and I'm not sure if I'll have time to eat in between.

I make a quick call to find out which room Serena is in at the hospital, and the rather cold-sounding woman informs me she's in 714 and that visiting hours are from 11:00 to 8:00. That means I have some time to kill, so I turn on the laptop and Google Freezer Dude again. I don't learn anything new though. Then I search for Thomas Sterling and the Sterling Company.

Turns out that Thomas Senior, the father, died eight years ago from a heart attack. The company...everything was left to his wife and son. Mrs. Sterling lives in Lido Beach, the next town over, and surprisingly, there are no pictures of any of them. Not the parents or Thomas, the son. That's strange. How can such a wealthy family not have their picture snapped? Are they not famous enough for the paparazzi to care?

Weird thoughts spring into my mind. Like are they on the run from organized crime and in the witness protection program? Maybe they're spies and don't reveal their identity in fear of being recognized by the other side.

I chuckle and keep searching. There's one photo from Thomas Senior's funeral. But it's at an angle where I can't make out faces. I assume the woman in front is Mrs. Sterling, but she has her face in her hand, sobbing, and there are several men huddled around her. One of them could be Thomas, but it's hard to tell. With a sigh, I turn off the laptop and check the time. If I drive slowly, I'll arrive at South Shore Beach Memorial just in time.

I head to the hospital and have to park way too far from the entrance. The air is slightly muggy, and it smells like rain. This time of year is known for it, so it's not a big surprise. I just wish I remembered to buy an umbrella. My last one was cheap and broke during a windstorm last spring.

I smile at the security guard seated behind his desk. Dark hair and eyes, a buzz cut, and a friendly smile. He's cute.

The elevators are around the bend, and I hit seven when I step inside.

Once on her floor, I have to pass the nurse's station to get to Serena's room. A woman in light blue scrub pants and a white, blue, and green floral top stands behind the desk, reading a clipboard. She doesn't acknowledge me, but she had to hear my squeaky rubber-soled sneakers on the highly polished tile. I'm extremely grateful when I pass by, and she doesn't call out to me, wondering where I'm going. I don't know if she's the one I spoke to earlier, but in case, I'd rather not withstand her chill.

The room is at the end of the hall, directly facing me. The interior is dim. The lights are off, but the TV in the far corner is on low. The first bed is empty, and the curtain between it and the next is drawn. I peek around it, and Serena's asleep in the bed closest to the windows. At least I think she's asleep.

There's a woman in pink scrubs seated in the chair, staring at the television. She gives a small start when she sees me. I wasn't expecting her, so I'm sure I look surprised too.

"Hi," I say. "How is she doing?"

"Are you family?" Her expression becomes stern. She's not giving out information to strangers. She knows her HIPAA laws.

"I'm a friend. I'm the one who found her last night and called the paramedics."

She smiles. "Good thing she has friends like you. She will be fine. At least physically."

Yeah, no need to add that it's her mental state that may need curing. Or her broken heart.

I move closer to the bed. Both side rails are up, in case she falls out. She looks so peaceful. So still. So dead.

The woman stands and moves away from the chair, so I can sit. "I can't leave though," she says. "Twenty-four-hour watch for anyone who attempts suicide."

Oh, wow, that's a sucky job.

I nod and stare at the chair. I'm suddenly not so sure I want to stay, to watch her while she sleeps, and I don't want to wake her. She doesn't know me. Maybe sleep is exactly what she needs right now. "I'll come back another time."

The woman nods and offers a slight smile.

I thank her and head back to the elevators. Now what? Where else can I get information about Serena and who would plant a bomb in her house? There's the friend, Zoe. I can drive by her place and see what she knows. I mentally smack my forehead. No, that won't work. I know the building she lives in but not which apartment. Thomas never told me, and I doubt he'll appear if I call out his name. Ghosts are unreliable that way.

I walk across the parking lot to my car. What about their job? Maybe Zoe's there. I glance at my phone. I have two hours before I need to be at the deli. Just enough time to nose around a restaurant. Of course, the luck of the day may have the place closed. I Google the address anyway.

I park across the street from Sparks, and run across the busy street to the shiny green painted entry doors. Sure enough, it is closed. According to the sign hung in a side window, the place opens after four. No lunch. And Mondays they are closed all day. Great. But before I brave the traffic on Park Place and get back in my car, I notice a couple of women dressed in heels and miniskirts heading to the side of the building. I decide to follow.

The back door to the restaurant is held open by a brick. The women walk in. They must work here.

I step over the threshold and immediately feel blinded. The area is so dim it takes almost a full minute for my eyes to adjust.

When they do, a man steps out of nowhere and slaps me on the chest. It knocks the breath out of me. What the...?

"That way," he shouts and points to a hallway up ahead. Just as fast, he walks off, and I'm left confused, angry, and possibly bruised.

Gosh, that hurt.

I look down and realize he wasn't hitting me for his sheer enjoyment. He slapped a sheet of paper to my top. It's white with a big black number. Three. That just adds to my confusion, but I decide to follow his instructions to see what's going on. I step into the hallway and head toward the light.

Yeah, that's not really funny in my line of hobbies. But it is accurate.

Voices sound closer, and there's a bright, shining light up ahead. I pass a kitchen, which is dark and empty, and another couple of shut doors. When I reach the end, I'm in the main dining room. Straight ahead are tables and more tables. To the right of me are the women from outside and a small stage. A man is polishing glassware behind the bar, which sits on the other side of the room, and seated across from the stage are a couple.

The woman has jet-black hair, cut up to her chin, with full bangs. Her dark purple lipstick looks amazingly good on her tanned complexion. Beside her, the man is slightly older with graying temples. His dark hair is thick and short, and a thick mustache makes me think of Tom Selleck. Ma enjoyed some show he was in.

Voices sound behind me, and a handful of women sprint down the hall to our location. Each of them have been slapped with a number. Four stands behind me.

"Any time now," the man at the table says.

The first woman steps onto the stage, hands a sheet of paper to another man at the piano—the piano I just noticed—and walks over to the microphone. What's going on? The piano man strikes the first chord, and chills explode throughout my limbs as the woman sings her first note. Not because her singing is bad. It's pretty good in fact. But because I realize I'm about to audition. To sing. To share my flat notes and off-pitchiness to the world. Or at least this room.

How on earth do I get myself into these situations?

I turn, ready to book the heck out of here, but Five, Six, and Seven are blocking the doorway. I hear finger snapping and turn to see the woman staring at me. She points to all of us and then to the tables behind her.

The women scramble to take seats, and this is the perfect moment to run. I take one step and stop. This is what I wanted though. Well, actually, I was hoping to just talk to Zoe. Not entertain. But I haven't run away screaming yet. Even though I came here to chat, this is an opportunity to get to know the people in Serena's life. What's the chance Zoe will spill something helpful? She probably doesn't know anything. And if she does, who says she'll share it? The best way to learn intel is directly—to infiltrate the people and places with the knowledge. Julian taught me that. I doubt I'll get a singing gig, but I should at least try. When I fail miserably, I can then apply to be a server. The great thing is they're open at night, and it won't interfere with my deli job. And I can't say no to extra income. I gather my courage and head to a table.

Before I have time to develop a plan, the first two girls finish, and it's my turn.

"Three," shouts the man, sending waves of panic through my body.

I stand up and walk to the stage, careful to not bump into the tables and chairs. And considering my nerves, they're not easy to avoid. As I climb the stairs, all I can think about is projectile vomiting and covering the front row à la Linda Blair in *The Exorcist*. But that's not exactly the best thought to have in mind while needing to open your mouth, so I push it away and think of puppies. They're small, cute, and man's best friend.

When I reach the standing microphone, I pull my thoughts together and find a spot above everyone's heads that's in the shadows. I can concentrate on that and pretend I'm in the shower.

"Do you have sheet music?" says a voice to my side.

I swallow hard and regrettably look away from my spot to the voice. It's the pianist, and he's staring at me hard.

"No," I whisper and stare at the bald spot on the top of his head. It beats looking him in the eye because acknowledging I'm not alone makes my stomach gurgle more.

"What are you going to sing? Maybe I know it.'

I think of Ma's love of musicals. I know them all by heart because of her, but there are so many choices, my brain becomes fuzzier.

"If you're not going to sing, you need to leave the stage," says the man in the audience. He turns and whispers something to the woman.

I straighten my back and shake my head once, bouncing my curls before my eyes. No, I'm going to do this. To the pianist, I say, "Do you know 'Shake It Off' by Taylor Swift?"

Hey, what can I say? Ma may love her Broadway hits, but I'm definitely a pop girl.

He strikes several keys, and the upbeat chords fill the room.

I turn to the mic, stare at the shadow, open my mouth, and sing the first line. Then the next. And before I know it, the first verse is out, and I haven't lost my voice or this morning's breakfast.

When I reach the first chorus, I spot movement and look away from the shadow to the audience. Numbers four through seven are dancing in their seats. I smile and don't miss a beat. Soon my nerves dissolve, and I pull the microphone out of its stand.

As soon as I sing about being lightning on my feet, my feet start moving on their own—left to right and back again. When I reach the spoken verse, numbers five and six say it with me.

The man glances back at them, and they immediately shut up, but I ignore it all and continue having a blast. By time I sing my last note, my heart is pumped, there's a line of perspiration on my forehead, and I need a cold beverage.

"Thank you," says the man. "Leave us your résumé. Number Four."

That's it?

I glance to the pianist who's smiling and place the microphone back in its stand. I kinda wanted a "great job" or even "you suck." Some kind of opinion. But they hadn't given one to the girl before me, so I guess I shouldn't be disappointed. I return to my seat and grab my purse. I glance up at Number Five who gives me a thumbs up, and I notice she's holding sheet music and a picture of herself. The big, glossy kind that actors bring to auditions. They want a résumé. Crap.

I dig through my purse and find another deli brochure. It'll have to do. I grab a pen and write my cell number and name on the back. Then, so they remember me, I add the song title. I hand it to the very confused man and make a beeline for the door. If they don't call, I'll have to just shake it off.

* * *

A few hours later, I'm behind the deli counter humming that song and scooping chopped salad into a half-pound plastic container. Chopped salad is something Izzie and I created years ago. We thought it was completely original, but then several years after that, I saw something similar online. So maybe we weren't that unique after all.

Sick and tired of Ma's usual lettuce, cucumber, and tomato variety, we went about dicing celery, carrots, black olives, green olives, avocado, red onion, radishes, and zucchini and added it to thinly shredded Romaine lettuce. Tossed together with a balsamic vinaigrette, it became a hit for the entire summer. Even Ma, Pop, and Enzo devoured it. I never thought Ma would add it to the deli's menu.

I ring up the cup of salad with a proud smile and thank the young woman after she pays.

The bell above the door rings, and I turn to see Carly walk in. My smile widens.

She's wearing jeans, sneakers, and a red sweater. Her blonde hair flows over her shoulders, and she looks about as happy as I feel. "Hi," she says and bounces over to me on the balls of her feet.

"Hey, what are you doing here?"

"I was hoping I could convince you to go out dancing tonight." She tugs the side of her bottom lip in between her teeth.

I wrinkle up my nose. "As in the third wheel on a date with you and Enzo?"

She giggles. "No, we're not dating."

I distinctly hear a *yet* at the end of her sentence.

"Just you and me."

Before I get a chance to respond, Ma walks out from the kitchen. Her blank expression immediately hardens at seeing Carly. Damn.

"Mrs. Mancini, how are you?" Carly must not notice the slight foaming of Ma's mouth because her tone remains perky.

"Carly, what are you doing here?" Ma practically growls the words.

Carly's smile flattens.

I step up because it's not fair the way Ma sometimes morphs into the protective mama bear role. "We're going out tonight. Isn't it great, Ma? You keep telling me to find a life."

Ma raises a solitary eyebrow. "I mean with Julian."

I roll my eyes. Beggars can't be choosy.

"Oooh, do you have a boyfriend?" Carly asks. "Any pictures?" She wiggles her brows, and Ma turns away with a scoff.

I'm torn between getting Carly out of here as fast as possible (who knows what Ma might say about the past?) and whipping out my phone and showing the pic of Julian fresh from the shower, that I took when I first moved into his apartment in

Connecticut. 'Cause the man is super sexy and needs to be displayed."

Ma huffs as she slams the lid on a display case, so Carly's safety wins out.

"I'll show you tonight," I say. "Where do you want to go?"

"How about D'Angelo's in Island Park? I can pick you up around nine."

"Sure. That sounds great."

She leans closer and whispers, "Are you living at home?"

I smirk at the idea of her being afraid to drive to Ma's, as she should be from the looks of Ma's glare. "No, I live in the apartment upstairs. Just pull in back, and I'll meet you down there."

"Sounds great. See you later." She starts to leave then stops and turns back. "Good-bye, Mrs. Mancini. It was nice seeing you again." Carly doesn't wait for a reply before walking out, which is just as well since Ma grunts.

I place a hand on my right hip and turn to my mother. "You were rude. All my life you scolded us if we were rude, and you now need a scolding." Not that I plan on giving her one. She is still Ma, and I know where to draw the line.

Ma's mouth is pursed tightly, but as the bell rings again, it relaxes into a smile. Carly obviously hasn't returned. "Julian," she says in a singsong voice.

I turn, and my breath hitches. He's dressed in regular old black jeans, a tan sweater, leather jacket, and black boots—nothing special—but my body involuntarily reacts just the same. My pulse quickens, my face heats up, and so do other regions of my anatomy.

Ma rushes around the counter and opens her arms for a hug.

Julian wraps his arms around her and gives her a kiss on the cheek. "You look as stunning as ever, Mrs. Mancini."

She giggles and swats his arm. I want to vomit at how much she likes him. It would be cuter if she wasn't so obviously trying to keep us together. I bet she's plotted out the names of our kids already.

"What did I say about you calling me Ma? And you'll be coming to dinner tomorrow, right?" she says as she steps back around the counter.

"Absolutely, Ma. I wouldn't miss it for anything." Then to me, he says, "Hi." It comes out low and slow and sexy, and my insides melt. Damn his ease at casual flirting.

"Hi," I say wanting to sound nonchalant, but I hiccup halfway through.

He steps over and leans on the counter in front of me so we're the same height and can look into one another's eyes without me straining my neck. He's thoughtful that way.

"Are you hungry?" I ask.

His gaze roams down my body, and his eyes go from light gray to steel.

Warmth creeps up my neck because Ma is close enough for her to see.

He must realize this because he shakes his head and looks away for a moment. "I was hoping you'd have dinner with me tonight."

Ma huffs and walks past me and into the kitchen.

"I can't. I'm going dancing."

He stands straight. "With who?" His tone has an edge to it. Is he jealous? How cute.

"An old friend."

He quirks a brow.

I can't help but smile because I know he's so off base. "An old female friend. Enzo's high-school girlfriend, to be exact. I'll see you tomorrow though."

He nods but doesn't look as satisfied as when he first walked in.

CHAPTER NINE

I wipe perspiration off the back of my neck with a cocktail napkin and then sip my ice water. Despite Carly being our designated driver, I don't feel like drinking.

D'Angelo's is a weird dance club the next town over. Weird because it's so bare, with a long bar at one end, up near the doors, and then nothing but white walls and speakers for the rest. It's so physically unappealing that I don't understand how they've stayed in business for over a decade. But every time I've been here—and it's been years—it's jam packed with sweaty, gyrating bodies. Like now.

"Are you pooped out already?" Carly shouts over the house music.

We've been dancing for the past twenty minutes, and I need a moment to sit. "Yes. I'm not twenty-one anymore."

She laughs. "You make it sound like you're fifty. You're not even thirty yet."

She doesn't know about my passion for Cheetos and sitting around doing nothing.

A petite girl who doesn't even look eighteen turns to us. She holds an unlit cigarette between the fingers of her right hand. "Do either of you have a light?"

We shake our heads. "Sorry," Carly says. "I quit."

As the girl walks off, I say, "That's right. I vaguely recall walking in our backyard one day and smelling smoke. You and Enzo were back there, and he told me that if I told Ma, he'd put spiders in my bed." What an awesome brother.

Carly chuckles. "I remember that. He wasn't always nice to you."

"You think? I'm still trying to get even."

"That's what you were doing in his bathroom. Trying to scare him? I can't believe you guys still do that."

I shrug. "Yeah, it's become routine. So was quitting smoking as hard as they say?"

She widens her eyes. "Oh yeah. I started at sixteen and only stopped a couple of months ago. It is the hardest thing I've ever done."

I'm very glad I never started.

The song changes, and I consider going back in for another dance, but Carly sets her drink on the bar right beside mine and jumps off her stool. "I gotta go to the bathroom. I'll be right back."

I turn back to my water as she hurries off.

A couple of young women step to the bar, around Carly's stool, and order drinks.

One of them glances at me, looks away, and then turns back and stares at me. "I know you," she says. Her words slur, so this round obviously isn't her first.

"Do you?" She's probably come into the deli, but unless you're a regular, I don't always remember faces. She has straight, black hair that almost reaches her waist and liquid dark eyes. She's slender and petite and wears a white minidress with spaghetti straps and three layers of fringe that shimmer when she moves. It looks amazing against her deep olive complexion.

She grins, and it lights up her whole face. "'Shake it Off' today at Sparks."

Oh gosh, she witnessed my humiliation. "You saw?"

I must look as horrified as I feel because she giggles. "Yeah. I work there and heard you as I came in. You were good."

I sit a bit straighter. "Really?"

"Oh yeah. And everyone seemed to enjoy it. Sparks is a great place to work, and Natalia, the owner, is really fair."

That must've been the woman in the audience. "Great to know. Thanks. I'm Gianna, by the way."

"I'm Zoe."

It feels like the floor pulls away, and my body is free falling for a moment.

Zoe looks to her friend, who's frowning at me. Zoe asks me, "Are you okay? You suddenly don't look so good."

I blink and refocus. "Oh, sorry. I'm just surprised. You're Serena's friend, right? I...uh..." I'm not sure how close they are or if she knows about last night. And I don't know if Serena wants her to know, so I keep hush about it. "I worked for Thomas for a short period of time."

Her mouth turns down. "It's horrible what happened."

The bartender approaches and hands her and her friend a drink. She gives him money and tells him to keep the change. Then there's this awkward silence where the friend is nudging her along.

This isn't the time to grill her, so I say, "Well, it was great meeting you."

Her smile returns to her face, and the sadness falls away so quickly and easily. I doubt she knew Thomas, which suggests she and Serena aren't that close. "You too. Good luck with the job. I hope you get it."

"Thanks."

She nods and walks off with her friend.

From the corner of my eye, I see someone walking closer. I don't know why I become very aware of their presence until I turn and realize it's Detective Kevin Burton. The last thing I want is to speak to him, so I jump off my stool and plan to meet Carly near the bathroom. But I only make it three steps from the bar when Kevin is so close I can smell the gallons of cologne he poured on and the stale beer on his breath. Great. He's drunk. He was drunk during our last altercation too.

I start to walk around him, but he grabs my arm and holds me still. In my ear he says, "I haven't forgotten."

Unfortunately, neither have I. To truly understand our hatred for one another, one would have to know that Kevin used to hang with Izzie's ex, Alice's father. So Kevin spent time at my house when they were teens. When he made a pass at me, Enzo stepped in to protect me. Ever since then, it's as if Kevin's had it in for me. I can't imagine why one rejection over a decade ago fueled our feud, but it has. Over the years, other incidences kept it ignited, but marrying my ex-best friend last month—the day I arrived home to South Shore Beach—and bullying me in my own apartment stepped way over the line. Oh, and let's not forget how he tried to falsely incriminate Izzie when she was arrested. Although that one I can't prove.

Suffice it to say, my desire to see him burn is pretty high. And even though he has more power and physical strength than I do, I never back down to him. I can't give him the satisfaction. But part of me assumed he'd leave me alone after the two ghosts gave him a scare. Maybe it's time Julian learns what happened that night in my apartment.

"Let go of me." I yank my arm free of his grip, which tells me he isn't all that serious about tormenting me.

Suddenly, Carly's by my side. "You okay?"

I nod, not really able to form words. Seeing Kevin and having him slur all over me again has me shaken up more than I thought it would. Last time I had a couple of ghosts to help me. This time there's a roomful of people, but I feel more vulnerable.

"Let's get out of here," she says.

I'm not about to argue. I nod and lead the way outside.

* * *

Sunday dinner is like a holy event at Ma and Pop's house—at least according to Ma. There's a dress code—somewhere between business casual and black-and-white gala—and a strict timeline. If you show up late and it's before dinner, she'll give you a stern eye and keep tossing the salad. If you show up during dinner, have fun choking down the baked ziti while she brings up story after story about how if she'd been late in her day, she wouldn't be able to sit for a week. I guess my great-grandparents were tyrants. And if you're not going to make it to dinner at all, don't bother showing up and get a doctor's note that you contracted an almost fatal strain of malaria.

Okay, so Ma isn't violent, and she and Pop never hit us growing up, but she gives an evil eye so menacing you'd wish you were a passenger on the Titanic.

The early afternoon starts like every other Sunday since I've been home so far. I arrive, and Ma and Pop are cooking. The

TV in the living room blares because Pop is either going deaf and won't admit it, or he likes to pretend he's actually at the football stadium. Izzie, Paulie, and Alice are already there. My brother-in-law is always eager for Ma's cooking. I love spending Sundays with my family. I'm just not super eager for the dress code. I love boots and bracelets, and sparkly manicures make me sing, but I don't own a lot of dresses, which Ma prefers. I decided on a black ruffled skirt, a black and gray, long sleeve turtleneck, black tights, and leather, Gucci knee-high boots.

Yes, this part-time deli worker owns Gucci, but to be fair, they're super old, and the zipper catches sometimes. I didn't pay full price for them. I found them at Goodwill. I don't know if the previous owner gave them away by accident or if they're one of those rich people who buy new even though the old isn't old yet, but I totally lucked out.

I walk into the kitchen as Ma takes the pan of baked ziti out of the oven. She looks over my attire choice with approval. "You're almost late," she says.

"Sorry." I won't tell her that Carly and I had a late night dancing. I do, however, rush forward and grab the pan from her hands and set it on the pot holder on the dining room table. We're using Ma's fancy dishes today. The white ones with the white leaf pattern etched along the rim. This means Izzie set the table. She has Ma's flair for "dress up."

"Where's Izzie?" I ask Ma when I return to the kitchen.

"She's upstairs in the bathroom. Alice spilled some grape juice on her dress, and Izzie's trying to get it out. Where's Julian?" She asks as if I'm his keeper.

The front door opens, and I smile. "That's probably him now."

She sighs in relief.

"You sure you don't want to date him?" I ask in fun.

She swats the air. "That is disgusting. I do, however, think he and you will give me beautiful grandbabies."

I inwardly groan. Babies are the last thing on my mind. Julian and I haven't even gotten this dating thing down right. Time to change the subject. "So where's your son?"

She picks up her wooden spoon and points it at the clock. "I don't know, but if he's not here soon, he's in trouble."

I smirk and head into the living room. Pop is shaking Julian's hand while keeping his attention on the television. Paulie gets up, greets Julian, and then walks toward the kitchen arch, where I'm standing. Julian follows.

"How is your friend?" Paulie asks.

"I only saw her for a moment this morning. She was asleep, but they say she'll be fine."

He pushes a hand through his thick, brown hair. "That's good. I hate suicide attempts. They shake me up."

I grin. Paulie's a good guy. Yeah, he screwed up royally last month, but he's still a caring person with a big heart.

Izzie and Alice come downstairs. My sister looks uncomfortable in a navy dress that stretches across her chest and stomach. She doesn't have a belly yet, but her boobs have almost doubled in size already. My niece is in a black skirt and shoes and a pumpkin orange top that's so blinding it could only be from Halloween.

She walks over to Julian, who gives her a hug, and then Alice lingers by him with a cheesy smile on her face. Izzie says her daughter is smitten with my boyfriend. What is it with the females in my life getting all googly eyed around him?

"We should wait a few more minutes to eat," Ma says. Annoyance settles in the lines around her eyes.

We all step farther into the living room, and the front door opens. Ma sighs in relief and smiles. Enzo steps inside and doesn't shut the door behind him. He looks over his shoulder, and suddenly Carly peeks her head around the door.

I glance to Izzie, who raises her brows, and then to Ma, whose face tightens. This should be fun.

Carly walks in all the way and shuts the door behind her. She smiles at everyone but doesn't look at Ma. I'm sure that's not an accident.

"Hey, everyone. You remember Carly, right?" Enzo says.

Pop gets up and gives her a hug. As Enzo introduces her to Paulie, Julian, and Alice, Ma grabs my wrist with her super-sharp talons and drags me into the kitchen.

She lets go of me, and I look down to my arm to see if I'm bleeding. Luckily the skin is still intact.

"Ow, Ma. That hurts. You should've become a wrestler or something."

She walks to the counter where she sliced a loaf of Italian bread, picks up the long serrated knife, and whirls around. "Did you know he was bringing her?"

I put up my hands as if I'm under arrest. "Whoa, Ma. No."

Carly never mentioned it last night, and I can't imagine why she'd keep it a secret, so they must've decided today. Did that mean they met up for coffee and bagels this morning, or did she go to his place after she dropped me off? Was Enzo getting jiggy with it? I won't share these thoughts with Ma. That's for sure.

She's not waving the knife around or even close to me, and I'm not scared, but I'm taken aback she's this upset. I need to sit down with Enzo and find out exactly what happened between him and Carly all those years ago. I wonder if it's as bad as Ma and Izzie remember, or if they're just being overprotective. If his heart was crushed into a million pieces, he wouldn't be hanging with her now. Right? And even if it was, he's a mature guy. Chances are he's forgiven her and moved on. So why can't Ma and Izzie too?

"But you knew they were spending time together again?"

"Well..."

"Gianna Rose Mancini, don't you lie to me."

"I will answer that question when you put down your weapon." I'm hoping my goofiness will take the edge out of her.

She glances at the knife, sighs, and sets it on the counter. "Spill."

"I saw her at Enzo's the other day. I don't know how close they are." I don't bother telling her that I first saw Carly when she was naked in Enzo's shower.

"Why didn't you say anything?"

I frown, feeling like I've done something wrong and am getting scolded. "I told Izzie. Besides, you were so pissed yesterday."

"I have every right to be," she says in a low, even keel and walks past me into the dining room.

This should be interesting.

Ma is especially quiet during the meal. In fact, she doesn't speak at all. When she wants me to pass the salad, she nudges my arm and points. I'm sure everyone notices because Ma's usually the one asking a million questions and making us share our lives. Without this guidance, the conversation lulls several times and most of it is spent talking about sports. Boring.

Afterwards, Pop, Paulie, Enzo, and Carly go into the living room to watch a game while Ma, Izzie, and I clean up, make coffee, and get the dessert ready. I find this wholly sexist, and I'm about to tell Enzo and Paulie to get their butts in here to help, but that would probably bring Carly in, and the kitchen is where the knives live.

I turn to get the empty breadbasket and see Julian bringing it to me. Warmth spreads inside me, and I smile. It's nice to know that not all of the men think it's our job to clean up.

He then goes to the kitchen table and sits beside Alice, who's reading a fashion magazine.

Ma sets the last utensil into the dishwasher, adds soap, shuts the door, and turns it on.

"You okay, Ma?" I ask. I'm starting to get worried since she's so quiet.

"Yes. I have a headache. I'm going to go lay down for a minute. Can you handle this?"

"Yeah, of course."

"I'll come get you when it's ready," Izzie says.

Ma nods and goes upstairs.

I turn to my sister. "Is this all because of Carly?"

Izzie quirks her brow. "I told you that woman is poison."

Those weren't her exact words, but I'm starting to wonder if I'm the one who's wrong. Maybe Carly will hurt Enzo again. Maybe she's the devil incarnate. But maybe this is none of our business just like Julian and I are none of theirs.

I pour coffee grounds into the permanent filter and glance at the table. Alice holds open the magazine and asks Julian, "Which outfit do you like better?"

He points. "This one."

She giggles at his choice. "But those shoes are so yellow."

"That why. It makes her look like Big Bird. I loved Big Bird as a kid."

Alice laughs harder.

I smirk. It's cute watching him with my niece, especially since he's so much taller than her.

"What about this one?" She flips to another page.

He widens his eyes and points. "Oh, definitely this one. The green and red make this other girl look like a giant Christmas tree."

Alice cackles. "That's what I told my best friend."

They laugh, and Izzie smiles at me. "You definitely should snatch him up. He's good with kids."

I want to roll my eyes at the mention of our relationship, but she's right.

"Don't wait too long. Someone else may beat you to it," she whispers then runs up to the bathroom.

I watch the way he not only answers Alice's questions but also seems genuinely interested in her opinion, and my heart fills. I see the wonderful things about him. I'm not blind. He loves me, and I love him. This should be easy. A no-brainer. Am I really going to let his job stand between us? Yeah, how he left Izzie hanging was awful, but he had no intention of letting it get to court.

Can I live with knowing that he may not be as generous to a stranger though? Whenever I think this way, I wonder about the choices I've made. No one is perfect. I haven't allowed anyone to be framed for murder, but I tell my share of lies to help ghosts move on. I'm not exactly applying for sainthood anytime soon.

Julian glances up and catches my eye. He gives me that slow, smoldering grin that sets my groin on fire. Suddenly

Thomas appears in my line of sight, and the feeling melts away.
"What are you doing?" he shouts.

I flinch and point to Mr. Coffee. "Brewing."

That's when I notice Julian's frown, through Thomas.

"You can't drink coffee. You need to help me," Thomas says, his voice still higher than usual.

I cock my head to the side then turn my back on Julian and Alice. Thomas follows around. "I am helping. With Serena in the hospital, there's not much for me to do, but I went by Sparks yesterday."

"And?"

"And I auditioned as their singer."

"This isn't time for a new job."

I roll my eyes. "You think I mortified myself just for a little extra cash? If I wanted that, I'd go strip."

His gaze roams my body. He raises his brows and nods.

"Hey." If he was corporeal, I'd slug him in the arm. "I auditioned to get closer to the people who work there. To find out if she has any enemies."

"What audition?" asks a voice behind me. It's Julian.

I turn and find him standing directly behind me.

"Ooh, I didn't hear you sneak up."

"I didn't sneak. You didn't hear me because you were busy talking to your invisible friend."

I glance to Alice, who isn't paying attention to us. Thank goodness. She's the only immediate member of our family who doesn't know about my abilities. Well, her and Paulie. Izzie doesn't want Alice knowing until she's much older. I don't know if my sister ever wants her husband to know.

"Asking people questions isn't enough," Thomas says. "You need to be with Serena. To sit with her and tell her she's not alone. That kind of thing."

I roll my eyes. "I told you. I'm not babysitting. I'll help figure out who killed you so you both can have peace and you can move on. But the hand-holding needs to be done by the professionals."

"I'm not crazy about the idea of you looking for a bomb expert, but I'll help," Julian says.

Thomas disappears with a huff, and I give my full attention to Julian. "Why do you want to help him and Serena?"

"I want to help you," he says. "I want to prove to you that our worlds can work together and that I'm not a bad guy."

"I never thought you were a bad person."

He steps closer and closer until we're just touching. "Good, because I never want you to think that."

"Okay, so how will you help?" I ask, suddenly anticipating his knowledge and expertise.

"Well, let's go over it. What do you have so far?"

"A bomb, a dead man, and a suicidal woman."

"That's not much."

That's nothing. "Last night I ran into Serena's friend, Zoe. They work at Sparks together."

"When you were out dancing with an old female friend. Was that Carly?"

"Yes." I smirk. This would be a great time to bring up Kevin, but I no longer want to get into it. At least not here, not now. I don't think Julian will handle it well. He'll want to go beat Kevin's butt, and while I would love to sell tickets and pop popcorn, Kevin's a cop, and I don't want Julian in legal trouble.

"Then maybe you should speak with Zoe. And I'll dig around and see what I can find out."

"Great. I guess I can go to Sparks and have dinner."

"You can bring a date," he says with a wink. "How about tomorrow night?"

That sounds like a plan. And I love a good plan and a free meal.

After we have cheesecake from Ma's favorite bakery and coffee, everyone starts to leave. I don't want to be the last person left because I know Ma will suck me into an hour-long rant. As much as I love the woman, I can't do it again. Besides, Izzie's the one who also hates how Carly treated Enzo a zillion years ago. She should be the one to endure. So as soon as Enzo and Carly leave, I grab my coat, kiss everyone bye, and fly out. If Julian thinks it's weird, he doesn't say anything.

Instead of going home, I drive to the hospital. Thomas has me feeling guilty, so a visit is in order. I walk through the automatic double doors and hope for another smile from that cute security guard, even though the chances of him working days and nights is slim.

I'm not nearly as lucky. The guard is a woman. Attractive. Blonde. Big blue eyes with hard lines feathering the corners. But still a woman. Not my type. I head to the elevators and jump on one just as the doors are shutting.

Before they close all the way though, I think I spot Freezer Dude.

CHAPTER TEN

I lean forward, ready to hit the button for the doors to open, when the man beside me frowns. "We're already moving," he says.

I pull back, not wanting to screw up the elevator mechanisms. The big boxes scare me enough as is. I'm not sure why, but I've never been a fan of elevators. Then again, I'm also not fond of escalators. It's getting on them that makes me nervous.

I step back and tell myself to not worry about Freezer Dude. Maybe it wasn't him. A lot of men have shocking white hair, right? And I may have thought the guy was gliding, but it was hard to tell as the doors were shutting. Besides, he has nothing to do with me, and if I just leave him alone... Oh, who am I kidding? I have no intention of doing nothing. But it will have to wait. I'm here to see Serena, and that takes precedent.

I exit on the seventh floor and go to Serena's room. This time the overhead lights are on, the TV is louder, and there's a woman in the first bed. She's sipping from a pink, plastic cup and listening to the woman in the chair beside her talking about the latest episode of *General Hospital*.

"Sonny learned the truth today," the woman says.

They both look to me as I enter the room.

I smile and walk past the bed to the drawn curtain. I step around it and smile at Serena, who's awake, and the babysitter-slash-nurse person. It's the same woman as last time. I try to not show surprise that Thomas is lying on the mattress, right beside Serena.

Serena's cheeks have color in them, and there's a slight smile on her face due to something they're watching on TV.

"Hi. I hope this isn't a bad time."

"Hi," Serena says and pats down the side of her hair. The nurse starts to stand, but I hold up my hand.

"I can't stay long. How are you feeling?"

Serena shuts her eyes and leans her head back. "Like an idiot."

"Oh?"

She covers her forehead with her hand. "I was so upset, so alone. I wasn't thinking clearly."

"You lost the love of your life. That is devastating." I understand exactly what she's feeling. The first love of my life was Craig. He was killed by a drunk driver. That pain had been so raw and lasted for some time. That was the reason I left South Shore Beach and moved to Connecticut to live with my cousin. And how I met Julian. I'm glad things worked out the way they did, but I wish Craig hadn't died.

"I didn't, and don't, want to die." Serena lifts her head and stares at me. "The police tell me that you called the paramedics. Thank you."

"You're welcome. I'm just glad you're okay." And want to stay that way. "I'm sure Thomas would be glad that you're okay as well."

Thomas nods. He's staring at her with a worried expression on his face.

Chatter on the other side of the room is at a lull. I'm sure Serena's grief is more interesting than Sonny and whatever he just learned.

"When will you be going home?" I ask.

"They said probably soon. I need to speak with the shrink again. He's been a lot of help already. I know last night was just a momentary lapse in judgment. They recommend therapy. I agree."

"I want her to be happy, healthy, and whole. And eventually, I'll want her to move on and find love again," Thomas whispers.

My throat tightens. Darn. I hate when ghosts make me want to cry.

I dislodge the lump in my throat by clearing it. "When you're feeling stronger, we'll need to talk."

Her overly plucked eyebrows draw together. "About what?"

I glance at her babysitter, not sure how much I should say in front of her. She's watching us as if we're actors on the TV. "Figuring out who did this."

Serena sits up, and her frown deepens. "Who are you?"

The nurse stares at me, and I hear one of the women behind the curtain whisper, "Oooh."

Maybe I should have approached this subject differently or waited until Serena is released and out of here. "I'm Gianna Man..."

"No, I know your name, but you said you're Thomas's assistant. Why would you get involved in this? Isn't that the cops' job?"

Thomas has stopped staring at her and is now nodding at me with his lips pursed, as if to say, "I told you so." What's up with these two?

"Well yes, but they can be slow about things at times." I scramble to think of a logical explanation. I can't very well say it's because I promised the ghost of her dead fiancé. Luckily Enzo isn't around to hear me disparage his comrades.

"Even so, you no longer work for Thomas. Don't you have another job to look for?" She seems annoyed that I want to help. And I can't help wondering why.

"Actually, I just went out looking yesterday." I smile bright, hoping to keep her off guard.

"Okay then." She breathes a small sigh of relief.

What exactly is she hiding?

"But this is what Thomas would want, so I'm going to look into it. Do you have a problem with that?" I glance to Thomas and bug out my eyes a bit. Why is he so damn quiet? He needs to speak up, to tell me what's going on. I'm here because he begged me to help her. Now that he doesn't like the way I'm assisting, he doesn't get to check out.

She shakes her head. "I don't want to know."

I can't believe this. "You don't want to know who killed your fiancé but was aiming for you?"

"No."

The nurse widens her eyes and glances at me. She looks confused and dumbfounded. I know how she feels. From Thomas's sullen expression to Serena's tense jaw, I know something is going on here, and I'm more than determined to figure out exactly what that is.

After saying an abrupt good-bye, but I'll be in touch soon, I take the elevator to the lobby. And as luck would have it, when the doors open, I spot Freezer Dude. That was him earlier.

I follow him through the double doors that lead to the Emergency Department waiting room. Half the room is full of people either asleep, doubled over in pain, or staring blankly at the televisions hanging up near the ceiling.

Freezer Dude jumps into the first person—a man holding his head. The man shudders and I bet feels worse than he did beforehand. Freezer Dude leaps back out and goes to the next person.

I watch him play leapfrog through half the room before he staggers over to a sidewall and appears to be leaning against it, gasping for breath. But ghosts don't breathe. Ah! He's exhausted from all the jumping. Good. Serves him right.

I walk over to him, hold my cell to my ear, and ask, "What the heck are you doing?"

He barely lifts his head. His crazy stare practically melts my eye sockets. How creepy. I half expect him to fly at me again, but he's too tired for that.

"Well?" I ask again. My patience is waning, and I want to get out of here.

His bright blue eyes light up, and I follow his gaze over my shoulder to the triage desk. A man in a blue-and-white checkered top and beige pants walks in. He's holding his wrist, and blood is spurting and dripping.

A nurse yells, "He's bleeding everywhere."

Panic sets in as someone races to get him a towel or something.

Freezer Dude wastes no time and jumps into the man. The man shudders and reacts in the usual way.

I hold my breath, not quite sure what's going to happen, but suddenly Freezer Dude is thrown back out. He lands on the bloody floor, on his butt. The bleeding man is ushered through a door.

Finally, Freezer Dude looks to me and says, "I'm trying to find a body that's weak enough to let me stay. I'll keep looking. There must be one around someplace."

With a wink, he disappears.

Now *I* need to lean against the wall as his words fully form in my mind. Holy crap!

* * *

Freezer Dude's disturbing comments keep me awake half the night. What if he succeeds? Then what happens? He just takes over someone's life? There has to be a way to stop him, to send him back to the hereafter. There has to be some sort of checks and balances system for the other side, like ghost police.

When I go to my shift at the deli, Ma's still being quiet. I really thought she would've given up the silent treatment last night. She asks me to hand her the spatula for the lasagna and to fill up the tortellini salad bin, but she doesn't talk. Not like usual. She doesn't even sing or hum. I'm starting to miss my chatty, musical mother.

She leaves as soon as Pop shows up, and at least he speaks to me. He doesn't initiate conversations—that's not Pop's style—but when I initiate, he responds. Work goes by slowly and is as boring as heck, so I'm very grateful when I get off and head upstairs to my apartment.

I step out of the shower, after scrubbing away the scent of vinegar and prosciutto, when my cell rings. I don't recognize the number. I swipe the flashing green phone receiver. "Hello?"

"Is this Gianna Mancini?" asks a female voice I don't recognize.

"Yes?"

"This is Natalia Kane from Sparks. I'm calling to let you know that you got the gig."

I got it? No.

"Seriously?" Despite the swarming of bald eagles in my stomach, I'm thrilled and feel like jumping up and down.

She gives a light chuckle. "Yes. I'd like you to come in and fill out the paperwork and get your schedule. Are you free tomorrow around 4:30?"

A schedule? That means more than one performance. Oh my gosh, what have I gotten myself into?

"Yes, I'm available. I'll be there. Thank you." I'm off from the deli tomorrow, so it works out perfectly.

"Great. See you then."

The line clicks in my ear, and I'm frozen to the spot. I got the job. Yay! I'm going to be singing in front of an audience. Ugh! The eagles subside long enough for my stomach to flip repeatedly. What if I vomit on stage?

No. I push my shoulders back. I was fine during the audition. I'll be fine when I perform. Besides, now I'll have time to practice. My thoughts go to Ma. She's the singer of the family. Will she be upset that I'm getting a chance to do this and not her? Should I even tell her about it? I don't think I can keep it a secret for long, especially not when I'm actually performing. I'll want to share it. Despite my hesitations, I'm really excited. I wonder how much it pays.

My cell rings again. Is Natalia calling back to say she made a mistake? The number is different but still one I don't recognize.

"Hello?"

"This is Mystic Aurora. Is this..."

"Yes, it's me. What's going on?" I'm so excited to hear from her I forget my manners.

"Can you swing by my shop?"

"I'm on my way." I hang up and run to my car.

* * *

When I enter her shop, I have to blink several times due to the dimness. Mystic Aurora greets me at the door with a sullen look and deep creases along her brow. Oh, this isn't going to be good. She takes my hand and leads me to a table in a back room.

I'm expecting brightly colored scarves draped on top of the tables and over light shades, to give a mystical atmosphere.

That's how it looks in the movies anyway. Instead, it's a pretty, sterile room with a round white table big enough to seat four and chairs. A deck of tarot cards lies on the table, and several are spread out. There's a desk along the far wall, a filing cabinet, and an oversized armchair that looks super cozy. A few plants, lamps, and a couple of framed photographs I can't make out from here finish the small space.

"What's going on?" I ask as panic starts to enter my body. "You're scaring me."

She lights a white candle. "I'm sorry. I don't mean to, but I must admit that what I saw the other night scared me as well."

"Ah-ha! So you did see the ghost."

She stares into my eyes. Hers are wide, and fear surrounds her light green irises. "I don't know what I saw. I've never seen one before."

"How is that even possible? You're a psychic. Don't the dearly departed come in to talk to their loved ones?"

She shook her head. "I mostly clear chakras." Her voice is low and squeaky.

I am clueless about chakras, and my psychic knowledge is limited, once again, to TV and movies, but it sounds like she's not going to be as helpful as I hoped. "So how do I get rid of him?"

"I don't know."

I sigh, starting to lose my patience. "Then why did you call me?"

"I'm looking into it, but in the meantime, I read your cards." She waves her hand over the deck laid out on the table before her. The cards are colorful and pretty, but I don't have a clue what any of them mean.

"Don't I need to be here for you to do that?" If not, I really know nothing.

She picks up the brochure I left with my number. "I used this for your energy."

Well, that's cool. "And? What do the cards say?"

"There are two men who keep showing themselves. There are changes in your future. Some will be good, something to do with a man, a partner who holds your heart."

That's Julian, and it's good news? Great. I don't think I can deal with any more heartache with him.

"But not all of the changes are good," Aurora says. "The other man is dark and dangerous. You have to watch out for him. He's in your way."

That has to be Freezer Dude, but in my way for what? "Can you be more specific?"

"No. The cards are more impressions, and they show what could happen. Nothing is guaranteed. You make choices every day, and all of this could change tomorrow depending on what you do today."

That's promising. It means I'm in control of my life. Just the way I like it.

She glances back down to the cards and points to one off to the side. "Please be careful though. There's a lot of darkness and danger in your near future."

* * *

Since I got the gig, there's no reason to go to dinner with Julian at Sparks. I am going in tomorrow and will catch up with Zoe and speak to the other employees soon enough. Plus, I forgot that Sparks is closed on Mondays. So after leaving Mystic Aurora's, I call Julian, and we switch restaurants to my favorite seafood joint in the East End.

I choose a simple black dress I bought years ago but rarely wear. It has short sleeves, a square neckline, and comes to just above my knees. The darts sewn into the waist area means it accentuates my full curves and doesn't just hang. My Gucci boots feel like the perfect foot choice. I pull my curls up and pin them loosely so they hang and dangle around my face. My makeup is heavier than usual, and I add a glimmer copper shadow to my lids and a bright fuchsia lip. Large, rhinestone studs and a simple silver chain with an open heart complete the look. I don't want to overcrowd it all with bracelets and rings. I'm going for elegant but still me. Aurora's words about a partner that holds my heart has me thinking lovey-dovey thoughts.

I meet Julian downstairs. I don't want him to come upstairs because if he looks as sexy as he usually does in a suit, and hence those lovey-dovey feelings, we may not make it to the restaurant. And I really have my heart set on some shrimp. So I run down and stand outside just as he pulls in.

I walk around the front of his car. The headlights make me squint, and when I open the passenger door, he whistles. It makes me giddy, and I laugh. I climb up into the seat.

"We should go to dinner more often," he says. "You look happy."

I turn to him full smile. "I am." Then I frown. "Do I normally look unhappy?"

He chuckles softly. "No, but you're usually preoccupied with something."

I pull at the seatbelt. He's definitely right about that.

He puts the car in reverse. "By the way, you look amazing."

My smile deepens. This is turning out to be a great night.

We arrive at the restaurant, Coastal, and surprisingly, it's packed. I hadn't expected a crowd on a Monday night. Luckily the host is able to seat us right away, and we score a table by the front windows. Coastal is this weird rustic fine-dining place where wood paneling accompanies white tablecloths. It's this mix of fancy and casual. The dining room is medium-sized with probably fifteen tables that are closer together than they should be. There's a separate bar area, which is small but cozy, and a patio with full service that's open on warmer days and nights. The absolute best part about Coastal though is the food. There's nothing casual about that. Succulent crabs and lobsters, and the scallops melt in your mouth.

I stare at my menu, immediately decide on the Pasta Coastal, and set the menu back down. It's a no-brainer. Shrimp and sea scallops nestled over linguine in a butter-garlic-white-wine sauce with mushrooms and shallots. How can I think of eating anything else?

"So, have you learned anything about Serena?" I ask.

Julian sets his menu down and opens his mouth to fill me on all the juicy details when suddenly I hear someone call my name.

I turn my head and see Enzo and Carly walking over.

"Oh, my gosh, what are you guys doing here?"

Enzo shakes Julian's hand. "We're having dinner too."

Carly points to a table on the other side of the dining room. There are two glasses of water, and the setting is messed up, but there aren't any plates.

"Are you done?"

"No, we just ordered, and I saw you walk in,' Carly said. "Enzo didn't want to bother you in case you want to be alone, but it seemed silly to just sit there and pretend we don't see you."

"You should join us," I say and look at Julian.

He doesn't hesitate when he agrees.

"We don't want to impose," Enzo says.

Julian gets up and sits beside me so they can sit together across from us. "No, man. This is fine. It'll be great.'

Enzo holds out Carly's chair. She sits down and giggles. "A double date. This will be so much fun."

Enzo frowns at her but doesn't say anything. "Let me go tell our server."

I have a feeling their server isn't the same as ours, so he or she may be pissed they're missing out on a tip. I want to make sure Julian is okay, so I lean into him and whisper, "Are you sure you don't mind?"

He places his forehead against mine. "Not at all."

I want to move my neck a few inches and press my mouth against his, but since we have an observer and I don't want to confuse poor Julian, I decide against it. But he smells so good. Like leather and something woodsy.

Enzo returns with our server, and Julian and I order.

We spend the next twenty minutes with small talk. Carly works as a receptionist at a used-car lot, and her days are long and boring. She's living in a small apartment in Island Park. It's actually the basement rental of a three-bedroom house. It's quiet, so she likes it. Enzo doesn't comment on its decor or the area, so I'm led to believe he hasn't seen it yet.

Our food arrives, and it looks and smells amazing. We each ordered something different, and if Izzie had been across from Julian instead of Carly, I would stick my fork in each of their plates, with their permission of course. I pick up a shrimp with my fork and bite into it. I'm pretty sure I moan as the garlicky flavors caress my tongue. Then again, I can't be sure because everyone else seems to be moaning too.

Julian ordered the crab stuffed sole with rice pilaf and broccoli, Carly got the butter soaked lobster tail, and Enzo is chowing down on his steak frites, which is a NY strip with thinly cut French fries but sounds more special when you say it in French. He was never one for delicacies from the sea. There aren't enough delicious adjectives in the world to describe my taste buds right now.

"How's the Sterling case going?" I ask after several mouthfuls. I hope I sound nonchalant. At least to Carly. She doesn't need to know I'm a meddling buttinsky. Enzo and Julian know exactly who I am and why I'm asking.

Enzo smirks and says, "It's funny you ask. I was meaning to..." He allows his words to trail. "Um, actually, the detectives discovered the dead man wasn't Thomas Sterling."

I allow my fork to slip out of my fingers and clank against my plate. "Excuse me?"

We're all silent while Enzo puts a large chunk of beef into his mouth and chews. He's not pulling my leg. The ghost isn't who he says he is? That can't be. I glance to Julian, who looks almost as stunned as me with his brows forged together.

I glance to Carly too, who's frowning as well, but she doesn't have a clue what we're talking about. She looks at me and asks, "Is that a bad thing? Doesn't it mean that this Thomas Sterling is still alive then?"

I can't very well tell her that the dead guy told me he's Thomas, and this means he's a lying sack of crap.

"Yes," Enzo says. "The real Sterling is in Europe. He has a second home there."

I'm trying to keep my composure and not act like I've been sucker punched, but that's how I feel. He lied to me. Does that mean Serena's been lying too? Was that why they didn't want me looking into his death? The creeps. But why the charade? It can't matter who *I* think he is. There has to be more going on here.

"What about his mother?" I ask. "She was at his house. Wouldn't she know where her son was?"

Enzo shakes his head. "I don't know that. All I know is that Sterling has been in Europe for the past six months with his wife."

"He's married?" I ask, doubly stunned.

Enzo nods.

Julian places his hand on my thigh, under the table, and gives me a reassuring squeeze. I wish Carly would excuse herself to the bathroom so I could rant out loud. I have a major bone to pick with a ghost.

Enzo changes the conversation to movies, and the double date becomes lively, but I don't want to think of the latest production of *Magic Mike,* which the guys do not find appealing, but Carly does. I'd rather continue to stew about the Fake Thomas. I don't want to spoil the evening though. So I bring up the third installment of *Insidious,* and the rest of the evening is filled with chatter and laughter.

Forty minutes later, we're walking to our cars, saying good-night and how we need to do this again soon.

With my seatbelt fastened, I lay my hand on Julian's, which is on the gearshift and about to put the car in reverse.

He looks into my eyes and starts to smile.

"Will you do me a favor?" I ask.

"Anything." One word so simple and he has me weak at the knees. Not in a sexual way, although that's always just around the corner with us. This is different though. This means he really is here for me. It's not that I haven't known this, but it's been on a mental level, and this is pure emotion right now.

"Can you please look into all of these people and find out who the fake Sterling and his mother are? You may as well throw in Serena Tate as well."

Julian smiles, and his eyes light up. My asking him to use his skills is important to him. I can see it all over his naturally tanned, gorgeous face. "Absolutely."

There goes another one-word, simple reply again. And my knees.

CHAPTER ELEVEN

———

A shrill ringing scares the bejeebies out of me and makes me snort in a breath, as if I forgot to breathe while I was sleeping. I open my eyes a hair's width, reach for my cell on the nightstand, and silently curse the caller. It seems to be light out but not very bright, which means it's either going to be a gray, rainy day or this mean person is calling at dawn.

"Hello?" I say without looking at the caller ID. That would require using my eyes, and they want to shut again, which I happily oblige.

"All of my jeans are too tight," Izzie says with disgust. "And don't get me started about my heels. I can't wear them anymore. What am I going to do? I can't wear flats and be...five-four." She whispers her height, like the short police are standing behind her. As if five-four is short.

"What time is it, and why has this become my problem?"

"Because you're my sister, and you care enough to not have me walking out of the house naked and short."

I snort twice and then have to cough. "So you want to go maternity clothes shopping?"

She gasps. "I'll just buy a few things in a larger size."

I try rolling my eyes with my lids still shut, but it just makes me dizzy, so I open them. "If I'm getting out of bed to go shopping, you're getting maternity clothes. Don't be vain."

Suddenly Thomas is sitting beside me, on the edge of my mattress. "I can't find her."

I scream.

Then Izzie screams. "Okay, so I'll buy maternity clothes."

"No, not you. Look, I'll call you back." Before she can protest, I click off. Clothes shopping can wait a bit. I'm sure she's not actually sitting around naked. She has that ratty robe.

"What are you doing here? Why are you scaring me? And who are you?" I sit up and cross my arms over my chest. Partly because I want to look tough and mostly because this white tank top is kinda see-through, and I don't want to give the ghost a peep show.

"Serena's missing."

"What do you mean she's missing?"

"They released her from the hospital, and she's not at my place or Zoe's. I don't know where else she could be."

A hotel and park bench come to mind, but as pressing as this may be, it's not as important as who he is. "I'm sure she's fine. So who are you?"

He frowns and looks at me as if I'm the crazy one. "It's me, Thomas Sterling."

"Yeah, no. The real Thomas Sterling is in Europe with his wife. Who are you really?"

He stares at me for a second. Then poof, he's gone.

How rude.

I quickly dress in leggings, combat boots, a black tank, and a super soft red-and-black plaid, oversized shirt and pick up Izzie. On the ride over the bridge, onto the main part of Long Island, she rambles about clothes while I think of everything I know so far.

Thomas the Ghost isn't Thomas Sterling. Serena doesn't want me to figure out what happened to Fake Thomas. And Freezer Dude is playing musical bodies. Welcome to my crazy world.

"Hey, are you listening to me?" Izzie asks as I pull my Kia into the mall's parking lot.

"Yes, you're fretting over clothes with a stretch waistband and a few extra pounds caused by the pregnancy of your beautiful, future child." I stare straight into her brown eyes. "Is that about right?"

First she narrows her gaze. Then she rolls her eyes. "Fine. I'm a horrible mother because I'm thinking about my wardrobe and figure. You know, guilt and shame are only supposed to work for mothers."

I inwardly grin and think of Ma. "I learned from the best."

After several hours of sulking, pouting (me), and spending way too much time in dressings rooms (Izzie), we finally drive back to town. Instead of going to her house, I pull into Grande on West Park Street. It's quaint, Mexican, and I'm starved.

We are seated by the front windows and order virgin strawberry daiquiris, fish tacos for me, and beef burritos for her. Then we dive face-first into the bowl of chips and salsa and don't come up to breathe until they're empty, and the server brings us replacements.

I sip my drink. "That blue-and-white striped dress is cute."

She nods. "They really did have adorable maternity clothes. I don't know why I was being such a boob."

I glance down to her chest. "Maybe because yours have almost doubled in size."

She smirks at my lameness. It's about time for her to be more than just grouchy. I can't wait until her hormones get back to normal.

"So how's the fam?" I ask.

She cocks her brow at me. "You really want to talk about Paulie and Alice, or do you want to discuss Ma's cold shoulder Sunday?"

I open my mouth wide and scoff. "Right? She didn't say a word at work yesterday either."

Izzie shakes her head continuously, as if she has a nervous tick. "I don't get it. I mean I can't stand Carly either but..."

She stops talking and stares out the window. What's wrong with her? I follow her gaze and see a blue Ferrari. A blonde woman has just gotten out of the passenger side and is shutting the door. She waves to the driver, who speeds off, then turns toward us.

That's when I realize why Izzie is speechless. It's Carly. Our gazes catch, and I wave at her. She freezes for a moment and looks dumbstruck. Then she glances to the side, and I realize she's looking at her car. I hadn't even noticed it when we pulled in. Then Carly turns back to us.

"What is she doing?" Izzie whispers.

"Contemplating running off without saying hi." It's my first thought, and I'm not very proud of how cynical it sounds, especially since I've been Carly's biggest supporter thus far.

But Izzie laughs, obviously enjoying my wicked side. "So you finally see who she is too?"

"I didn't say that. It's just obvious that she wants to leave."

Carly gives us a half smile and decides to come inside. When she gets to our table, I notice a flash of gold beneath her mid-calf-length trench coat. Izzie must notice it too because she grabs the hem and pulls it aside, revealing the bottom inch of a gold, sequined, minidress.

"Wow, you're dressed up," Izzie says. "Where have you been?"

Carly may think that smile on Izzie's face is friendliness, but I see the evil glint in her eye.

I start to say she doesn't have to answer that. Obviously Izzie's in a mood, but not only does my curiosity get the better of me so does my sisterly protectiveness. It's almost noon, and she's dressed like she spent the night dancing. Was she out with girlfriends, or is she seeing someone beside Enzo?

"Some friends and I were out late last night. I crashed at Ella's, and she just dropped me off."

"Here and not at home?" Izzie asks.

Carly points to her car parked on the other side of the lot. "We met up and had dinner here and then went out dancing. We went to D'Angelo's."

Izzie quirks her brows.

"Carly and I went there the other night. And guess who I ran into? Although technically he ran into me."

Izzie shakes her head.

"Kevin."

She widens her eyes then looks back to Carly. 'Do you want to join us?"

"Oh, no. I need a shower and caffeine. Plus something for my headache. I'll see you guys later."

We say our good-byes and watch her get in her car and pull out.

"Dude, I barely got an acknowledgement from you about Kevin," I say and pick up another chip. By time the food gets here, I'll have eaten my weight in fried corn tortilla goodness.

"She's stepping out on Enzo," Izzie says.

That's when I realize my lunch is now ruined, and I'll be lucky if we spend more than five minutes not talking about Carly and Enzo.

And I was right. While the lunch wasn't completely ruined because my tacos were out of this world, like interplanetary delicious, Izzie rambled about our brother and his bad taste in women the entire time. The only reprieve was when she asked for the check. Come to find out Enzo dated less women than I dated guys. I'm slightly disturbed because I'm two years younger than him.

After I drop Izzie and her new wardrobe home, I spin by the real Thomas's house, but there are no cars in the driveway, and no one answers when I knock. I even go around back and peek through the kitchen window. There's no movement. It's empty. So where is Serena?

It's not that her supposed disappearance isn't important. I just assume she's fine. But I think to the night she almost overdosed, and panic starts to set in. The problem is that I haven't a clue where Serena would go, and I don't know her cell number.

Note to self: get cell numbers from every person you meet that's involved with a ghost from now on.

I spend the afternoon driving around town and pacing my living room. There has to be a better way to contact a ghost. All of my calling, screaming, and pleading doesn't make Fake Thomas appear. He's deliberately ignoring me. I can feel it.

I quickly change the top half of my body, put on a royal-blue tunic, and drive over to Sparks for my 4:30 meeting with

Natalia Kane. I park in the side lot and enter through the back doors. Instead of heading up to the front though, I ask one of the cooks where Natalia's office is located.

He's young, probably early twenties, with a head full of dark, thick hair. His smile is mischievous, and he has a slight Puerto Rican accent. He points to the corridor that leads to the front of the joint and says, "Third door."

I thank him and walk off. For some reason I glance back and find he's still smiling at me. Or my butt.

As I reach Natalia's door, I spot Zoe coming toward me. I smile way bigger than I intend. It just feels great to actually know someone here, although "know" is a strong word.

"Hey," she says. "I hear you got the position. Good for you."

"Thanks. So do you make good tips here?" It's none of my business, but I figure it's better to ease my way in to the more personal questions. Starting with, *do you know who wanted to kill Serena* isn't the best option.

"Weekends are amazing. The rest of the nights are decent. Do you also wait tables?"

"I did a bit of it a while ago. I can't say it's something I love." It was during my time living in Connecticut with my cousin. The hours on your feet were long, and it paid a barely livable wage, but the people were great. And there were no dead bodies.

"I originally planned to apply for that job."

"It's a good thing you have a great voice then. I'm sure singing pays better than serving."

That would be a total bonus.

"I need to get ready for my shift," Zoe says. "Good luck, or break a leg."

"Thanks."

I knock on the office door, and Natalia's sultry voice says, "Come in."

I step inside an immaculate room that consists of a long, glass-topped desk, shiny, black filing cabinets, as well as a few matching side tables, a black loveseat off to the side, and a couple of white chairs across from the desk. The walls are painted stark white, and with a couple of plants and bright lighting, this room feels very different from the front, dim dining room.

"Gianna," she says with a half smile. "Please have a seat."

I sit across from her desk and get a good look at her.

She has jet-black hair, cut into a chin-length bob with thick, full bangs. A natural tan and chiseled cheekbones makes her look regal and stylish. She could easily pass for a fashion designer in black trousers and a sand-colored blouse.

She opens a manila folder and hands me several sheets of paper and a pen from an acrylic holder beside her computer screen. "I just need you to fill these out."

I complete the standard forms for employment and tax purposes. It's all straightforward. When I'm done, I lay down the pen and am given another moment to watch her as she types on her keyboard. She keeps her nails moderately long and has on a nude polish.

There's something very attractive about this woman but not in a beautiful way. On second glance, her facial features are harsh. But I think it's the way she holds herself. She's certainly confident, and that's incredibly appealing.

She finishes what she's doing, takes my paperwork, and looks over the pages. Then she offers a slight smile and meets my gaze. "Everything looks to be in order. How about you come in Friday afternoon for your first practice? I will have to approve song choices, so why don't you return with some suggestions, and we'll take it from there?"

Still surprised and giddy about the idea that my singing was good enough to land this job, I smile and feel like giggling. That won't happen again though. "Thank you. That sounds great."

Instead of leaving through the kitchen, I head up front in hopes of catching Zoe alone. I'm hoping she knows where Serena is. The dining room is brightly lit and empty except for a bartender placing glasses into a rack and Zoe and Serena setting salt and pepper shakers on tables. Jackpot!

"Hi." I approach.

Zoe smiles, but Serena looks surprised to see me. The feeling is mutual.

"What are you doing here?" she asks.

"She works here now," Zoe says. "Nat just hired her."

Serena's look of confusion changes to suspicion. Her eyes narrow, and she cocks her head ever so slightly. "I thought you were an assistant."

"Yeah, well, there's no job there anymore. Besides, come to find out he wasn't who he said he was, right?" I carefully watch her expression for a telltale sign that she knew Fake Thomas wasn't a Sterling.

But it seems like I've caught her off guard because a frown forms. "What are you talking about?"

She doesn't know. How could she not? I mean, I guess it's possible, depending on when she met Fake Thomas. I assumed it was longer than the past five or six months, however long the real Thomas has been in Europe, but maybe not. The more I think about it, the more I realize how little I know about any of them. I've gone mostly on assumptions. And if I remember back to Thomas Sterling's place, there wasn't one photo in his living room or bedroom that was personal.

I stare into Serena's eyes. Since I haven't been able to reach her today, it's likely the cops haven't as well, which means, assuming she's telling the truth and doesn't know about Fake Thomas, she's more clueless than me. I decide to not be the bearer of bad news. At least not yet. Time for an abrupt subject change. "Are you back to working here?"

Natalia walks into the dining room. "Zoe, Serena, I need to speak with you. Zoe, first."

Zoe walks over, but she seems hesitant in leaving our conversation. I don't know how much she knows about Serena's life, but I gather it's not as much as she'd like.

Serena remains tight-lipped until Zoe's out of earshot, and then she says, "Yeah, I need to find a new place to live, and I need to find a way to survive. Alone."

"Where are you staying in the meantime?" I try to sound like I'm asking 'cause I care, which I do, but I also need to know where to find her in the future.

"At Zoe's. It's small, but she has a pull-out sofa."

That's definitely more than what I have.

"Look, I don't want Mrs. Sterling finding out that I'm working here," she says.

Now I'm confused. "Why not?"

She swallows hard, and tears gather in her eyes. "She doesn't want me at the funeral."

I suck in a gasp. How awful. What kind of a witch is she? Wait a minute. This must have something to do with Fake Thomas not being a Sterling, right? Mrs. Sterling has to know her son is married and living in Europe, so who was the woman I met?

"She's pushing me away."

That makes sense if Fake Mother doesn't want Serena discovering the truth about them.

"I'm so sorry." Regardless of who Fake Thomas and Fake Mother really are, it doesn't change the fact that Serena loved him, and he tragically died. This does, however, alter suspects. Is it possible the killer was after Fake Thomas?

Gosh, I need some actual names because I am starting to confuse myself.

"What does that have to do with this job?" I ask.

"I don't want to give her any extra ammunition for contesting Thomas's will."

If I were a cat, my ears would be visibly perked. "Excuse me?"

Zoe reentered the dining room. "Natalia wants to see you now, Serena."

Serena nods to her friend and says to me, "Thomas left me a lot of money, and his mother is fighting it. She says that the will shouldn't be legal because Thomas meant to leave me that money after we were married. He wasn't planning on dying. But it's there on paper, so it must be legal, right? I gotta run."

Before I can question her further, she takes off and heads to Natalia's office.

What does all of this will talk mean? Clearly Fake Thomas and Fake Mother aren't wealthy. Fake Mother isn't really concerned that her daughter-in-law-to-be might inherit their family wealth. It can't be. If they were rich, why pretend to be someone you're not and break into their home to do it?

But Serena believes them, and that's what I can't shake as I walk to my car. Just how much money does she think she's getting, and is it enough that she'd kill for it?

I decide the best place for answers is Enzo's, and it's about that time of evening when he should be home. When I get there, his car is parked out front. I knock on his door, but he doesn't answer. I don't see Carly's car, so he can't be too busy. Maybe he's in the bathroom or changing. I try the knob, and it turns. He's getting very careless about locking up. He knows better. If Ma learns of this, she'll be livid. You always lock your doors behind you on Long Island.

I step inside. It's quiet. I consider hiding in a closet, but that feels too boring. The living room is empty. The TV off. That's unlike my brother. He likes background noise. I start to go back to his bedroom, but the last thing I want is to get an eyeful of a naked Enzo.

"Yo, brother, it's your sister."

When he doesn't answer, I listen. I don't hear the shower running.

I turn into the kitchen and realize the light's on. I step over the threshold and see him lying on the floor. My heart jumps into my throat, and I run to his side. There's a knife sticking out of his arm. Blood is covering the wound and has seeped to the floor.

Oh, my God. No, no, no, not my brother!

CHAPTER TWELVE

"Enzo," I cry out, get to my knees, grab the front of his shirt, and shake him. I know that's stupid to do. It's not like he's napping. How can shaking an unconscious person help? But I'm doing it anyway.

What the heck happened? Did someone break in? A random person off the street or was this related to some criminal he apprehended? My mind races with thoughts. My fingers go to his wrist to find a pulse, but I was never good at that, so I can't tell if he's dead or not.

"Oh, gosh, Enzo. Hold on. I'm calling for help.' I reach into my purse, which I dropped beside me. I push the side button to bring the phone to life, and I catch movement.

I look down, and Enzo is convulsing. Oh my God, no! What am I supposed to do? I think I need a wooden spoon so his tongue...

The corners of Enzo's mouth creep up, and I realize the seizure is actually laughter. The jerk is faking it.

I slap him in the gut. "Are you kidding me? This is a prank."

He opens his eyes and lets out a rumble of laughter. Then he raises his arm, and I see that the knife was only positioned in his armpit.

I get to my feet and softly kick him in the shin. "I hate you. You know that, right? Why are you trying to give me a heart attack?"

He gets to his feet and grabs the roll of paper towels. "I saw you coming and figured I'd have some fun."

"Yeah, I'm in hysterics. This is the best time of my life."

He wipes the fake blood off his shirt and then the floor. "You owe me a bottle of ketchup."

"You give me a near fatal stroke, and I owe you?" I grab my purse and storm to the front door.

"Wait," he says and runs after me. "Why did you stop by?"

"I wanted to talk about the case, but I'm still having trouble breathing."

He giggles and then tries to make a straight face, but he sucks at it. Truth is, it's an awesome gag, and had he done it on someone else, I would be in stitches. But he seriously had me scared to death, and I can't fully forgive him just yet.

"Stay, and we can have dinner."

"I hate you. Why would I want to eat with you?"

This makes him laugh more.

"Besides, since when do you cook?" I ask.

He shrugs. "Carly's taught me a few dishes."

He and Carly are cooking together? I definitely need to stay. While I believe that Carly was just out with girlfriends last night, I can't help wondering if maybe Izzie is partially right, and Enzo could get hurt again. There isn't anything for me to do to stop it, but I can listen and be here for him if needed.

"Fine. What are we having for dinner? It better not involve ketchup." I toss my purse onto the counter.

He tries to hold back a chuckle, but he doesn't do a good job. He reaches into his fridge and pulls out a rotisserie chicken container from the grocery store. "How about leftovers?"

I raise a brow to his choice of cold chicken but think twice about protesting when he next pulls out macaroni and spinach salads. Separate, not combined.

"There's also a Carvel ice cream cake for dessert."

Oh, heck yeah. I'm staying. While the layers of vanilla and then chocolate ice cream are good, it's the chocolate crunchies in between that are the best.

He pops the top on the chicken. "Cold or heated?"

"If you plan on microwaving it, cold." Nuked poultry has an icky taste to me.

We each make a heaping plate and settle down in the living room, across from the TV, which Enzo finally turns on.

"Ma won't be happy you're not going to her house for dinner."

"After Sunday's cold shoulder, she'll be fine."

I hadn't thought about how that fiasco affected him. He had a smile on his face during dinner and dessert and seemed so untouched by it all. "Izzie and I saw Carly at lunch today."

"Oh yeah?" He shoved a forkful of chicken into his mouth, completely uninterested.

"Did you hear me?"

He frowned at me. "Yeah. What's wrong with you? You're sitting a foot away from me. I'm not Pop."

So I'm not the only one who's noticed Pop's audio issues. "Well, don't you want to know who she was with or where we were?"

He shrugged and scooped up some macaroni salad. "It doesn't matter."

"Why not? The two of you are cooking together. She was in your shower, and you brought her to Sunday dinner, which is the same as *meeting the parents*."

"You're sounding like Izzie. Carly and I are just friends. We're not getting married. Besides, you bring Julian to Sunday dinner."

I shake my fork in the air, back and forth. "Oh, no. Ma brings Julian to Sunday dinner."

We both snort because we know it's true.

"So, just friends? You sure?"

"I would know," he says.

"Izzie told me about high school. Was it as bad as she says, and why wasn't I aware of it all?"

"You were a kid. And I wasn't going to confide in my little sister. At least not back then."

Aww, that means he confides in me now. And that would be so much cuter if he was doing any confiding.

"So, confide."

He sighs and sets his fork down. "You're not going to let me eat until we paint each other's nails and talk about boys, huh?"

I grin as wide as my cheeks will allow. "Uh-huh."

"Fine. No, Carly and I are not together nor are we getting back together. I'm not interested in going down that road with her again. She's just a friend. And right now, she needs one."

"Why? What's wrong?"

"She recently broke up with the love of her life."

"Ouch, and that doesn't bother you?"

He stares off into the distance then shakes his head. "No, it doesn't. It would have if I was still eighteen, but I forgave her and moved on. You know, I have dated in the past eleven years."

I smirk. "Yes, I'm aware, but sometimes our first loves stay with us for a very long time."

"Is that the case with you?"

"My true first love died. There's nothing for me to hang onto. But no. I'm happy with Julian."

"Are you? I never know if you're back together or not. I still don't know why you broke up this last time."

Didn't we have this conversation a few days ago? Does he simply not remember, or is he pumping me for intel? I just shrug. "I'm not sure either, but he makes it hard to keep him at arm's length."

Enzo scrunches up his face. "Okay, before I learn about my sister's sexual habits or appetite, can we stop this slumber party now?"

I laugh. "Yes."

He lifts his plate and starts shoveling his food in as if he hasn't eaten in days. When he finally comes up for air, without turning his gaze from the TV, he asks, "You said you wanted to talk about the case. Do you know something more?"

I wish. "No, I was wondering if you learned anything new."

"Nothing more yet."

Darn.

* * *

When I leave Enzo's, it's dark, and I'm full of ice cream. I'm so glad I'm wearing elastic-waist leggings and not something with buttons or zippers. I pull my car onto the gravel driveway that leads to the back of Mancini Deli and park.

It's dark back here. There's a streetlamp by the street, but it's dim and only lights the entrance. I've been meaning to mention it to Pop. He's all about his kids' safety, so I'm sure he'll put up a flood lamp or something equally blinding, but it will be safe. I'm thinking about my darn brother and his prank as I get out, so I totally miss the silhouette of a person until I'm too close to be at a safe distance away.

"Crap," I mumble under my breath and stop in my tracks. I'm afraid that if I turn and try to make it back to my car, the assailant will grab the back of my hair and drag me to my death. Yes, I watch way too many episodes of *Criminal Minds*. But isn't it better to be prepared? Plus, I've already been around one murder victim and got way too close to her killer. And I know what death feels like up close and personal.

The mass murderer makes a stifled sound, and I gasp.

Screw this. I turn and run to my car when I hear my name.

"Gianna, what are you doing?" the voice asks. It's female.

I turn and hope I'm not making a mistake. "Who are you?"

She steps out of the intense shadows until I can make out her dark ponytail, high cheekbones, and bow-shaped mouth. "Gianna, it's me, Serena."

I take a deep breath and clutch my heart. Well, more like I lay my hand on my chest. Clutching my actual heart would be a bit messy and probably fatal.

"You scared me half to death. What are you doing here?"

She steps even closer, and I realize she's sniffling, crying, and that was the sound she made. "The police came by Sparks to tell me about Thom..." Her voice trails off.

She knows. They told her he was a fake. My chest becomes heavy, and I feel for her.

"Come on. Let's go upstairs."

I lead the way and unlock the downstairs, outside door. Pop recently added the lock to it. Then we climb the long, narrow flight of stairs, and I unlock my apartment door. I fling my purse onto the floor near the breakfast bar, turning on lights as I go.

"Have a seat," I say and point to the lumpy sofa. "Do you want coffee? I also have water, orange juice, and vodka."

Not that I want her drinking and driving... "How'd you get here? Where's your car?"

"I parked on the street. I didn't know your apartment was in back until I got out and walked around. And no, I don't want anything. You know, right? About him. That's what you were saying earlier."

I sit beside her and nod. "Yeah, I heard that your fiancé wasn't the real Thomas Sterling. I'm sorry."

She sniffles again. "How is this possible?"

I wish I knew. And if Fake Thomas would show his ghostly face I could maybe find out. The coward.

"The police think I'm lying and that I know who he really was, but I don't." Her sniffles turn to full-fledged sobs. They're too heavy, too real to suspect she's faking it. It's nice to know she wasn't involved in that farce.

I get up, go into the bedroom, and come back out with a box of tissues. I hand them to her and return to my seat. "Is there anything I can do to help you?"

I'm still not sure if she's guilty or not in his death though, so maybe I shouldn't be offering, but she looks so miserable. And I know what it feels like to lose someone you love. Granted, my first love died in a hit-and-run. It has to be harder when it's murder meant for her. Supposedly.

She shakes her head to my offer of help. "The police didn't have anything to hold me. Lying isn't exactly a crime, not like obstruction. But I haven't done anything wrong. They suspect I have my hand in this mess somehow though. I'm totally innocent, but what if they fabricate something? You hear about dirty cops."

I'd love to tell her that's a myth, but Detective Kevin Burton did exactly that last month with Izzie. I also don't want to needlessly worry Serena, so I say nothing and hope she won't notice.

"What do you know about Fake...about the man you were engaged to?"

She shrugs. "Just what he told me. Everything was about the real Thomas Sterling. The police told me things about Mr. Sterling, and they're identical to what my Thomas told me."

"Like what?"

"That he grew up with his parents in a big house up in Lido Beach and that he went to Columbia University. It's as if my Thomas memorized all of Mr. Sterling's information."

I stare at her, wondering if she's really this clueless or if it's the grief talking. "He did, Serena. It's a con. He was probably pretending to be the real Thomas Sterling for some reason, and he didn't mean to fall for you. Unless you're wealthy. Are you?"

She widens her eyes. "No way. If I was, I wouldn't be back at the club working."

I hear that.

"But why lie to me?"

"I can't answer that." But if Fake Thomas was here, maybe he could. "What about his mother, Brenda? I'm assuming she passed herself off as the real Mrs. Sterling. I wonder if anyone's spoken to her." That was a silly question. Of course the police spoke with the real Mrs. Sterling. That's probably how they learned the real Thomas was alive and well in Europe.

Serena buries her face in her hands and groans. "This is just crazy."

That is not a lie.

"How did you and he meet? Where?" I ask.

"It was at a party. A quick introduction from friends. And then I ran into him again one day, and he asked me out. Just like that. We instantly fell in love."

"And what about the fake Brenda? Did you ever meet her at her *mansion*?" I do air quotes and softly chuckle.

Serena doesn't think it's funny though because she just continues to stare wide-eyed. "Yes. A couple of times."

My brain does a rewind to what I asked. "Wait, what? You met with her at her mansion? The one up in Lido Beach?"

"Yes, that's why this doesn't make sense."

Another nugget of truth.

I stand up. "Take me there."

* * *

I follow Serena's white Toyota through the East End and past it into Lido Beach. The Sterling mansion is huge and white and seems to shimmer in the moonlight. The drive from the street to the house is all lush, manicured shrubs. Some short boxy ones but others that are tall and shaped like cones.

I park behind Serena, who stops a few feet from the front steps. I get out and follow her up those glistening steps, wondering how anyone keeps white so clean. Ma would be impressed but the poor Sterling's staff. I hope they get paid well.

Serena uses the heavy brass knocker on the door and glances at me. She seems to be biting the inside of her cheek. I interpret the look as nervousness. Or maybe that's just due to the swarm of butterflies in my own belly. I have high expectations we'll get some answers here, and I can't wait.

The door opens to a man in black pants and vest and a crisp white shirt. I wonder if he cleans the stairs.

"May I help you?" he asks.

"We're here to see Mrs. Sterling," Serena says.

"I'm sorry, but the lady of the house can not be disturbed." He starts to shut the door, but Serena sticks her foot in the threshold, preventing him from closing it all the way.

"Don't you remember me?" she asks.

He doesn't respond or show any sign of recognition.

"I was here last month. I was her future daughter-in-law."

"Mrs. Sterling already has a daughter-in-law."

Serena sighs. "That may be so, but I was here, and so were you. You passed the living room to the right." She points as if he needs to know which way is right.

"I was sitting in there waiting for Mrs. Sterling. You asked me if I wanted tea or coffee, and I didn't. You don't remember, or you don't want to?"

I can't help but grin widely. Part of it is because of how Serena plays hard ball. I like it. And the other reason is because this is my first time meeting an actual butler. Pop would be so impressed. Every time we played the game *Clue*, he always said "the butler did it," even if he knew it was Colonel Mustard in the study with a lead pipe.

"Look, we're not leaving until we speak with Mrs. Sterling, and if you don't let us in, then I'll go to the press and tell them how I've been in this house, that I know how the entire living room is white, from the rug to the furniture and walls, and how the imposter knew everything about the Sterlings. Things I'm sure they don't want made public."

When Serena is done with her awesome monologue, she takes a step back, removing her foot from the doorway.

The butler says, "One moment please." He shuts the door and leaves us staring at it.

"If I ever need to win an argument, I'm calling you," I whisper.

She lets out a light giggle and smiles at me. It looks good on her.

The door reopens, and the butler waves an arm for us to enter. Part of me wants to say, "ha" as I pass, but I was raised better than that. Besides, I'm sure the butler is a very nice man. He's just doing his job.

I follow Serena into the white living room, and she wasn't kidding. Oh my God, it either costs a fortune to keep this room so brilliant, or it's hardly used.

But before we get cozy, as much as one can get cozy sitting gingerly on the edge of a cushion while hoping you don't leave behind a body imprint, the butler clears his voice. 'This way, please."

I turn to see him pointing in the opposite direction. To the left. Wonder what's behind these double doors. He opens them to reveal a smaller room in various shades of blue, from the pastel walls to the navy sofa and a muted blue Tiffany lamp. I suddenly want to explore the rest of the house to find the yellow, red, and green rooms. I'm sure they exist.

A woman around Ma's age is seated on a settee. She wears a long, floral gown, which must be the rich equivalent of a housedress, with a matching scarf around her head and jeweled slippers on her feet. Is this Mrs. Sterling, or are we about to get our fortunes read?

She eyes each of us suspiciously, which, under the circumstances, I completely understand. "Thank you, Jeeves. That is all."

I choke back a laugh. No way. His name is Jeeves? Just wait until I tell Pop.

She must notice the half smile I'm desperately trying to hide because she says, "His actual name is Benjamin, but we have a running joke about the Jeeves thing around strangers."

Ha, they have a sense of humor. How cool.

"Now which of you young women is the one wanting to cause trouble for my family?"

Serena raises her hand to cheek level. "I don't want trouble. I just want to talk to you."

Mrs. Sterling points to the sofa across from her. "Well, sit down because I don't want to strain my neck, and tell me what you want to talk about."

We sit and Serena looks at me. She suddenly seems at a loss for words, so I begin. I tell the woman about the fake Thomas and how he died and how he and Serena were engaged.

"Yes, I heard about that. I am terribly sorry someone is dead, but that man was impersonating my son. I hadn't any knowledge this was even going on or that my son's home had been used for this ruse until the police spoke with me. It's all very upsetting, but surely you aren't here because you feel entitled to something?"

Serena looks taken aback. Poor girl. Even if she is a murderer, which I kinda doubt, she's had a ton of crap fall on her lately.

I take the lead again. "We're here, Mrs. Sterling because we simply want to understand. Serena met the fake Mrs. Sterling here, in your home. In the white living room."

Mrs. Sterling frowns. "That's not possible."

"But it is," Serena says. Her voice is strained, as if she's on the verge of tears again. "The last time was just last month. It was on a Tuesday. I remember this because Thomas and I went to dinner afterwards, and I don't work Tuesday nights."

Mrs. Sterling raises her chin and stares at us down her nose. "Tuesday? What time of day was this?"

"Around three or four. Thomas and I left after we discussed wedding plans with his mother. She was not happy."

"Why is that?" Mrs. Sterling asks.

Serena shrugs. "She didn't think I was good enough for her son."

What if the fake Mrs. Sterling was trying to kill Serena and accidentally killed her own child? Then again, were the imposters even related?

"I am not home at that time of day on Tuesdays," Mrs. Sterling says. "I have a weekly luncheon with friends at the Rose Garden."

Ah-ha! Now we're getting somewhere.

"What does this *fake me* look like?"

"Um, brown hair down to her shoulders. She's slightly thick but not fat, just not slender. And there's a beauty mark at the corner of her left eye," Serena says.

I hadn't noticed the beauty mark.

Mrs. Sterling inhales a sharp breath. Then she picks up a small brass bell and jingles it.

Oh my gosh, I've seen it all. You'd think there'd be a more appropriate, or at least respectful, way of calling for your servant. Maybe this is part of their humor, but I get the feeling Mrs. Sterling doesn't feel like laughing.

Almost immediately, Jeeves appears in the doorway. "Yes, Ma'am?"

"Can you please ask Cynthia to come here? And don't say why."

He gives half of a bow. "Yes, Ma'am."

After he leaves, I ask, "Who's Cynthia?"

"My assistant." Mrs. Sterling now sounds curt, and her top lip is stiff, so I don't ask anything more.

We sit there for a minute or two and hear footsteps coming closer. Then a woman says, "You called for me?" We can't see her from our angle. She isn't fully in the doorway yet.

"Yes, I'd like you to meet my guests." Mrs. Sterling points to us.

The woman steps into the room, stares at us, and widens her eyes.
I mimic her expression when I realize Cynthia is Fake Mother.

CHAPTER THIRTEEN

My foot fell asleep while sitting here waiting for the police, and now I'm flexing it to return it to normal, but it's not helping much. Of course the jitteriness in my stomach doesn't help my overall mood much either. It's not that I'm anti police. I'm just anti Detective Kevin Burton, and guess who showed up when Jeeves called?

Mrs. Sterling's assistant, Fake Mother, aka Cynthia, took off as soon as she spotted Serena and me. I mean, she turned around and booked out the front door without a sound. No purse, no "see ya." She just hauled butt. And now Kevin and his partner, Detective Sanchez, are here, and they're asking Mrs. Sterling a bunch of questions. It's only a matter of time before I have to smell Kevin's hostile breath.

I can't hear what Mrs. Sterling is saying because she's in the foyer with them, standing beneath the seventeen-ton crystal chandelier. I mean, how does anyone clean that thing? I guess it's pretty telling the kind of life I lead when all I can think about is the manpower necessary to keep a fortress like this running.

Serena and I are still seated on the blue sofa, still in the same spots. I haven't moved because Serena seems to be existing in a state of frozen shock, and I figure she could use any support I can give. Even if it's the butt-numbing kind.

When the detectives have pumped all the info they can from Mrs. Sterling, Kevin and Sanchez move on to Serena. This conversation I hear perfectly. Especially the part where she tells the cops that I'm the Fake Thomas's assistant.

"Is that so?" Kevin asks, shining his death-ray glance on me. If glares could singe, I'd be ash right now. "You seem to be everywhere."

Serena blinks a few times. "You know each other?"

"Unfortunately," I say under my breath, but everyone still hears me.

Sanchez goes as far as to smirk. That puts me a bit at ease. He seems like a really cool man, so he has to see his partner's ridiculousness.

They spend the next fifteen minutes grilling Serena about Fake Thomas. Unfortunately, Mrs. Sterling doesn't know Cynthia's son's name. She's only seen him twice from afar and hasn't been introduced to him. So referring to him as Fake Thomas will continue until the darn ghost decides to show himself again. As for poor Serena, her face has turned red, and she looks like she's either going to start crying or screaming due to the questions. It's not because they're hard to answer but because they keep asking the same thing over and over but in slightly different ways.

Like, "When you met, how did he introduce himself?" and "He approached you at the party and said what?"

It's exhausting to listen to.

After they've drained her, they turn their faces to me. Kevin's mouth moves slightly, like he's scratching his teeth with the inside of his lips. He's dying to ask me something but holds back. As if they share some form of telepathy, Sanchez pats his partner on the shoulder. Kevin obediently steps back and allows Sanchez to get closer.

The older man sits on the edge of the coffee table. He's a big guy, kinda stocky, so our knees almost brush against one another. This means I have to stop shaking my leg and sit still.

"Ms. Mancini, you worked with the Thomas Sterling impersonator? How long have you known him?"

"I don't *know* him and 'worked with' is a stretch."

"Yeah, he died shortly after he hired her," Serena says, telling them the lies I told her.

How exactly am I going to get out of this mess? If I admit that I don't know him at all, I won't have a way to explain how I knew things that Fake Thomas told me. And then I have to deal with Serena knowing I lied to her. She won't help me, even if inadvertently, figure out who killed her fiancé. Although I'll admit that I'm starting to wonder if I should even bother. I'm so confused as to who is who and what's going on. I need a scorecard.

If I lie to the cops and tell them everything Serena believes then they'll assume that I know more than "nothing" about him, and that's not true. Besides, Fake Thomas isn't here, so I can't even fake it. I sigh. I'm screwed no matter what I do, so I decide on pleading the fifth and keeping my mouth shut. More or less.

"How well do you know him?" Sanchez asks.

"What's his name?" Kevin asks.

"I don't know his name."

Kevin crosses his arms over his chest, obviously not satisfied with my answer. Hey, I wouldn't be satisfied with it either, but for once, I'm not lying.

"There has to be a way for you guys to figure out who he is, especially since you now know who his mother is."

Sanchez nods a couple of times and says, "We will, but in the meantime, it would help us greatly if you told us everything he ever said to you."

I think back to our conversations, to see if there was anything pertaining to his life before death, and the only thing I can recall is, "He loved Serena a lot."

"That's helpful," Kevin says. The sarcasm is thick, and if anyone else had said it, I would chuckle.

Serena smiles, and the red on her face starts to dissipate. It's helpful to someone.

"What work was he having you do?" Sanchez asks.

Technically he wanted me to help Serena, but I can't say that. Great. Here's the part where I have to look uncooperative.

"Well, that's hard to say."

Kevin scoffs. "Try harder."

I stare into Sanchez's big brown eyes and wonder what he thinks of me. This is the second dead person case we've spoken about. Does he find it odd that I seem to be involved in this one too? I don't bother wondering what Kevin thinks because then I'll probably need a good hosing down.

I shake my head slightly. I really can't help them. "I don't have anything to say."

* * *

Suffice it to say, they don't take my refusal to talk well. They say a few more words with Mrs. Sterling, tell Serena they'll be in touch, and drag my butt downtown. Sheer glee explodes on Kevin's face when Sanchez suggests I go back to the station with them. I think he's going to start dancing a jig. They insist I leave my car at the Sterling estate and ride with them. Joy.

When they usher me into one of the interrogation rooms, Sanchez offers me coffee, but I decline. My jitteriness has catapulted into a near seizure so the last thing I need is caffeine.

Kevin pulls out a chair from across the metal table. Its legs scratch against the tile creating a nails on chalkboard effect that even Sanchez grimaces at.

"I understand there may have been things you didn't want to say in front of his fiancé," Sanchez says while taking a seat directly across from me. "So now we're alone, and you're free to tell us whatever you know."

I look into each of their gazes quickly. Part of me hates what I'm about to say because I know they won't believe me, and this will only escalate until Kevin is breathing down my neck, but what other choice do I have? I know nothing.

"There's nothing to tell. I wasn't being evasive back there. I simply don't have answers to your questions."

Kevin clenches his jaw. "That's a lie."

Sanchez glances to his partner and then back to me. He uses an extra calm voice. "I don't know what you're afraid of..."

"I want to talk to my lawyer." I cut him off.

Kevin's eyes gleam. "You have something to hide?"

"Only that you're dumb. Oh wait. Everyone already knows that." Okay, so that might've been unnecessary. Thank goodness Sanchez is a reasonable man, or one day Kevin might arrest me for smarting off. I fold my arms over my chest and slink into the seat, trying to find comfort on the aluminum chair. I have no idea if Julian's boss, Mr. Hamilton, will come down here. He helped out Izzie last time, so I'm hoping.

"You're not under arrest," Sanchez says. "You don't need a lawyer."

"I do if you're going to make me sit here and discuss things I can't because I don't have answers."

Kevin jumps up and starts to protest, but Sanchez cuts him off by placing his cell phone in front of me. "Make your call."

I stare at the black rectangle and think about my perfectly good phone that's sitting in my purse at my feet. Does he want me to use his so there's a trace of the call, or is he not thinking and just being polite?

Either way, I pick up his phone and dial Julian. Luckily he's not screening his calls and picks up the unknown number. "Hello?"

"Hey, it's me. I need your help. I'm at the police station. Can you get in touch with Mr. Hamilton?"

There's silence, and for a moment, I wonder if the call disconnected.

"Are you there?" I ask.

"Yes. Are you alright?"

"Fine. It's just routine questions." I glance at the detectives. Sanchez is simply watching me with no expression I can decipher, and Kevin looks like he ate something bad. What else is new?

"On my way." The call clicks off before I can remind him I need Hamilton more than him, although I'll be much happier to see Julian. I put the phone on the table and slide it to Sanchez.

Then we all settle in for a staring contest.

* * *

Twenty minutes later there's a knock on the door, and a uniformed officer peeks his head in. "Her attorney is here."

Sanchez and Kevin rise. I stay seated.

The officer widens the door and steps back. Mr. Hamilton and Julian walk in.

"He's not a lawyer," Kevin says as he glares at Julian.

Mr. Hamilton looks extra sharp in a black suit with a silver tie. "Is my client under arrest?"

"No," Sanchez says. "We're just trying to find out some information that she may have."

"Then there's no reason why Mr. Reed can't join us for a moment."

With that said, Julian hurries over and takes the chair beside me.

Sanchez motions for him and Kevin to leave. When the door shuts behind him, Julian asks, "What's going on?"

I fill them both in on everything that happened tonight.

Mr. Hamilton sits in Sanchez's seat and listens intently. But when I get to the part about not being able to give them the answers they need, I stop. How do I explain that I can't because Fake Tom is a ghost that's been talking to me?

I look to Julian and plead with my eyes, but since he can't read minds, he hasn't a clue as to what I want to say in private. So I take a risk and say it out loud. "This has to do with my friend."

He immediately understands that and looks to his boss. "There are things involved that can't be explained."

Mr. Hamilton raises his slightly bushy brows. "You're going to have to do better than that if I'm to help you."

I nibble at the inside corner of my mouth and contemplate blurting out the truth. My truth. But then I remember where we are and how there's a camera in the wall. I don't know if it's on or not. It shouldn't be, but I can't take that chance, so I grab Julian's hand and squeeze it. "Go somewhere private, and tell him everything."

He doesn't respond at first. He seems to be considering what I said, so I just continue to hold his hand. It's warm, and I wish he was holding me close to him. "You're sure?" he asks.

I nod and let him go.

He and Mr. Hamilton step out of the room, and I just sit here and wait. And wait.

A mix of emotions run through me. I hate sharing my secret. It's left me friendless in the past. Not that Mr. Hamilton and I are going to braid each other's hair anytime soon, but it still makes me feel itchy. Like I'm a snake shedding my skin. I've never gotten over my ex-BFF and now Kevin's wife, Hilary, blabbing my secret in high school. It's also through Hilary that Kevin learned the truth, the reason he arrived at my apartment drunk that night. He doesn't know for certain that I can see the departed, but he suspects. And I'm sure my ghost pals scaring him didn't help. I laugh at the memories. Ah. That was a fun time.

When the door reopens, my heart feels like it's beating inside my throat. Mr. Hamilton is running his hand through his hair over and over again. His faraway gaze makes him look a bit stunned. I don't blame him. If Julian told him I see dead people, he has every right to be stunned. He sits beside me. Julian doesn't reenter, but Sanchez and Kevin come back in.

Mr. Hamilton pats my hand and offers a half smile. The look on his face is blank. I have no idea how much Julian told him or if he believes him.

Sanchez asks, "So now that your attorney is here, can you please tell us what you know about the Thomas Sterling imposter?"

I glance to Hamilton who pats my hand again.

"Ms. Mancini doesn't know anything about him."

Kevin rolls his eyes and opens his mouth to say something when Hamilton raises a hand to cut him off. "Before you start ranting and raving, Detective..."

I choke back a chuckle. Even Hamilton knows what a jackwad Kevin is.

"Let me explain," he continues. "Ms. Mancini told Miss Tate that she was this imposter's assistant, but that is untrue. Ms. Mancini has never met the imposter. She only heard of his death and existence after the explosion, which occurred a few blocks from her home and family business."

Sanchez frowns and scratches his temple. "But why would you lie about that?"

"She's been working for me," Mr. Hamilton says without any indication that he's lying.

I stare at him and hope my face doesn't look as surprised as I feel.

"Excuse me?" Kevin asks.

"I employed Ms. Mancini to help us with a case. I cannot discuss it in detail—attorney-client privilege. But I can say that Ms. Mancini was going to apply to be the imposter's assistant. She just never got the chance."

Darn, he's really good at the lying. Not even a muscle twitched.

The detectives just sit there and digest this information. Finally Sanchez asks, "But why lie to Miss Tate?"

I wait for Hamilton to say something, but he must be out of fibs because he just glances at me and nods. Oh, so it's my turn?

"Um, because I was trying to find out what I could from her. I didn't know if she knew the truth about him or not."

That seems to interest Sanchez because he leans forward, resting his forearms on the table. "And what did you learn?"

"From what I can tell, she had no clue. She's been extremely upset since his death. You know she almost overdosed. Julian...my friend and I found her and called an ambulance. That wasn't fake. She was admitted to the hospital and held for observation."

Sanchez nods and looks into the distance for a moment. I seem to have stumped Kevin too. Good.

"Is that all?" Mr. Hamilton asks. He pushes his chair out and rises to his feet. Guess it doesn't matter if it is or isn't because he gingerly touches my elbow, guiding me to my feet as well. "If you have more questions for Ms. Mancini, please call my office."

He doesn't leave his card or anything. He opens the door and allows me to walk through first.

I glance back one last time. Both of the detectives have risen as well. But while Sanchez isn't paying us any more attention, Kevin is staring at me. That shouldn't be a big deal. It's becoming his permanent expression, but I admit it unnerves me for a moment. Is it possible he's figured out that my undercover case with Hamilton has something to do with Fake Thomas's ghost?

* * *

Julian and I sit in his car outside my apartment. He blasts the heat, and I'm toasting my fingers over the vent. Somewhere between this afternoon and tonight it's become cold, as if it's winter and not the middle of fall.

"How did Hamilton react when you told him I can see ghosts?" I still can't believe he knows the truth and acted as if it was an everyday thing in the interrogation room.

Julian smirks. "I think I blew his mind, but he's very good at not showing his emotions."

Makes sense. He's a lawyer and needs a poker face for court.

"He didn't question it. He didn't seem to think I was crazy. He just accepted it and told the detectives you and he are ready to continue. I'm not sure if he believes it, but he acted like he did."

It's a lot to ask of someone, especially a stranger. I think my family deals so well partly because they've had years to digest it and because they love me. They don't have a choice.

"Thank you," I say. "Not just for talking to him but for finding him and showing up."

His brows move closer to one another. "Of course I'd show up. I'd do anything for you. You know that, right?"

When he talks like this, I start to forget the reason I'm mad at him. Not fully. I know his secrecy almost cost Izzie her freedom, but I need to believe he would've come forward in the end. He made a mistake. How long am I going to hold it over him?

My thoughts jump to Ma and Carly. It's been over a decade since Carly hurt Enzo, and Ma still treats her like the plague. I don't want to be like that.

Without another thought, I unbuckle my seat belt and lean into Julian's space. I place one hand on the console between us so I don't fall onto him completely. I'm not ready for that. Then I awkwardly place my other hand on his thigh and softly press my lips to his.

He sighs ever so gently and pushes toward me, deepening the kiss, but he doesn't take control. He allows me to say how far it will go, and that makes me linger longer.

When I pull back, I stare at his shut eyes. He opens them and smiles.

I return to my side of the car fully and grab the door handle. "I should get going."

If he's disappointed, it doesn't show on his face. He's still smiling. "I'll drop off your car first thing in the morning. I'll get a buddy to help me."

I frown. He's never discussed buddies before, and I haven't asked. "You have friends?"

He chuckles and fills his car with that delicious sound. "Wow. Do you think I'm a loser?"

"No. I just don't have any friends, so I'm a little envious. Besides, that means there's a part of your life I know nothing about."

He brushes the back side of his knuckles down my cheek. "They aren't actually hang-out friends. At least not yet. Just a couple of guys from Hamilton's office. Coworkers."

"Oh. That's cool."

"And I'm not hiding anything from you. Never again."

Now I smile. "Me too."

I hop out of his SUV and go up to my apartment, locking the doors behind me as I go. I head straight to the bathroom and get ready for bed. My stomach is grumbling some, but I'm so tired from being woken this morning and then the day's turn of events that food will have to wait until tomorrow.

Dressed in a tank and shorts, despite the falling temps outside, I climb under my sheet and comforter and lay my head against the pillow.

"Is she okay?" says a voice.

I spring up and gasp. Standing at the foot of my bed is Fake Thomas.

Holy ghosts!

CHAPTER FOURTEEN

"Where have you been?" I shout. I don't mean to, but he scared the crap out of me, and I'm ticked off that I'm not sleeping. But that will wait because I have a ton of questions, and he better be in the mood to answer.

I get out of bed, grab my hoodie off my closet floor, and go into the main room. If I'm going to be awake, I'm going to eat. I head straight to the fridge.

"Around." He sounds sullen.

I turn to him, and it dawns on me. "You figured out how to be around but also be invisible to me. You've been watching everything."

He looks guilty and nods.

I breathe in deeply. "Okay, so talk to me. You have nothing to lose by my knowing the truth. Right? In fact, I won't help Serena anymore if you don't tell me everything right now. So spill."

"I don't know where to begin."

I go back to the fridge because my stomach is going on strike. I find potato salad and pull it out. "How about your real name?"

"Frank Mason."

I stare into his brown eyes. "Hi, Frank."

The corner of his mouth lifts but just for a second. "Hi."

"So, is Cynthia your actual mother?"

"Yes. She's been pulling cons her whole life. I was raised on them. I guess that's not an excuse." He lowers his head as if guilt wracks him. Then again, maybe he's conning me right now too.

"If you know they're wrong then no, it's not an excuse. But I'm not the morality police. I simply want to know what's going on." I stick another forkful of potato into my mouth and feel the beast in my belly start to calm down.

"Okay, well usually it was mail or check fraud, but this time it has to do with a man."

Don't most things?

"He wanted to meet her family, so she begged me to play Thomas. It was supposed to be one dinner. One night." He did that downward head thing again.

"But..." I say and take another bite of salad. Darn, this is good. Ma uses just enough mayo that it's wet but not drenched, and there are bits of onion, hard-boiled egg, and relish, with a sprinkle of paprika. It's the relish that sets it apart.

He shrugs. "He invited me to parties and dinners, sometimes with Mom and sometimes without. Then one night, I met Serena as Thomas Sterling. When I ran into her again, was I supposed to tell her that I'd lied the first time?"

Well, yes, that would've been awesome. But I don't say anything 'cause what good will it do now? It's already happened, and we can't change it. Plus, I don't want to interrupt. I want to hear every syllable he has to say and finish my salad.

"She was so beautiful, and I couldn't believe she was talking to me. She laughed at my jokes." His voice sounds dreamy and far away as if he's remembering the night vividly.

"Okay, so you kept quiet. But what about when you proposed? Were you planning on marrying her as Thomas Sterling?"

He looks at me sharply. "No. Never. I waited longer than I should have. I know this. But I just wanted to make sure she loved me first and not my so-called money."

"Even after you proposed?"

He shrugs again. He obviously wondered about her sincerity, which tells me I may be right about suspecting her.

"We were having dinner that night, and I was coming clean. That's why I was at her house the day of the explosion." His voice cracks.

Holy bomb! What kind of coincidence is this?

"Why were you there before Serena? Were you early? Where was she?"

What if Serena is behind this? Maybe she wanted the inheritance, but what if she found out the truth and was angry? I don't know if that's probable though. She seemed awfully upset earlier. She'd have to be one great actress to pull that off. And why bother showing up at my place at all if she knew all along? Why stage a suicide attempt? Unless that was real because she was feeling guilty for what she did.

Gosh, I have too many darn questions.

"I don't know where she was. I never got the chance to ask."

Hmm, things aren't looking great for Serena.

* * *

I'm outside. The sky is a vivid blue, and the sun is bright. A woman says, "Your brother is calling." I start running down the hill, but the voice continues. I can't escape it. It's everywhere. It's...

I open my eyes, stare at the ceiling, and realize it's my cell. The caller ID says it's Enzo, which I already knew by his special ringtone. It's 6:00 a.m. Why is he calling me so early? I sit up while swiping the throbbing green circle. "What's wrong?"

As soon as I say that, there's pounding on my front door. It's loud and continuous and panic sets in. Maybe this is another dream.

"Enzo?" I say while kicking off my covers and waddling into the living room. "I'm coming," I shout to whoever is trying to break in. I should probably look for a weapon, but I'm too groggy to see my surroundings in detail.

Enzo sighs and says, "I'm sorry. I thought they knew."

Knew what? Who knew?

"What are you talking about?" I look through the peephole and see a distorted Ma. I step back and walk into the center of the living room as realization hits me. "You told Ma about the police questioning me last night, didn't you?"

It's the only reason Ma would be up here and not down in the deli at this hour. Unless someone died, but then she'd have tact and wouldn't be beating down my door.

"Like I said, I thought they knew. I found out through the grapevine, so I figured it wasn't a big deal," he says.

It wasn't, but that's not the point. I didn't plan on telling the folks because I don't want them to worry. I also don't want 6:00 a.m. confrontations. "I am revoking your brother card," I whisper.

Suddenly I hear the lock click, and the door is opening. Of course. Why didn't I think of that? Ma has a key. She steps inside with a wide-eyed stare that makes her look crazy. It doesn't help that her dark hair is full and frizzy around her face. It must be humid outside. Instead of her slamming the door shut behind her, Izzie steps in. She woke up my pregnant sister too?

"I gotta go," I say into the phone and click off our call. I am so getting Enzo back for this and the fake-death-ketchup thing.

Izzie looks almost as crazed as Ma, but her raised brows and wide eyes read more concern than fear and outrage. At least that's how I'm interpreting it.

"Do I have time to pee before we get into this?" I ask.

"Why didn't you call me immediately last night?" Ma asks.

I guess that's a nope. I'll just hold it in. At least this means Ma is talking again.

"By the time Julian dropped me off, it was late. I didn't want to wake you up. And it wasn't a big deal. Just some questions."

Ma's face completely changes, and the angry look is replaced by calm, serenity, and a half smile. I swear she has Jekyll and Hyde tendencies. "Julian was with you?" she asks.

Of course that makes all the difference in the world.

I sit on a stool at the breakfast nook. "Sometimes I think you like him more than I do, Ma." Which is saying a lot since I love him, even when I hate him.

She giggles and swats away my words. "Don't be ridiculous."

Izzie rolls her eyes. "This is all adorable, but I'm still annoyed at you. I was worried when Enzo said you spent the night at the police station. My own ordeal is still very present in my memories, and why'd you tell him and not me?"

Now it's Ma's turn to roll her eyes.

I try really hard to not do the same because I know Izzie went through major stress when the cops arrested her, and I don't want to make light of that. But the sibling jealousy thing is silly. "I didn't tell Enzo. He must've found out through a cop buddy. Only Julian knew because I called him to get in touch with Mr. Hamilton."

Izzie and Ma gasp, which causes me to frown. What did I say?

"You needed an attorney?" Ma asks. "Then this is serious."

Not as serious as my need to pee. But I don't make a break for it because I still have another good hour of sleep in me. I want this conversation to end so they'll leave.

"No, it was just questions, but I didn't know how to answer them, so I called Julian." I expect to see Ma smile at the mention of his name, but she's back to frowning.

"You didn't know *how* to answer them?" Izzie repeats. Then she raises her brows. "Oh, is this another ghost thing?"

"Maybe."

Izzie lets out a deep breath, and her whole demeanor immediately calms. "Okay."

Ma looks to her eldest with a deeper frown. "No, this is not okay. The last time you helped some ghost you almost died. You can't help them."

Well now, that's just plain crazy. "I can't ignore them. They need me, and I'm good at it." Okay, so I'm more like decent at it, but I'm sure with practice I'll be the next Jennifer Love Hewitt from *Ghost Whisperer*.

"No, you find a great career, you get married, and you have kids. Do something normal."

My body freezes for a moment as I process the insensitive words she uttered. Even Izzie looks stricken by them. I can't believe Ma said that. "But I'm not normal, or this is my normal. And all the wishing in the world won't change that. I can't just walk away from them. I was given this ability for a reason, and it would be selfish of me to not help them."

Ma huffs, storms past Izzie, and walks out.

I hate when she does that, but I'm glad she's gone too. She really hurt my feelings.

Izzie gives me a reassuring smile. "Don't worry. She'll come around. She's just scared for her baby." She rubs her growing belly.

Good thing neither of them know about Freezer Dude.

When Izzie leaves, I lock the door behind her and wait until I feel they're completely gone. Then I run to the bathroom, do my business, and jump back into bed. As I lay my head on my pillow, our conversation replays through my mind. I consider doing what Ma suggests and not helping them anymore.

But I'm not sure I can walk away from Frank and Serena right now. Wow, calling Fake Thomas Frank is sure weird. No. Ditching them would be mean. And what would I do when he comes around or the next ghost appears? There's no way I can ignore this.

* * *

Late that afternoon, I'm behind the deli counter, watching the clock tick by. It's been slow since the lunch crowd, and there's nothing worse than standing around doing nothing. When I arrived at work, Ma clicked her tongue at me a few times but didn't bring up this morning's conversation. When Pop arrived, he didn't mention it either. He has to know though. Ma tells him everything. And I'm pretty sure she ranted to him when Izzie or Enzo told her. I'm still not sure which of my siblings deserves a time out.

Before I arrived for my shift, I went looking for Serena, but I couldn't find her. I'm not sure what she's thinking about me. Does she realize I'm almost as big of a con as her dead fiancé? I hope not. I just wanted to help. I never meant to deceive her. Hmm, I guess that's how Frank feels too.

I checked Zoe's house, finally getting the apartment number from Julian. No one was home, not even Zoe. I tried the real Thomas's place, just in case. There were cars parked there, but none was Serena's. I imagine they belonged to Thomas, his wife, and possibly Mrs. Sterling. I even swung by Sparks, but it was too early for anyone to be there. I have no other ideas where she goes during the day. I plan to look more tonight. She has to show up somewhere eventually.

Then I called Julian and gave him the name Frank Mason. He promised to look into it and call me when he has something. Thank goodness I have people in my life who can find out this kind of information. And with Julian, as opposed to Enzo, I don't have to worry about him losing his job if caught. Finding the goods on people is his job. Maybe Julian's line of work isn't the worst. Sometimes.

My shift is finally up. I untie my apron, kiss Pop's cheek bye, and head out back to the fresh air. I go up to my apartment and jump into the shower. As I towel off, my cell rings. It's Julian.

"Hey, what's up?"

"I have that information. Can I stop by after work?"

Wow, he's fast.

"I'm free now."

"I'm not. I'm on a stakeout. But I should be wrapped up soon. There are only so many hours one can sit in their car watching a house."

"Oooh, sounds like fun. Can I join you?" I swear I don't mean to make that sound sexual, but my sultry, sex-kitten voice emerges.

"Sure." He sounds way too eager. He rattles off the address.

"I'll be there as soon as I get dressed."

"Are you naked now?"

I glance down to my towel. "Maybe."

He moans into the phone. "I'm waiting."

I hang up feeling tingly from head to toe.

* * *

I pull up to the location and park half a block behind Julian. I'm not a spy, but I've watched my share of television, and common sense says that parking right behind him and then getting into his car may call too much attention to us. So I try to be as stealthy as possible. Plus, there's this thrill associated with sneaking around that puts goose bumps on my arms and chills down my back in a giddy sort of way.

I grab my purse, lock and shut my door, and step up onto the sidewalk. At first I'm hunched over, trying to blend into the parked cars, but then I realize I must look like a thief. So I stand straight and try to act nonchalant, like I'm simply walking down the street. No big deal. I know how to walk.

When I reach Julian's car, I pull up the handle and climb into the passenger seat. I wanted to slide into the seat like a snake, but at five-two, I need to climb into his SUV. I shut the door behind me and turn to him.

He has a smirk on his face that makes him look like he's guilty of something, and his eyes travel from my face to my chest. He's probably still picturing me naked.

"Did you see me coming?" I ask.

"Yeah, but I was looking out for you."

"Aren't you supposed to be keeping your eyes on your stakeout?"

His smirk grows.

"Which house are you watching?"

He points to the one-story, brick bungalow across the street. A light blue tricycle sits sideways by the front walk, and they have an American flag swaying in the breeze by their door.

"Can I ask why?"

A shadow clouds his expression for a moment. "I shouldn't say."

"It's okay." And it truly is. I don't expect him to answer. I probably shouldn't even be here. I'm grateful for this. "So, what did you find out?"

He reaches to the backseat and pulls up a notepad. He flips a few pages and says, "Thomas Sterling, the real one, comes up clean. He and his wife, Vivian, have been in Madrid for the past six months. As it turns out, they spend every year there from right after Mother's Day to mid-November."

Must be nice.

"I did a background check on Serena Tate. She also comes up mostly clean. No arrests, a couple of parking tickets. The usual stuff, but there are some financial discrepancies."

Really? This is sounding juicy.

"Like what?"

"She makes more money than she should. On her bank statements, deposits she makes weekly are higher than her recorded salary from Sparks."

"She's a server, so it's probably tips," I say, but a nagging feeling in my gut tells me that's not right.

Julian agrees with my gut because he's shaking his head. "No, this is a lot more money. Thousands."

Holy dollar bill!

"Do you have any idea where it's coming from?"

"Not yet. As for Mrs. Sterling, she checks out too. Cynthia Mason, her assistant, however, is not so squeaky clean."

I tell Julian what Frank told me about growing up the son of a con artist and how he met Serena. All of it.

When I'm done, Julian stares out the windshield with a faraway look on his face. I'm not sure if he's thinking about the life as a con or that I talk to ghosts. I don't bother asking 'cause part of me doesn't want to know. He still needs time dealing with all of this, like I need time dealing with his job.

He clears his throat. "Okay, so Cynthia Mason appears to have been clean for the past decade, but prior to that, she was arrested for a lot of small crimes. Shoplifting is her earliest and most frequent offense, but there's also some light check fraud. I'm surprised Mrs. Sterling hired her."

"Maybe she didn't run a background check."

Julian glances at the house he's supposed to be watching. "That seems a bit reckless, no? Especially with her kind of wealth."

Considering the outcome, yes.

Serena's extra income makes me mentally bold her name at the top of my suspect list. Well, she's my only suspect too but still. I have every intention of hunting her down and getting answers. Coming out and asking won't get results. I know this. Hmm, I wonder if Frank knows about it. Any chance he's working with her? It didn't sound like it. What if she was conning him as much as he was conning her?

My head begins to throb. I rub my temples.

"You okay?" Julian asks.

"Yeah, fine. I'm just trying to figure out how to get answers out of Serena."

Julian smiles. "Well, my grandmother always said that people can't resist kindness."

I doubt that works with criminals, but it can't hurt. My best chance of tracking her down is at Sparks. "How about dinner tonight?" I ask.

He narrows his eyes. "This isn't a sexy date but a work one, huh?"

I laugh. "You're so perceptive."

CHAPTER FIFTEEN

I take another shower 'cause you can't be too clean, especially for a date, and I really want to use the new strawberry-and-champagne scented soap I recently bought. A small treat to myself one day at the mall with Izzie. She was complaining about her feet hurting, and I needed to reward myself for putting up with her. I'm now so grateful I splurged.

After drying off, diffusing my hair with the blow dryer so my curls don't drip down my back, and applying nighttime makeup—gray shadow, eyeliner, mascara, blush, and a deep-red lipstick—I stare into my closet. I am definitely a flats kinda girl, but this feels like a dress and heels night. I will end up being the one complaining, at least in my head, about my feet, but it might be worth it. I decide on a navy wrap dress and navy heels with a peep toe. He hasn't seen me in this one because Ma bought it for me when I moved back to South Shore Beach last month. It was after the charges were dismissed against Izzie and after I almost died. Ma took us shopping and bought each of us a dress. I assume Ma thought I'd wear it to Sunday dinner, but I haven't yet. It feels too special for just dinner under the aging chandelier.

I slip into the dress, figure out how to wrap it around correctly, and my cell rings. It's Carly. "Hello?"

"Hi, Gianna. I really enjoyed our double date the other night. I was wondering what you and Julian are up to tonight?"

I hesitate, not sure what to say. I had a great time too, and I want to do it again, but I'm extra fancy tonight, and I *kinda* just want it to be the two of us. But we did have fun. It wouldn't be so bad to have another couple with us. I guess.

"Actually, Julian and I are going out. We're headed to Sparks for dinner. Why don't you and Enzo join us?" I push my feet into the heels.

"Oh, we don't want to intrude if you already have plans. Besides, I was thinking we could all have dinner at Enzo's. I'm not really in the mood for anything fancy."

I glance at myself in the full-length mirror hanging on my closet door.

"We can do it another night," she says. "We'll make plans ahead of time."

"Sounds great. I'll call you."

I hang up, grab my purse, and hurry out the door. I'm on the last step when I get a text from Julian saying he's here. Perfect timing.

* * *

The club is packed when we get there. Most of the tables are filled, as are the barstools. Four servers are running around, and the speakers softly play jazz music. It's such a different vibe now from the other times I've been here. There's a buzz that seems to have filled the room. The chatter is lively but not too loud, the servers smile as they approach each table, and there's laughter, like everyone is just happy to be here and enjoying the food. I hope it's not too busy for me to get a chance to speak with Serena.

I grab a menu at the hostess station and glance at it. Why hadn't I checked out the menu before? Food is an important part of my life, and it seems I've been missing out on the fried ravioli and portobello mushrooms stuffed with crab and white wine. In fact, all of the items are appetizers, salads, and sandwiches. My kind of place.

The man who sat beside Natalia during my audition steps up. He's wearing a white suit and looks as annoyed as he did that day. No—more like constipated.

"Two?" he asks while grabbing a menu and eyeing the one already in my hand. He doesn't seem to recognize me, which tells me he isn't aware I'm now officially an employee.

"Yes," Julian says, and we follow the man in white to a table in the middle of the room but directly across from the stage.

He holds out one of the chairs for me. How nice. I take a seat, and he places the other menu in front of Julian. "Someone will be with you shortly. Enjoy your meal."

I look around the room, hoping to catch sight of Serena. And there she is, taking an order at a table closer to the stage.

She smiles at the older couple, and she looks carefree. I'd never guess all the trouble she's going through by her clean, organized appearance. Her hair is pulled back into a slick bun. Her black blouse and pants are pressed, and she looks relaxed but professional.

After she makes a note on her pad, she takes their menus, and starts to walk away. She looks up, and we lock stares. Instantly her smile fades just enough that I can see the pain and sorrow in her eyes.

I nod at her. She does the same and heads to the kitchen.

"This is a nice place," Julian says, glancing around. "Is it new? You never mentioned it all those times you talked about your hometown."

"Yeah. It wasn't here the last time I lived here. I don't remember what this building held, but it couldn't be important."

Zoe approaches our table and smiles wide when she sees me. "Hey, what are you doing here?"

"Showing the boyfriend my new place of employment," I say and immediately realize I referred to Julian as my boyfriend.

He smirks and says hi to Zoe.

"Very cute," she whispers to me, but he totally hears because his smirk grows. Then she asks, "What can I get you this evening?"

I want to ask for a quiet moment to talk to her, to pick her brain about her friend, but instead I order the stuffed mushrooms, a grilled shrimp salad, and a seltzer with lime. I'm not in a drinking mood.

Julian gets the sliced steak, grilled onions and mushrooms, and melted Swiss on garlic bread with fries and a beer on tap.

The man in white seats a young couple at the table behind me.

Zoe gives them a quick smile then rushes off. She doesn't have time to talk. Today may end up being a bust for me after all.

As it turns out, it really doesn't matter. The food is divine and the company even better. I slide a mushroom onto Julian's plate, and he leans toward me, holding his sandwich so I can take a bite. It would be easier for him to cut a piece off for me, but I think he just wants me to have to lean so he can get a better look down the top of my dress. It's totally worth it because the caramelized onions are to die for.

I'm halfway through my 'shrooms when the man in white approaches our table.

"We need you," he says in a panicked tone.

"Excuse me?" I choke down a lump of crab stuffing.

"You are the new hire, G-something, right? Natalia said table seven."

How does Natalia know I'm here? I didn't see her. Then again I have been concentrating on my plate and Julian. I glance to the doorframe leading to the back, but it's empty.

"Yeah, I'm Gianna."

He looks only slightly relieved. "Good. Our other singer called. He's going to be late and will miss his first song. You have to go on in his place."

"Me? I'm not ready. I haven't practiced yet."

He frowns and sighs. "Do you want the job? Then get on stage. Now." He walks off.

I stare at Julian. "He's serious."

"He doesn't look like the kind of man who plays practical jokes."

No, he does not. Damn. That means I either need to get up there again or lose my gig. I place my napkin on the table and stand up. Okay, you can do this, Gianna. I glance to the kitchen doorway. The man in white is standing near it on his phone. Then I glance to the pianist, who is looking at me. He offers a smile. It's the same guy from the audition. That's good. I take one final look at Julian.

He smiles. "You can do this. Imagine everyone naked. I know I've been doing that all night."

I chuckle, and my face heats up. That doesn't help.

I make my way over to the piano. "Hi, I don't have anything planned. Can you play..." I glance back to my table and stare at Julian's eager expression. Gosh, I hope I don't humiliate myself.

I tell the pianist my song choice and get up on stage. No one pays much attention to me, other than Julian and the man in white, who is now off his phone and staring at me. I look away from him because he's making my nervous stomach jump.

The opening chords play. I can't look at the same area as last time since there are people sitting there, so I look at my empty chair. I open my mouth and start singing "All of Me" by John Legend. Considering this is interrupting a date, a lovey-dovey song seems to be in order.

I catch movement from the corner of my eye and glance over. I don't know why this is any different than the servers coming and going from the kitchen, but I look just the same. It's Natalia. She's standing beside the man in white, nodding and smiling at me. She must approve. She's in a hot-pink pencil skirt and white blouse, looking professional and stylish. When I look back to my seat, I realize there's a lull in the crowd, and everyone is watching me. Oh my!

I shut my eyes for a moment and listen to the beat. It's the only thing that doesn't upset my digested mushrooms.

The song line about how hard it is risking your heart for love hits home, and I stare at Julian. That's what all of this is about. Whether or not I want to risk my heart to be with him. All of him.

When I sing my last note, I take a step back from the microphone and think about risk.

The audience applauds, and I'm taken aback for a moment. I momentarily forgot there were so many people here. I smile, and a man in a red top and black pants walks onto the stage. He's in his midthirties with blond hair and light blue eyes.

"Hey, thanks for covering for me," he says. "I'm Alan."

"Gianna." I smile my thanks to the pianist and step off the stage.

Natalia walks over to me. "I was right. You're good."

The man in white looks slightly less pinched than earlier. I go back to my table as Alan says, "Everyone, that was Gianna. She'll be back another night."

I slip into my seat and want to hide under the table. I'm not used to this kind of attention.

Julian grabs my hand and squeezes my fingers. "You were amazing. I'd like to say that every time that song plays on the radio, I'm going to think of you, but I already do. It's kinda ironic you sang it."

Not irony. Fate.

It's a beautiful song about love. How can I not sing it to him? And knowing he thinks of me makes my chest swell.

* * *

I don't bother trying to get Serena alone. There's more time for that. Not much more. I want this case solved, and I want to help Frank move on, but for tonight, I want to be ghost-free.

Julian pulls into the parking lot behind the deli. "I had a great time."

So did I, and now I don't want it to end. I know if I invite him up there's a good chance it'll become romantic, and I suddenly look forward to that.

"Do you want some coffee?"

His grin is sincere and not too eager. "I'd love some."

He parks his truck, and we head up. One night of tenderness and love, and I'll get back to Serena and Frank first thing in the morning. Upstairs, I start a pot of coffee, but I don't plan on actually drinking any.

I turn to him and step so close the knot of his tie brushes against the tip of my nose. "Thanks for dinner."

"Thanks for the entertainment." His voice is low and gravely. Good. That means tonight is affecting him as much as it is me.

I look up into his eyes and tilt my head back as seductively as I know how. It must work because Julian leans down and presses his mouth against mine.

I close my eyes and breathe in his scent. His lips are soft and warm, and his tongue tastes salty. I lean into him, and his hands mold my back, my hips, and my butt.

I moan softly and hear, "Excuse me."

I open my eyes, frown, and wonder when Julian became a ventriloquist. But then he frowns too, and I realize he didn't speak. I pull away and see Frank standing in the center of the living room. For crying out loud!

"We should talk," Frank says. "But I can come back."

If that was the case, why didn't he just leave and not interrupt us? The fact that *he* feels we should talk makes it sound super important.

"What's wrong?" Julian asks.

I sigh and step out of his embrace. "I'm sorry, but we have company."

He looks around as if he can actually see the departed. Silly man. Then his chest puffs up, and he slowly exhales. He gets it. "Oh. Should I leave?"

I hope I don't regret this. "Actually, yeah. You're welcome to stay, but I think it'll be easier to chat if I don't have to relay everything he's saying. I'm really sorry. I want to be with you, but tracking this guy down has not been easy."

Julian's expression goes from confused to frustrated. Boy, do I understand. He kisses my forehead. "I get it. I don't like it, but duty calls. I understand. And you'll call me tomorrow?"

"Absolutely."

I walk him downstairs, lock the door behind him, and run back up. Frank is still in the same spot. I walk over to the Mr. Coffee and pour myself a cup. Guess I'll be drinking it after all.

"So, spill," I say.

"You're mad."

Is he seriously concerned about my feelings?

"Yeah, 'cause I'm tired of the runaround and the lies. If you were honest from the get go... Never mind, just tell me what you want to say." And it better be good.

His brows draw together. "You have to convince Serena to not go back to her old job."

Too late, buddy. "She's already waiting tables. And why?"

He bows his head. "She deserves better, and I can't stand to know she's with them."

I feel like I just walked into the middle of a conversation. I don't know what's going on or even who the players are. "With who?"

He turns and glides over to the front windows. "When I first met Serena, it was at a party."

"Yeah, you told me. You were out with your mother's latest con."

"Yeah, well, I didn't mention that Serena was at the party working."

I shrug. "Okay, so she was one of the servers?"

He looks at me. "No, one of the escorts."

"Excuse me?"

"She was there with a man who hires women to go to parties and events with him. Among other things." He bows his head again.

Like sex? Oh my God!

"In fact, the man I was with, my mother's latest con, and I also had escorts for the evening."

I gasp and leave my mouth hanging open. I'm certainly not a prude, but I'm surprised. I've heard about the whole business obviously. I'm not living under a rock. But I never knew anyone who worked as an escort or hired one. Then again, I don't usually run around in circles with friends who can afford one.

I take my cup of joe to the sofa and sit cross-legged. "Tell me everything."

He blinks. "You're not offended?"

"Pfft. Why would I be? In fact, I'm curious." Plus, this totally makes sense as to where Serena's extra income comes from.

"Okay, well, Don, my mother's latest con…"

I chuckle at the rhyme.

Frank smirks. "He said he had dates for us for the charity event. All of the proceeds were going to cancer research."

How nice.

"Don introduced me to Serena's date—a friend of his. Some old geezer who looked like he was in his eighties. I could tell that all of the women, Serena, my date, Kit, and Don's date all knew one another. I didn't think much of it until the next day when Don told me that his date and Kit were escorts.'

I sip my coffee and make encouraging sounds to let him know I'm listening and he should continue.

"When I ran into Serena again, we hit it off immediately. We started dating, and she stopped working as an escort. Money was tight, and she couldn't afford to quit, but she did it for me. And she thought I was loaded, so I could help her out."

This doesn't make Serena look any less suspicious.

"Why didn't you just tell me all of this when we first met?"

"I was afraid that if you knew the truth you'd think less of Serena and maybe not help us."

I set my cup down on a side table, untangle my legs, and walk over to the kitchen. "Dude, that's not me. I don't care what you or Serena do on the side. I need all the facts to do my job."

He nods. "I get it."

I return to my seat with a small note pad and pen. The pad used to belong to Ma until I borrowed it. "Now that I have more information, I can widen the suspect pool. I hope. So it's possible that the bomb was placed by an ex-client?"

He shrugs and scrunches up his face, obviously not liking the memory that his true love had clients. "I guess it's possible."

That's not encouraging, but I'll take it. I write *Ex-Clients* at the top of the page.

"What's the name of the guy she was with when you first met?"

"Um, Charles Warren."

I jot down his name. "What about her other clients. Know any of their names?"

He shakes his head. "No. I didn't ask."

I'm sure he doesn't want to know. "That's okay. I can ask Serena."

He looks stricken.

"Dude, I have to talk to her about this. It's a missing piece, and whoever planted that bomb may have done so because of it."

"I guess." He doesn't look pleased.

A thought strikes me. "Oooh, any chance one of her clients was pissed she was quitting?"

"I don't know, but wouldn't planting a bomb be extreme?"

"Yeah, probably." But people kill for the stupidest reasons. Just ask Ma. She has a basement full of their artifacts. Speaking of which... "Any chance I can get a souvenir of our time together?"

"Like what?"

"I don't know. Where are your belongings? Did you live at Thomas's all the time?"

He nods. "I moved into his place after Serena and I got engaged. Most of my things are with my mother or in storage."

That must be a hard way to live.

"We can deal with that later. What else do you know about her escort job? Wait. You said she's going back to it."

He grimaces. "Unfortunately."

"So she could still be in danger."

He widens his eyes, and the realization hits him. "You have to protect her."

I roll my eyes. What exactly do I look like? A SWAT team? A personal bodyguard? I'm not Kevin Costner, and she's not Whitney Houston. "I'll do what I can."

Which means I'll find information, process it, and pass it along to the proper authorities. I heard Ma this morning. She's worried I'm dealing with another murder. I'm concerned as well. The last one almost didn't end well for me. So I have no desire to play hero or place myself in the path of a bomb. But uncovering the details surrounding someone's death is exciting. Who knew?

And the first place I'll start with is this escort service. Pen poised, I ask, "Where is their office?"

"Office? You mean the escorts?"

I nod. "Uh-huh."

"I don't know. I don't think it's a public place."

I bite my bottom lip. Yeah, probably not.

"I know her boss though."

That's good. It's a start in case Serena isn't forthcoming.

"Oh, is this why she doesn't want me looking into your death? Because I'll find out she's an escort? And why you didn't seem forthcoming too?"

"Yes."

It all makes sense now. This could mean she's not guilty after all, which means my suspect pool goes from one to zero. That just means I have to dig deeper.

"Okay, who's the boss? Wait, doesn't that mean this person is a madam? Is it a woman?" The excitement in my voice is undeniable. I probably shouldn't sound so darn happy considering the circumstances, but this is my first madam.

"Yes, it is. It's the owner of Sparks. *Natalia Kane.*"

CHAPTER SIXTEEN

Once again, sleeping is futile. I get out of bed bright and early and drive to Enzo's house—sans breakfast, a cup of morning joe, or fixing my hair, which isn't easy when it's curly. I can't just brush it without looking like the Bride of Frankenstein. I have to rewet it, comb it through, and allow it to naturally dry. Who has time for that? At least I put the unruly mess into a ponytail, and I brushed my teeth.

I'm not surprised Enzo's door is unlocked again, but I am starting to get concerned. This early, he probably hasn't left the house yet, so did he forget to lock up behind him when he came in last night? That's not responsible, and if Ma finds out, she'll go ballistic. Oh, wait. This is her baby boy. She'd go ballistic on me or Izzie but would probably give Enzo a stern, but not too stern, lecture. Ma says she doesn't have favorites, but Izzie and I aren't blind. Ma treats him differently. I think that deep down she feels he's not as capable when it comes to "girl" things, like cooking, cleaning, taking care of himself. Ma can be sexist.

I go in and expect the unexpected, which has now become the expected, like him lying in a vat of ketchup. But the living room is empty, as well as the kitchen and dining area. The bathroom door is shut, and I hear running water. So I do the only thing a little sister should do. I run into his room, drop onto my knees on the floor, and slide under his bed feetfirst. Thank goodness his bed frame isn't one of those platform ones. I wiggle under until I get to my butt, then I have to push my pelvis into the plush, gray carpet. This would be easier if he had hardwood floors like at my place.

Another minute goes by, and the bathroom door opens. I pray he comes into his bedroom and doesn't just walk straight out the door, otherwise this is all for nothing. But because the sneaky, prank Gods are shining on me, he enters the room. I watch his black, sock-covered feet walk to the tall dresser, which is mere inches from the right side of his bed.

I don't hesitate. If I wait too long, he may move, and I'll lose my chance. I reach out my arm and grab his ankle.

He screams, in that high-pitched kind of way that makes the hairs on the back of my neck rise.

I laugh my butt off. Well, not completely off since wiggling out from under the bed is still difficult.

"Gianna!" His face is red, and his breathing is irregular. Just the way it should be after a successful scare.

I point at him and laugh some more. "You totally deserve that, and you know it."

He huffs and storms into the other room, but I notice the slight smirk on his face. He knows I'm right, but he'll never admit it. I follow him into the living room, where he sits on the couch to put on his shiny, black shoes. His uniform looks pressed. He'd never go to work with wrinkles. Unlike me, who picks up yesterday's clothes off the floor to wear today.

"If you're here because you need help, I'm never helping you again. Ever."

I chuckle. "But helping me helps you. You are the one who wants to make detective, and what better way to do that than with the help of our dead friends?"

"Dead people are your friends, not mine. And how did you get in here?"

"The door was unlocked. Again. You really should be more careful about that, what with you being a cop and all."

He huffs again and rolls his eyes. I'm so glad I can make his morning a little brighter. He stands and walks across the room to the shelves by the television. He opens his lockbox, pulls out his gun, and slips it into the holster at his waist. "If you need something, you better speak quickly. I need to leave soon. And since when are you up so early?"

There's so much animosity in his tone that I'm not sure if I want to share right now. Maybe I should wait until he's more prone to being open-minded. If I do it now, he may do something by the book just to get back at me for scaring him. Telling him about Serena being an escort was at the top of my list when I arrived. But suddenly I'm not so sure. I obviously didn't think this through well enough as I tossed and turned all night. I spent most of the time thinking about Natalia being a madam, trying to fall asleep, and punching my pillow because it's so flat. I need new ones. Maybe Izzie will be in the mood for another shopping trip.

Anyway, what I planned to tell Enzo didn't really come up while I was in my bed. I just figured his place was the first to stop at when I finally put on yesterday's clothes. But now that I think about it clearly, it doesn't feel right. If I tell Enzo the truth, he'll be obligated to either investigate or tell the detectives, and I'm not so sure that she and Natalia should be arrested. I mean, really, what harm are they doing?

I run a hand over my face, realizing that I just stepped into that gray zone Julian lives in. This is what he means about everything being not so black and white. His job requires him to do things that aren't always right, and now I'm stuck in the same place. Granted, he gets paid for his job. I can't put mine on my résumé, but in the end it feels the same.

"Well?" Enzo is staring at me, waiting for me to say something.

"Um, I wanted to tell you what I learned about the dead guy. His real name is Frank Mason."

Enzo nods. "Okay, great. Thanks."

And just like that, I lied to my brother, the cop, and enter the land of in between.

* * *

After leaving Enzo's, I head straight to Zoe's. I'm hoping that arriving early means Serena will be there, and that she'll be so tired and-slash-or surprised by my questions that she'll just regurgitate answers without thinking too hard about what she's telling me. I park in an empty space across from her building and head up to apartment 4A—according to the info Julian showed me the other day.

Zoe opens the door and squints at me. She's dressed in pink-and-white plaid pajama pants, and a long-sleeve, pink T-shirt. "Hi," she says and has to clear her throat to erase the scratchiness.

"Hey, sorry to knock so early, but I'm hoping Serena is here."

She doesn't ask how I know where she lives. See, the early morning element of surprise. "Sure. Come in." She steps back, so I can enter.

I step into the living room-slash-dining-slash-kitchenette. It's a lot like my apartment but with more space and much better furniture. Is Zoe an escort too? That could explain how she can afford a glass-topped coffee table, a royal blue sofa, a hot pink, armless armchair, and lots of plants that open the space up. Everything looks brand new, and the upholstery appears to come with a hefty price tag. Not that I feel envious at all, although I'm suddenly contemplating a career as an escort.

A folded blanket, sheet, and pillow sit on the end of the sofa. Serena must already be up. Zoe points to the pot of brewing coffee on the kitchen counter. "Do you want a cup?"

"No, thanks. I can't stay long." As soon as I leave, I plan on going home and raiding my fridge. I'm suddenly famished.

A door opens in the not-so-far distance, and I hear footsteps head toward us. Serena rounds the corner and steps into the room. She blinks twice at me. "What are you doing here?"

Good morning to you too. "I was hoping we could chat for a bit."

She yawns wide. "It's kinda early."

Zoe is turned toward Mr. Coffee, but I see her giving us sideway glances. This isn't going to be easy. I need to find a way to get her alone, just in case Zoe makes really good tips or has a rich Daddy.

"Yeah, sorry about that. Did you have a late night? Were you out with Don?"

The color pales from her face, and she freezes for a moment. Then she glances to Zoe, who's still pretending to ignore us, and finally says, "Zo, would you mind giving us a minute?"

Zoe faces us and opens and closes her mouth a few times. She looks like she feels out of place in her own home. "Oh, yeah."

"Sorry," Serena says. "This is your place. It's just that she and I need to discuss stuff about Thom...um, you know, my fiancé."

Zoe nods and heads toward the doorway. "No, yeah, that's fine. I'll go get dressed."

Serena watches her leave and waits until a door clicks before she turns on me and asks, "What are you talking about?" It comes out all sunshine-and-roses sounding.

I get why she's keeping it a secret. Really, I do. I wouldn't want to have to wear an orange jumpsuit either. But I'm so tired of having to pump information out of people.

I rub my right temple. A headache is already forming. It's too early for this. I want to ask her to stop lying and playing games, but I can't imagine that will endear me to her, so instead I say, "I haven't brought this up because I figured you wouldn't want to talk about it, but after everything that's happened, we should probably just be straight with one another."

She widens her eyes. She may appear innocent, but I know she understands what I'm referring to. "What do you mean?"

I start to say Frank but remember that she may not know his real name yet, and it may be too suspicious if I have that information as well. "Your fiancé told me about Don and your escort job."

She looks to the doorway Zoe disappeared through. "Sshh!" She says it so loud and fast, spittle hits my cheek.

I wipe it away with the end of my sleeve.

"Not everyone needs to know my business. It's bad enough you do."

"That means Zoe isn't an escort too?"

She frowns. "I didn't say that. But we don't share the details with one another. It's just better to keep that stuff quiet."

So Zoe goes on the suspect list too. It would be pretty messed up if Serena was staying with Frank's killer.

"I can't believe Thom...he told you. Why would he betray me like that?"

Crap. I don't want her to think he shared her secret with me. I don't want her memories of him to be more tainted than they already are. She has to be questioning everything he ever said and all the plans they made with him being a con artist. "He didn't mean to mention it. It kinda slipped out, and you know me. I'm nosy and ask a lot of questions." I chuckle to lighten the mood.

She nods and looks quite serious.

Gee, thanks.

She grabs my arm lightly. Her silvery glitter polish shimmers in the light. "Okay, but you can't tell anyone."

"I don't want to, but I'm thinking that maybe someone you know from that job is the one who placed the bomb."

She frowns and shakes her head. "That doesn't make sense. No one hated me."

"Are you sure? Maybe a wife found out what her husband was up to."

She continues shaking her head. "No, I'm not a mistress. Just a one-night hire. If I'm not available, he'll just hire a different girl. An angry wife would be better off killing her husband."

That's true. "Well, do you have any enemies? Anyone you fought with recently, or even not so recently?"

There goes that shaking head. I'm starting to wonder if she's having a seizure. She lets go of my arm. "No. No one I can think of."

Sleuthing looks so much easier on TV.

* * *

Later that afternoon, I'm at my shift at the deli, and Julian comes in. Warmth immediately spreads throughout me. Just seeing him makes me smile, and this time I'm not thinking dirty bits. I simply like seeing him. He looks casual today in fitted, dark blue jeans and a light blue, thin-knit sweater. It's somewhat fitted and stretches across his tight biceps. Gosh, I love those arms.

When I focus on his face, his smile is wider. He glances down at his arm area, to where I was staring. "Something fascinating?" he asks.

Yes, but I'm not about to gush over his arms in front of Pop. Awkward. I shake my head.

He walks to the register and puts out his hand for Pop to shake. "How are you doing, sir?"

I get giddy at his formality.

"Good. How's the PI business?" Pop asks.

My stomach tightens. Even though I've told my folks my fair share of lies over my lifetime, especially covering for Izzie in high school, I feel guilty doing so.

Pop walks into the back to give us our space. He's nice like that. There are no customers, and he probably doesn't want to see his daughter kissing a man—any man. Fathers are weird like that.

I step out from around the counter and walk into Julian's embrace. He kisses me lightly on the mouth, as if it's an everyday occurrence and we've been doing it all of our lives. I like it. Not just the kiss, although it's pretty special, but the comfortable feel of it all.

"Why are you here?" I lay my ear against his chest and listen to the steady rhythm of his heartbeat. "Not that I'm complaining."

He wraps his arms around me tighter and leans his chin on the top of my head. "I missed you."

I smile, close my eyes, and snuggle into his arms more. "That's nice."

"Maybe we should try this date thing after your friend passes on."

I look up at him and grin. "That might be best. Hopefully it won't be too long. I got Serena to admit she's an escort."

He raises his brows and pulls back. "How'd you manage that?"

"I can be very persuasive."

He chuckles. "Yes, you can. So now what?"

I wish I knew. "I'm going to see how close I can get to Natalia."

His surprised expression turns to disapproval with a deep frown. "Are you going to pose as an escort?"

"No." Actually I haven't considered that. "I don't think so. Maybe it would help. What do you think?"

He scoffs. "Do you really need to ask? I don't want my girlfriend working as an escort, whether it's undercover or not."

I smirk. "So I'm back to being your girlfriend?"

"You referred to me as your boyfriend last night."

I think back. "I did, huh, and you didn't call me on it."

"You were preoccupied singing."

"Ssshh." I glance at the kitchen door, making sure Pop can't hear us. "I haven't told anyone else yet."

"Why not? You were amazing."

I smile, and my cheeks warm. "I'm not ready yet, but I will." Eventually.

"Okay, well, I need to get back to the office. I'll talk to you soon, girlfriend."

Is this really it? Are we back together?

"Yes, later."

He pulls me up against him and gives me a proper, firm kiss on the mouth. I want to go deeper, but he pulls back and heads to the door.

I wave bye, and my finger starts tingling. Oh no!

Julian turns the corner, out of sight, and Freezer Dude appears in front of me.

I don't want anything to do with him, so I turn to go back behind the counter. "I don't have time for you," I whisper.

But he materializes directly in front of me again. I could run down the street, and he'd always be right there. "I need your help."

I laugh. "You're not serious."

"Look, I don't like this either. You're the last person I want to ask a favor from, but you're the only one who can see me."

I'm about to tell him that's not true, but it's not fair if I toss him at Mystic Aurora. Plus, she seemed pretty freaked out when she saw him. She's a newbie.

"I won't leave you alone until you help me, so you may as well do it."

I roll my eyes. He would annoy the heck out of me too. I'll never get time alone with Julian if I don't give in. "Fine. What do you want?"

The kitchen door swings open, and Pop comes out holding a loaf of rye bread. "Julian gone?"

"Yeah, he had to go back to work." I turn my back to Pop and pretend I'm checking the salad levels.

Freezer Dude floats to my side. "I want you to talk to my daughter for me."

Well, it's about time. I know I'm foolish to hope that he may move on once I do this, but I can't help it. It's the one thing every other ghost wants, and afterwards, they usually feel settled.

"Fine," I whisper. "Later."

Pop looks at me. "Did you say something?"

"Nope, just talking to myself."

Pop goes back into the kitchen.

I turn to see Freezer Dude is still here. I want him gone so my finger will stop throbbing. "What else do you want?"

He narrows his eyes and gets right up in my face. "You better not go back on your word."

Then he disappears, and I'm left standing there with an intense chill. At least my finger stops tingling.

CHAPTER SEVENTEEN

When I get off work, I drive over to Deborah Young's and park in front of her house. I'm not sure what I'm supposed to do without Freezer Dude filling me in, or how long I have to wait for him to show up. I never gave him a time. I close my eyes and think of his white hair and icy blue eyes, visualizing him before me. My finger throbs fast and furious. I open them and look over.

He materializes in my passenger seat. Did I just make that happen? That is so cool. Too bad I can't do that with the ghosts who don't freak me out.

"What do you want me to say to her?" I ask. "And how am I supposed to know this information?"

He's staring at the house. "I don't see any lights on, and her car isn't here."

I roll my eyes. Why didn't I pay attention to that? "Great. So I made the trip for nothing. You know, you could check these things out beforehand."

He faces me with his brows forming a unibrow. "She was home when I found you earlier."

"I was working. I can't just leave."

"It's your family deli. What are they going to do if you walk out? Disown you?"

"Clearly you have no idea how to be a family member. You don't just leave them high and dry."

He gets a stricken look on his face, and I realize this is exactly what he did when he went to prison.

"I'll have to come back another time," I say. "Just make sure she's home first."

"Just wait. I'm sure she'll be back soon." His impatience leaks with his snappy tone of voice.

"Were you ever nice?"

Suddenly Frank appears in the space between us, and my heartbeat leaps.

I yelp in a rather unattractive fashion. "Would it be too much to ask for you guys to wear cow bells?"

"I've been thinking," Frank says.

Freezer Dude glares at him. "Is that a miracle because if not, get lost. You're interrupting my time."

Frank scowls. "Who's this?"

"Long story. What did you realize?"

"I don't have time for this," Freezer Dude says with a long groan.

I scoff. "Where else do you have to go?"

Freezer Dude's gruffness doesn't seem to faze Frank at all. "I was thinking about Kit. She was upset when I canceled on her that last time. I didn't remember this until earlier."

I shrug. "Okay, so she was upset she wouldn't get paid for the night?"

Freezer Dude clicks his tongue. "You were with a prostitute?"

I start to point out Freezer Dude showered with men for years in prison but decide I don't want him pissed off and trying to get back at me. I want him out of my life.

Frank shakes his head, ignoring Freezer Dude. "No, this was more than that. She sent me a few romantic texts until I canceled, and then she got angry. She texted that I was dog meat and I would pay."

"And you forgot to mention that?" I almost shouted.

Freezer Dude starts chuckling and won't shut up.

"I didn't think much of it because it was months ago. I hadn't received a message in a long time. I figured she moved on."

I stare out my windshield, trying to ignore Freezer Dude's incessant laughter, and shake my head. It's possible that Kit let it go, but it's also possible she's spent these months figuring out her revenge.

"What?" Frank asks. "You think she wanted me dead?"

"No," I say.

Freezer Dude shuts up. Finally.
I look Frank in the eye. "But she may have wanted Serena dead."

* * *

After another thirty minutes without Deborah's arrival, my friendly ghosts leave, and I drive home. I climb the stairs to my apartment, and my cell rings. It's Ma. "Hello?"

"Gianna, I need you to get over here stat," she says in a rushed tone.

Panic swirls in my belly. "Is something wrong?"

"No. I need you here now though." Then she hangs up before I can find out the problem.

Even though she's says nothing is wrong, my stomach tightens, and I turn abruptly on the step, almost missing it and flying down them all. I run to my car and pull out of the lot quickly. I consider talking to Pop, but then he'd have to close the deli, and if Ma is right that this isn't as dire as it sounds, it will all be for nothing.

When I pull up to their house, Enzo's car is parked behind Ma's in the driveway. I brake right in front of the house and try to calm my racing thoughts as I speed race inside. Enzo is seated at the kitchen table, in front of a place setting, and Ma is scooping mashed potatoes into a serving bowl at the stove.

I blink, trying to refocus the scene to make sure I'm seeing things correctly. There's no blood, ambulance, or heart attack. Enzo is calm and practically drooling over the awesome aroma of meat and potatoes, and Ma is humming a tune I, surprisingly, don't recognize. It all becomes very clear.

"This is about dinner?" I shout.

Enzo shrugs but looks as snug as a bug in rug with a knife and fork close by. And how exactly does a bug get in a rug? "She made the same phone call to me."

If he knows this, then he was here when she called me. That brother card may get torn to little pieces. "Why didn't you text me to tell me to not break all speeding laws on the way over?"

He points to the brown wicker basket on the top of the refrigerator. "She took it from me."

I give an unexpected snort. Growing up, Ma used that basket as a form of punishment if we brought anything to the table besides our hungry bellies. Izzie was infamous for wanting to read magazines, and I went through a Bratz stage—fashion dolls with big eyes and lips and really cool accessories. They were way cooler than Barbies. Anyway, Ma would take our items and stick them in the basket until after dinner. And if anyone tried to take it back, especially Enzo when he grew tall enough, we'd be punished with a night of no television or dessert.

I doubt the consequences are still the same today, but Enzo is dutifully letting it go. My cell is in my pocket, and I have no intention of playing with it.

Ma smiles at me. "Wash your hands then have a seat. The food is done."

I let out an exaggerated sigh, drop my purse by the leg of the table, and walk to the sink. As I wash up, I spot the resting roasted chicken, bowl of peas, and a loaf of Italian bread that looks freshly made. It smells amazing. Ma's gone all out.

I take a seat at the table while she cuts into the bird. "What's the occasion, Ma?"

"There isn't one. I just want to spend time with my kids."

"Is Izzie coming?" Enzo asks.

I hope she didn't pull one of those phone calls on the pregnant woman.

"No. It's just us. She has her family. Plus, she won't be pleasant company for another month."

Enzo and I smile. It's so true.

"And Pop will eat when he closes the deli," Ma says. She carries the platters and bowls to the table. When Enzo and I start to stand up to help, she wags her finger, points, and orders us to remain sitting.

I'm seated beside Enzo, at the back of the table, and I feel like I'm ten again. He and Izzie would fight over the drumsticks, although I'm not sure why since there are two on every chicken. Ma and I like the white meat, which left Pop with the thighs. No one argued over the wings.

Ma places a generous portion of breast meat with crispy skin on my plate and then proceeds to give Enzo both drumsticks. His eyes light up, and a playful smile dances in the corners of his mouth.

I grab the spoon in the bowl of taters and take way too much. But I'm not complaining.

Enzo rips into the bread and hands me a chunk. I get giddy because it is warm, soft, and squishy. Ma fills our glasses with ice water, and for the next blissful fifteen minutes, we all eat in silence.

I sigh and sit back, stuffed beyond repair. Enzo goes in for seconds on the sides, and I watch in amazement. He has the best metabolism in the world. Lucky son of a gun.

The silence is broken by the trilling of my cell. I widen my eyes and stare at Ma.

The muscle at the left side of Enzo's mouth twitches.

Ma sips her water, sets the glass down, and without looking my way says, "Go ahead. We're practically done."

"That's not fair. She gets to use her phone when you've taken mine away," Enzo says as if he's five.

Ma raises her brows. "She's not dating someone I can't stand. My house, my rules."

I snort and pull out my phone. Speak of the devil, it's Julian. I stand and walk to the back door so they won't see my sheepish smile as I answer.

"Hey," I say and try to not sound cute and girly in front of the family, but it's no use. This man makes me feel very feminine all the time.

"Hi. I have time to kill on my stakeout and thought I'd nose around in your case."

I cover my mouth to prevent from laughing. He said "your case" as in it's mine. That's so adorable.

"Did you find anything?" I ask.

"I only have a first name to go by for Frank's escort. Were you able to get anything else?"

"No, just that her name is Kit."

"That's probably not real either. Okay, I'll dig around in Natalia's records and see if I can find anything. I'll talk to you later."

"Okay, bye. And thanks." I hang up and turn to find Ma and Enzo staring at me. "What?"

Ma narrows her gaze. "What were you talking about? You're not getting a cat? I don't think we should have pets around the deli."

"No, I said Kit, as in...Kit Kat. I love them."

Ma nods and gets up, gathering her plate. Enzo's still watching me though. He knows I'm lying.

* * *

After Enzo and I clean up the kitchen, we kiss Ma goodbye, promise to come by more often than just Sundays, and go our separate ways. I step into my apartment, and Frank pops up in front of me.

"Geez, you scared me."

"Sorry. I need your help. I found my mom."

"Great."

"I want to say bye to her before she runs off to God knows where. You need to tell her."

I inhale deeply and sigh. "I can't."

His eyes widen. "What?"

"I mean, I can't do this and not tell my brother where she is. It's one thing to help out and fudge things, but it's another to aid and abet. I'm not risking my freedom, and there's a very angry cop who would like nothing more than to send me to jail." At least I'm assuming that would give Kevin delight.

Frank looks into the distance for a moment. "Okay. Fine. But will you tell her bye before you alert the police?"

"Yes. That I can do."

Cynthia Mason is hiding out in a motel in Oceanside, two towns away. On the ride over, Frank tells me what he wants her to know, and I come up with a slightly plausible cover story. If she believes it, I'll be golden. If she doesn't, well, at least she won't threaten to call the cops on me.

I knock on her door and listen to scrambling inside. I knock again and take a step back in case she wants to peek out the window and check me out. I'm sure she'll recognize me, so I don't know if that will hinder or help.

"Cynthia?" I say. "I have a message from Frank."

The lock clicks, and the door creeps open. "What did you say?" she whispers.

I step closer and lower my voice. "I can speak to dead people, and Frank's standing beside me."

I don't like blurting that out, but I don't know how else to get her to talk to me. And the worst that happens is she tells someone. At this point, she has no reason to rat on me.

We stand there for another half a minute, and then she opens the door a little more.

"I never worked for him. I was at the house after the explosion, and I saw his spirit there."

She gaps and covers her mouth.

I fill her in without giving too much detail. She looks paler and paler as I speak, and I'm not sure how much she can handle. In this moment, I feel bad for the woman. Despite all she's conned, no one deserves to lose someone they love.

When I'm done explaining, she steps back and sits on the full-size bed. I enter the room and shut the door behind me. Frank sits, as best as a ghost can, beside his mother.

"She seems so frail," he says, and a lump forms in my throat.

Gosh, why did I have to care? This would be so much easier if I didn't.

"Did he suffer?" she asks with a sniffle.

He shakes his head.

"No. He wasn't even aware it happened when we met."

She nods her head and stares into her lap.

"He wants you to know that he loves you tremendously. With everything you both went through over the years, that love never faltered." I glance at Frank to make sure I got it all right.

He smiles at me, but it's not a happy grin by far. It's full of sadness.

I just sit there as Cynthia cries, and Frank stays close to her side. At one point, it seems as if she can feel him. She leans into him a bit, and he leans back. It's comforting to watch them.

After she calms down, I tell her the last part Frank mentioned on the ride over.

"Frank wants you to pick a new lifestyle, to stop playing games. Those were his exact words."

She looks me in the eye. With no makeup on, her hair back in a sloppy ponytail, and in a crumbled navy shirt and sweatpants, it's remarkable how different she looks from the first night I saw her.

"Thank you. I appreciate your coming here to let me know. Tell him he was the best son a mother could ask for."

"You just did." I point to where he's seated just in case she doesn't feel him.

She gives a half smile and turns to him. "I love you, Frank."

"I love you too, Mother."

I stand up, ready to leave before I start crying. Before I shut the door, I say, "Look, my brother is a cop, so I can't not tell him you're here. But maybe I can wait half an hour or so, give you some time to figure out what you want to do next."

Frank's grin is wide. He stays behind. I sit in my car and pull my phone from my pocket to check the time. Thirty minutes and then I'll call Enzo. Maybe it's not right but... Darn, this is that gray area again, huh?

I chuckle. "Way to go, Gianna. It's not like I can be a hypocrite for long."

"Have you finally gone crazy?"

I flinch and spot Freezer Dude in my rearview mirror. I turn my head and look back there. Yep, it's actually him. Then I look at my finger. It's tingly and throbbing, but there was no warning first. Well, darn. If that keeps up, I won't be able to get ready for him.

"Now what?" I ask, not wanting to ruin the tender moments I just shared with one ghost for the anger and pettiness of another.

"My daughter is home."

This is definitely a night for family.
I softly sigh. "Fine."

* * *

When I'm knocking on Deborah Young's door, I wonder if I should be upfront or not. I don't know this woman at all. She may believe in my abilities or think I'm a kook and call for the men in white coats.

The door opens, and Deborah stands there. She has light blue eyes like her father. Her blonde hair falls to her shoulders, and there are light laugh lines in the corners of her eyes. She's dressed in beige trousers and a thin, chocolate-brown sweater. "Hello, can I help you?" she asks.

"Hi. I'm sorry to bother you, but I sometimes get messages from the dead." I hold my breath and hope she doesn't slam the door in my face.

Her brows rise, and she just stares at me. "Okay."

Really? That's her response?

"And what does that have to do with me?" she asks.

Holy moly. She's a believer. This may not be as hard as I anticipated. "Your father, Mitchell Young, wants me to let you know that he loves you. He also says good-bye."

When she stands there with her mouth parted, looking numb, frozen, and perhaps scared, I wonder if she really is a believer.

"Look what you did to her," Freezer Dude shouts.

I bite the corner of my lip. "I didn't mean to blurt that out. I know most people think I'm crazy, but he won't leave me alone until you know."

Her eyes widen. "He's here now?"

"Yes."

She nods several times. "If he can hear me, I hope he knows that while I appreciate the concern, I don't care."

I'm not expecting that.

Freezer Dude's furry white brows knit together. "What?"

"Can you explain?" I ask.

"Sure. He was a criminal. He spent most of my life in prison for his crimes. I never knew him. Mom didn't want me to be the girl with her father in jail, so I never visited. I was once troubled by that, but after I grew up and had kids of my own, I realized she was right. That's not a way to live. So I'm glad I didn't know him, glad I had a wonderful stepfather who was truly there for me. I haven't thought of Mitchell Young as my father in decades. Thank you for coming by, but please don't return."

She carefully shuts the door, and Freezer Dude and I stand there gawking at her door.

"I have grandkids," he says.

Is that what he takes from all of this? I turn to him. "Are we done now?"

"We'll see." He disappears.

"That wasn't the deal," I shout at the air.

CHAPTER EIGHTEEN

The next morning, I roll over in bed, open my eyes, and listen for impending doom. My alarm clock says it's 8:00 a.m. There's no clanking from the deli, no phones ringing, no one banging on my door. I haven't been visited by ghosts young and old, and there aren't any emergencies. I slept deeply, without tossing and turning or feverish nightmares. Holy cannoli, the world is ending.

I chuckle, sit up, and rub the sleep from my eyes. Today is Friday, which means I'm off from the deli, but I need to go to Sparks to practice my repertoire. Ha! I have a repertoire. I'll get a chance to cozy up to Natalia and see if I can wiggle any information out of her. I also have a good feeling about Freezer Dude. He got what he came back for. He may not like what his daughter had to say, but there's no denying it. He can now move on.

As for Frank, I need to find Kit. And the best person to ask is the one who used to work alongside her. I leisurely get up because arriving at someone's house at the crack of dawn two days in a row is just rude. I shower, dress in black leggings, a *so long it could be a minidress* tunic, and my black boots with the spikes on the toes and then flip on the TV while I make breakfast. I fill the room with the Morning Show's chatter about the latest T. Swift song and aromas of coffee, toast, and two perfect over-easy eggs.

After much sipping, chewing, and moaning over the deliciousness that is food, I head out.

When I get to Zoe's, she's on her way out to run errands, and Serena is washing her coffee cup. I sit on the side of the couch sans the folded sheets, blanket, and pillow. I can tell she doesn't want to talk to me, what with the hunched shoulders and lack of saying hello. I got a grunt, and I'm certain that if this was her place, she wouldn't have let me in. Thank goodness I arrived before Zoe left.

"I know this isn't something you want to talk about," I say. "It must be hard, but I'm assuming your reluctance to want to find your fiancé's killer had to do with your job and not because you don't want to know. Right?"

She turns toward me while drying her hands on a green-and-white striped towel. "Of course I want to know. I want whoever did this punished so hard."

Good. At least we're on the same page.

"Why is it so important to you though?" she asks.

I've told so many versions of this truth that I'm beginning to confuse myself. "Last month my sister was accused of murdering a woman. It was very hard on her and the family. I helped figure out the truth. Now, it kinda feels like an addiction. How can I ignore that injustice?"

Okay, so that's full of holes and doesn't add up at all, but she looks thoughtful, so she must be buying it. Truth is that if it wasn't for the ghosts, I'd mind my own business. Although "addiction" may not be the wrong word.

She sits in an armchair perpendicular to the couch. "Why are you here today?"

"I want to know more about Kit."

She frowns and sits straighter. "How do you know that name?"

Yes, how do I? "I, uh, saw it doodled on some old papers of your fiancé's."

"Frank doodled her name?" Her pitch rises, and I sense jealousy in her tone.

So she knows his identity. Good. Talking around it isn't easy.

"Well, not a doodle so much as an angry scribble."

Her posture relaxes.

"He had jotted some notes, and it said *Angry Texts* with Kit's name beside it. Do you know about that?"

She shakes her head. "No. He never mentioned her to me."

"But he had seen her before the two of you starting dating?"

"Yes, but as far as I know it wasn't a thing. She was just a hire." She chews her bottom lip as if suddenly worried.

"And you know who she is?"

"No. We don't use our real names. I've heard her mentioned from a couple of the other girls and Frank, but I've never met her."

"How is that possible? How many girls does Natalia have?"

She smirks. "There are a lot of men on Long Island."

I take a moment to replay her words. There's a lot of wealth on the island, especially in the Hamptons. I bet Natalia's girls know the town well.

"What about at the party, when you met Frank? Kit was his date."

She nods. "Yes, but I didn't see her. It was busy, and she wasn't by Frank's side when I bumped into him. I caught a glimpse of them when they were leaving, but it was from behind."

I sit up straighter. "Well, that's something. What did you see?"

"A woman with long, bright-red hair in a skintight black gown. The color made me think it was a wig. No one naturally grows hair that color."

There has to be a way to find the answers. "What about Zoe? Maybe she knows Kit?"

Serena shrugs. I widen my eyes, and she copies my expression. "What?" she asks.

"What if Zoe is Kit? Is that possible?"

Serena hugs herself and rubs her arms, as if warding off a chill. "No. She can't... I don't know. It's possible, but I doubt it."

We need something stronger than doubt. There's no way I'd sleep in the same apartment with doubt.

Serena starts shaking her head vehemently. "No. Wait. Zoe was at Sparks that night. I remember because I was scheduled to work, and I asked her to take my shift."

"Why?"

"My date that night, he specifically asked for me, and Natalia told me to switch serving shifts with someone. So Zoe wasn't at the party. She can't be Kit." She lets out a relieved breath and a giggle.

I understand the feeling. For a moment, I got completely creeped out. But just in case Zoe got someone to cover the shift she covered for Serena, I ask, "What are your and Zoe's escort names?"

"I'm Reena. Not very original. I don't know Zoe's. Even though she's letting me stay here, and I call her a friend, we aren't that kind of close. Zoe hangs with the other girls, but that's not my style. I like my privacy."

Her life choice sounds lonely. This doesn't completely rule Zoe out. There are plenty of other girls too, but I'd like to narrow the list down enough to know that Serena isn't sleeping by a killer. "You're back at work now though. Have you seen Kit? Does she still work for Natalia?"

"I'm not sure. I haven't fully gone back yet. I haven't gotten up the nerve. When I quit, I never thought I'd have to go back. It's not a bad job. Natalia takes exceptional care of us, but it's..." Her voice trails off. "Anyway, I have a date scheduled for this weekend. I can ask, if you think that'll help."

I widen my eyes. "Oh yes, that would be awesome. Just make sure no one gets suspicious." I don't want her in danger again.

"Of course, but why Kit? You think that because of these angry texts she wanted to kill Frank?"

"I think she may have wanted you out of the picture. The flower bomb was sent to your house."

She gasps. "In the beginning, I assumed the bomb was a mistake. Sent to the wrong house."

That sounds a bit naive.

"And when I learned Frank wasn't Thomas, I figured it was meant for him. But to think it really was for me." She squeezes her eyes shut for a moment. Then she springs them open and looks terrified. "Do you think the killer still wants me dead?"

I have no idea. Except for the *wrong house* part, I had the same assumptions as Serena. And now I can't help but wonder what the police have been thinking. Why hasn't someone been keeping an eye on her in case she is the target? Isn't it better to be safe than sorry?

"I think that you shouldn't worry. You don't have any enemies, so chances are this isn't about you personally. And if this was the act of Kit, she probably wanted you out of the way so she could be with Frank. That's a moot point now."

Serena covers her face with her hands. When she puts her hands back into her lap, she says, "A bomb? Isn't that a bit extreme for a man?"

I've thought the exact same thing. Why not a knife to the heart or a bullet wound to the skull, something not so dramatic? "Yes, it is."

"And how would she know how to make one?"

"Unfortunately, you can find that information on the internet."

* * *

Shortly after I leave Serena, I get a text from Enzo. He wants to chat, so I drive to the police station and park in the same spot I did last time. I have no intention of going inside and possibly running into Kevin Burton or even Detective Sanchez. Partly because I never want to see Kevin and mostly because of the other night. I've been questioned by the cops three times in my life. The other night, when Izzie was suspected of murder, and when my boyfriend, my first love, died years ago. Kevin wanted to blame me for his death, a hit-and-run accident. All three times have left me with a bad taste in my mouth. Nope, I'm staying outside.

I text Enzo and tell him I'm outside. Then I step out of my car and lean on the hood. I kick a silver wedge out from under my foot. I see no one's cleaned up the gum wrappers. If Ma worked here, she'd order someone to get to it. I should take a picture and send it to her as a joke. She might get on Enzo's case until he cleaned it up. No, that will give him more fuel to prank me back, and I'm not sure I can stand another fake death.

Enzo walks out of the police station and sprints across the parking lot. His brow is furrowed, there are circles under his eyes, and his complexion is ashen.

When he stops in front of me, I ask, "Are you drinking enough water?"

His frown deepens. "What?"

"You look dehydrated."

"Thanks, I'll get on that," he says with attitude.

When we were little and Pop would have a tone in his voice, we kids would say, "What's with the snap and crackle, Pop?" We thought we were hilarious. It would make Pop smile and laugh. It worked every time. Now I open my mouth, ready with that same reply but decide not to. It won't have the same effect on my brother.

"So, why am I here?" I ask.

He scratches the back of his neck. "I want to know if you received any new information from your *friend*."

He says it as if he's referring to my period, all mysterious and secretive. Well, I do appreciate the secret part. I'd texted him about Cynthia and her location about forty-five minutes after I left her.

"How did it go with Mrs. Young?" I ask.

He purses his lips, shakes his head, and looks disgusted. "The room was empty when we got there."

Guilt grips my shoulders. "Sorry about that."

He shrugs. "It's not your fault."

Well...

"Have you learned anything else?" he asks.

"I haven't seen Frank since he led me to the motel." I think about Serena, Natalia, and the escort business. I want to share with my brother, but I don't want to tell the cop in him. It feels wrong to rat on them. No one's getting hurt, and it's not my business to share. Gosh, the gray area sucks!

"Okay. Well, I should get back," he says and starts to turn but stops. "Are you really getting a cat?" A small smile sits on his mouth. He knows Ma would have a conniption. Is he hoping I'll get in trouble since I scared him? Nah, he's not a petty brother.

"No. That had nothing to do with a cat. I said Kit."

He frowns. "As in the candy?"

Telling the truth would mean revealing the escorts. "Yeah."

"Okay. Talk to you later." He turns, and I walk to my car door. "Oh," he shouts.

I look up. He's standing in the middle of the parking lot facing me again. "Carly wants you and Julian to have dinner with us, at my place. How about tonight around seven?"

This isn't making plans in advance, but I don't have plans and always need to eat. "Sure. Sounds great. I'll let you know if Julian can't make it."

He nods and watches me get into my car.

I grab my phone and text Julian. *You. Me. Dinner @ Enzo's tonight. 7:00?*

When I'm done, I look up and catch the last few glimpses of Enzo walking back into the station. His posture seems heavy. Something is weighing on him. His job must be super stressful.

My cell chirps.

I'm all yours.

Oooh, just the way I like my man.

* * *

Later that afternoon, I drive to Sparks for my practice. I spent the last hour in my apartment sweating over which songs to rehearse. They can't be too depressing or raunchy, but they have to move the crowd too. I finally narrowed it down to a ballad, one that makes you want to move your feet, and something with just enough sass it should make people smile but not get me fired.

The tables are prepped with silverware and salt and pepper shakers, the lights are turned up full max, and the pianist is playing a soft tune I don't recognize. The bartender is slicing fruit, and one table by the stage has recently been in use. A chair is pushed out, the setting is off to the side, and a bottle of water sits ahead of a notepad and pen.

"Right on time," says a voice behind me. "I like punctuality." It's Natalia, and she looks ever chic in steel-gray slacks, a short-sleeve, ivory cashmere sweater, and gray pumps. She takes the seat at the table and jots down something before looking up at me. "What song choices have you prepared?"

Prepared is a stretch, but I hand her my sheet of song titles.

She simply nods and points to the stage. I guess that's my cue to begin.

Again, I feel woefully unprepared. I stare at the pianist with as much apology as I can muster. I forgot to buy music sheets. Where does one buy music sheets nowadays?

I give my choice of songs, and thankfully he knows all of them. Whew, major embarrassment number one averted. Now for number two. I cross my fingers, take a deep breath, and open my mouth. One song after another, with just half a minute to breathe and gather my thoughts between each, I sing my heart out.

The whole time, Natalia seems to give me half of her attention. Her foot taps to the beat though, so she must be listening somewhat. But she's also reading her paperwork, writing things down, and doing something on her phone.

I concentrate on the end of the third song and finish it with more emotion behind the lyrics than I thought I had in me. Hey, that was pretty great.

I smile at the pianist, who does the same. Then I look to Natalia for approval.

It takes her a second. Her foot stops moving. And then she looks up and offers a nod. "Sounds good. I like your choices, but I'd work on that second one. You were a little flat in the first verse."

I clear my throat. "Okay."

"Micah," she shouts and points her pen over her head to the bar. "Give Gianna a water, please." Then to me she says, "Take a five-minute break, and then try again."

I nod and quickly step off the stage and over to the bar. I smile my thanks to Micah who, up close, is buffed, blond, tanned, and not bad on the eyes. If I didn't notice this across the room, I need to have my eyes checked. Man, he's hot. That doesn't surprise me. A swanky place like this probably wouldn't hire unattractive people. Zoe is pretty, the pianist is attractive in an older-man kinda way, the other singer is nice looking, and Serena is drop-dead gorgeous. Wait. That means I fall into this category of pretty people in their eyes too. Score.

"Come here, Gianna," Natalia says, and my way in presents itself.

I wasn't sure how I'd cozy up to Boss Lady. She doesn't give off the *chat about your life and snuggle with me* kinda vibe. But if she's calling me over, maybe I'll find a way.

I go over to her table and take a seat. I glance at the paperwork. It looks like accounts-payable records from my angle.

She picks up her phone and types in something. "You seemed a little nervous at first."

I assume she's speaking to me, so I say, "This is my first singing gig." But after, I wonder if I should've kept my mouth shut. You never admit to the boss that you don't have experience in the job she just hired you to do.

She sets her phone down, leans back in her chair, crosses one leg over the other, and stares at me. Oh boy, I'm about to get it, aren't I?

"Yes, I assumed you were green when you gave us a deli pamphlet instead of a résumé." Her smile is surprisingly warm and friendly. She should definitely wear it more often. It totally softens her angular features.

"Yeah, sorry about that. I hadn't planned ahead of time. I found out about it at the last moment." Like when walking through the door.

She studies me for a moment. "I like your determination and hard work, Gianna. You've been there for Sparks twice so far. I admire that. So tell me, why did you audition that day?"

I don't expect that question. "Why?"

"You seemed shocked when you realized you'd have to get on stage and sing, so I doubt you knew what was happening until you stepped inside. The question remains, why did you step inside?"

Oh wow, she caught all of that. I don't even remember her glancing my way until I was on stage. She's very perceptive. "I, uh, was looking for a job. I just wasn't planning on singing."

I'm about to say how I thought I'd fill out an application for a server, but she narrows her gaze for a second, and I stop. It dawns on me that this is the perfect moment to do that cozying-up thing. So I keep my mouth shut and let her assume whatever she's thinking. Hopefully it's what I want her to.

"How did you learn about Sparks? Were you just driving by?" Her tone sounds suspicious, and I'm glad. There's no way I could drive by and assume this place was hiring. There are no signs out front. She knows this.

"Serena told me about it. We're friends." Okay, so that is a major stretch of the truth.

Natalia doesn't take the bait though. She uncrosses her legs, stands up, and gathers her papers. "She is an excellent employee and woman. You're in good company. You should get back to practice now."

That's it? It's silly for me to think she'd whip out a Natalia's Escort Service business card from her wallet or invite me to join. I'll just have to find the time to dig more, leave more clues. Eventually I'll figure it out.

CHAPTER NINETEEN

As I'm leaving Sparks, my cell rings. "Hello?"
"Gianna, it's Mystic Aurora. I think I found something."
It's all she needs to say. I shout that I'm on my way, click *Off*, toss my phone onto my passenger seat, and hightail it to the mini shopping mall. I park directly in front of her storefront, a little crooked, I might add, but my thoughts are on getting rid of Freezer Dude. Nothing else matters at the moment.

I jerk her door open too hard and practically dislodge my arm from my shoulder.

"Gianna?" asks Aurora from the back room.

"Yeah." I start to run but figure I'll likely trip, fall, and break something really expensive, so I walk.

I expect to see her at the table, reading her tarot cards, but instead, I find her standing at the back of the room. All of the furniture has been pushed out of the center and sits haphazardly on the sides. And front and center is a large circle created with...salt? I flash to an episode of *Supernatural*. Aren't fictional demons held or killed by salt?

Now that I think about it, salt is also used to melt ice, like in the winter, reduce a sore throat when gargled, season food, and ward off evil. It's some handy stuff.

"What is all of this?" I step forward but don't touch the edge of the circle. I don't believe in demons. I doubt this salt thing will work with a ghost. But in case I'm completely wrong, there's no way I'm touching it.

She points to a book sitting on a table to her right. The book is thick and old, with gold around the edges of the pages.

"What is that? A grimoire?"

She smiles. "I'm not a witch. It's just research. I think I found a way out of your jam. We need to gather the ghost into a protective circle and bind him to this world. Once that's done, we'll be able to banish him back to the other side."

Is she flippin' serious? "Oh, is that all? Sounds easy."

She looks up at me with wide eyes. "Yeah?"

And she's delusional. "No. I was being sarcastic. How the heck are we going to get him inside that circle? Should we ask, *pretty please*?"

She cocks a brow, and it instantly reminds me of Ma. "You're in a mood."

I take a deep breath and exhale slowly. I don't mean to be a witch, no pun intended, but she obviously doesn't know how ruthless this guy can be. He's not going to willingly do as we ask. "I'm sorry, but this won't work. He won't comply."

"Of course not. We will lure him in."

So she has a plan. Good. I can't wait to hear it. "Okay, how?"

"You'll be bait."

Oh heck no!

I turn and face the door, wanting to run out, but I know I won't leave. As crazy as this idea is, it's also brilliant. It could just work.

"You'll be safe," she says. As if she can actually promise me that.

I turn back. "Can you guarantee that?"

Her gaze wavers as her eyes dart to the side. She's not a hundred percent sure. Then what am I doing here? I don't think Freezer Dude will kill me, not on purpose. He needs me. He knows this. But he has the ability to make my life miserable—late night booings, constant throbbing fingers, and I'm not really sure he won't try to harm someone I love to get to me. Or maybe I saw that on a Lifetime movie last week.

"There are no guarantees in life, Gianna."

Don't I know it.

"Okay, look," she says. "I've never dealt with anything like this before, and this is the only book I could find that even mentions banishing ghosts. Not demons but spirits. So this is all we have. Do you want to try or not?"

I wish I had a choice. There is the possibility that he left after my speaking with his daughter last night, but I'm not betting on it. And I really want him gone. While his time here so far could be worse, the stress of knowing he's around is ridiculous. Not to mention the guilt. I feel responsible for his return. If I hadn't slipped, fell, and died in the freezer all those years ago, he wouldn't have latched on to me.

Latched on to me? I think to when I visualized him in my car, and he appeared. We are connected in some weird way. Perhaps this won't be as difficult as I think.

"Well?" Aurora asks.

I shrug. What do I have to lose? My sanity, a finger if it becomes frostbitten…nothing too important. "Fine. What do I do?"

She smiles. Freezer Dude isn't bothering her, so I can only imagine that her enthusiasm pertains to trying out this banishment.

"Stand in the circle," she says.

A cold sweat washes over me. "What? You want me in there with him?"

She walks over to the book and looks down at the open page. "Yes, but just long enough to call him forward. Once he materializes, you step out. He won't be able to."

Okay, that sounds easy enough. I step over the ring of salt and take center stage.

She holds up her hand. "Wait. Before you call him, don't let him touch you. If you do, he won't be bound to the circle when you jump out. He'll be able to hitch a ride with you."

Seriously? I hope she's read every word on those pages several times. "Great. Any more creepy details before we begin?"

"Be careful not to swipe away the salt when you jump out."

That goes without saying. "And?"

She shakes her head. "That's it."

I close my eyes and think of Freezer Dude. The white hair, blue eyes, foul mood.

It's only seconds before I feel my finger start to tingle. I open my eyes, wanting to know the exact second he's with me. There will be no time to waste. Once he figures out what we're doing, he'll do something squirrely, like jump inside me.

The tingling gets stronger, and it quickly turns to throbbing. "He's coming," I whisper.

From the corner of my eye, I spot Aurora shift. I bet her stomach is flipping and twisting as aggressively as mine.

Then, just like we hoped, Freezer Dude appears. But instead of floating inside the circle with me, he's across the room by the back wall. We stare at one another. This is not how it should be.

Aurora gasps, and he glances down at the salt circle.

For the briefest moment, his brows become one. Next, he chuckles loudly and obnoxiously, and then he vanishes.

* * *

There's no sense in trying again, so I leave Aurora's, with plans to figure out another way, and go home to shower and change for dinner at Enzo's. I plan to meet Julian at my brother's, and when I arrive, his black SUV is already parked out front. Carly's and Enzo's cars are in the driveway, so I park behind Julian.

I don't bother knocking. I turn the knob and walk straight inside. This time an unlocked door makes sense. As I step over the threshold, the tantalizing aromas of onions, bread, and beef greet me.

"Hello, dinner," I whisper.

It feels like Sundays at Ma's. The men are in the living room cheering and shouting at the television, where a loud sport is playing, and the women, or in this case Carly, is in the kitchen cooking.

I wave to the guys. Enzo gives me a head nod. I don't mind. He's my brother. But if Julian does the same...

He gets up, pulls me close, and plants a kiss on my face, which lands at the corner of my mouth. That's much better. "Hi," he says in a low, throaty way that makes my knees buckle.

"Hi. I'm glad you're here."

He smiles, and it radiates off him. "Glad you invited me."

Enzo jeers the TV, startling me, and calls Julian back to watch.

Julian kisses the tip of my nose and returns to his seat. Since I am not a fan of sports in any capacity, I join Carly in the kitchen. She's wearing a black skirt, pumps, and a red blouse. Over that is a full apron that she must've brought from home because I've never seen it here before.

"Hey," I say and set my purse on the only empty counter.

The rest are covered with various cooking items—bowls, peelers, knives, spoons, and empty boxes. From the looks of it, Carly has made a two-layer vanilla cake, which is cooling, and a can of chocolate frosting sits beside it. There must be a salad in the fridge because lettuce and tomato remains are on a cutting board behind her. She's currently pushing potato chunks through a ricer. Yum, mashed potatoes. And a huge pan of something covered in tinfoil sits on the back of the stove. It looks like we'll be eating soon.

"Wow, you really went all out, huh?"

She smiles, and from her profile, I spot her cheeks flush. "I like being domestic, and cooking is a lot of fun. Do you cook?"

"I don't usually do all of this, but I make a mean sandwich."

She giggles. "Sandwiches aren't the way to a man's heart."

Is that what this is all about? She wants Enzo's heart?

She must realize what she said because she widens her eyes for a split second and adds, "I don't mean with your brother. We're just good friends. But for you and Julian. He seems like a great guy. You don't want to let him get away."

Wow, she and Ma would really get along if Ma knew how to let go.

I change the subject 'cause I fear we'll be talking about babies soon. "Do you need any help?"

"No, I'm almost done. I just need to add the butter and cream to the potatoes, frost the cake, and get the dinner rolls out of the oven. Enzo can carve the roast."

Yum, a roast.

"And how's the job?"

"It sucks." She laughs. "Being a receptionist is boring as heck, but doing it for a used-car lot is probably the worst. The boss is one of those loud, over-the-top men. I guess he has to be to sell cars, but it gets annoying. Most days I leave work with a headache."

I lean my hip against the drawer of utensils. "But you stay?"

"The pay is decent, and the hours are cool, but I can't imagine doing this for the rest of my life."

"What would you rather do?"

She gives me a sheepish grin. "Get married and have lots of babies."

Ha, I guess I'm not escaping this topic. I'm just glad we're discussing her babies and not mine.

Carly's mouth downturns. "Not any time soon but eventually." She must be thinking about her breakup.

I'm about to ask her what happened when my cell chirps. I dig it out of my purse as Carly pours a small pot of heated cream and butter into the potatoes. My stomach growls at the sight. This is going to be a fantastic meal. I look down at my phone. It's a text from Serena. My interest piques a thousand percent.

It reads: *Going to ask Zoe about Kit tonight when she gets home from Sparks. Want to join me?*

Heck yes. If there's any chance Zoe is Kit, Serena shouldn't be alone with her.

I reply: *Absofreakinlutely!!!*

:) It won't be until late. Around midnight.

That gives me plenty of time to have a relaxed dinner and even a few kisses with Julian. And I'll have Julian wait outside, in case things get heated.

Perfect. See you then. Don't start without me.

"Something has made you happy," Carly says.

I look up, and she's smirking. Then I realize I have a huge grin on my face. I laugh. "It's a..." I start to say *friend*, but that's hardly what Serena and I are, and I'd like to not lie about everything just because it's easier than explaining the truth. "It's a coworker."

Carly frowns. "From the deli? I thought that was only family."

I slip my phone back into my purse. "Oh, it is. I have a second job."

She grabs an oven mitt, opens the oven, and pulls out a pan of dinner rolls all nestled close together. "To make ends meet. I totally understand. Where is it? And are they looking for help?" She chuckles and sets the pan on the front burners of the stove.

I look to the doorframe and listen for the guys' voices. They're still cheering at the TV. Just the same, I lower mine. "I got a singing gig at that club, Sparks."

She raises her brows. "I didn't know you sing."

A chuckle rolls up out of my chest. "Neither did I. It happened quite suddenly."

She cocks her head to the doorway. "And no one else knows?"

I lower my head, feeling shameful for keeping quiet. "Just Julian. I haven't told the family yet." I look at her from under my lashes. "I'm nervous that Ma may feel jealous."

"Of her daughter?"

"I know it sounds crazy, but singing was always her dream, and instead of going off and doing it, she got married and had us. What if she's resentful?"

Carly walks over to the cake and pops the top off the can of frosting. "Look, based off of the silent treatment from Sunday, as well as the glares she threw my way..."

Yikes, I didn't know it was that bad.

"Your mother loves you guys something fierce. Even if she had a moment of regret for her own choices, I doubt she'd place them on you."

I look up fully and smile. "That's sweet. I'm sorry she made you feel uncomfortable."

Carly dips her butter knife into the can and plops a wallop of frosting on top of one layer. "I don't like it, but I get it. I hurt Enzo many, *many* years ago." She emphasizes the second many and smiles.

"Yeah, you'd think she'd let it go by now."

"I might hold a grudge with my kids some day."

I watch her frost the rest of that layer, then carefully place the second one on it, and frost the top and sides of the whole thing. When she's done, she stands back and admires it.

With a wink, she asks, "Hungry?"

"Starved."

I help her carry the bowls to the dining room table, which is already set for four. She brings in the roast on a large serving tray, and I wonder if she brought over all of these serving bowls and platters because I'd swear Enzo didn't own this kind of stuff. She's so efficient.

We call the guys in, and the television goes off. Their eyes light up at the spread.

"It looks delicious," Julian says.

"Thank you. Enzo, will you carve the roast?"

It doesn't take long for Enzo to do his job and for the rest of us to pass and scoop enormous amounts of food onto our plates. Well, Carly takes dainty portions, but I think I may have one more spoonful of potatoes on my plate than Enzo has on his.

We fall into silence with several moans and sighs of yumminess for a few minutes. It's just too good to take the time to open my mouth to speak.

"This is incredible," Enzo says. "Thank you."

Carly bats her lashes and smiles. It's more cute than flirty. "You're welcome. I love cooking. It relaxes me. Plus, it feels good when people enjoy what I make."

"You always enjoyed cooking," Enzo says, then glances at me. "Do you remember those cookies she'd bring to our house?"

I think hard for a moment, really not wanting to take my concentration off the roll I'm mashing to bits with my teeth, and then I remember. "The peanut butter ones with chunks of chocolate. Oh my God, they were heavenly. I think I ate my weight in them one summer."

"You did. That's why Ma had to buy you all-new school clothes in August."

I playfully jab my fork toward Enzo's hand. He chuckles. "I remember that summer. I also had to get new clothes because my girls grew, and Izzie's hand-me-downs no longer fit in the bust area. That wasn't from food. Not all of it."

Enzo scoffs in disgust. "I do not want to talk about my sister's puberty during dinner."

Carly giggles, and Julian smiles. He gives me a dirty look. I know he doesn't mind talking about my girls. Warmth creeps into my cheeks. The last thing I want is to get him all hot and bothered at the dinner table. We can save that for later. So I change the subject.

"That same summer, Enzo proved he could sleep through anything."

Carly frowns. "What do you mean?"

"Ma burned bacon on the stove, and it filled the kitchen with smoke. The detector went off, and it wouldn't shut up. Izzie and I awoke immediately, but Enzo slept through the whole thing. It blasted for a good fifteen minutes."

"Good thing there wasn't really a fire," Julian says.

"Yeah, I'm pretty sure my sisters would've let me burn." I shrug. "Maybe for just a minute or two."

Carly's smile widens. "I love hanging with you guys. I miss how much fun you are. All those times you'd sit in a dark closet or bathroom waiting for the perfect moment to jump out at one another. I never laughed so much."

Enzo gives me a side eye. "Yeah, she got me the other day."

I'm surprised he's bringing it up. He usually doesn't like to admit when I get him good.

Carly wiggles in her seat, and her eyes light up. "What happened?"

He explains my reaching out and grabbing his ankle, and she and Julian start laughing. I join in because it's still funny as heck.

"I was only getting him back for the prank from earlier when I came by and let myself in and found him on the kitchen floor with a knife in his arm and blood under him."

The laughter dies, and Carly looks stricken. "What?"

Enzo's chest moves up and down with a few deep chuckles. "It was a joke. I held the knife in my armpit, and the blood was ketchup. I saw her park out front."

Carly giggles and places a hand over her mouth. "Oh my goodness, you're so bad."

"Yes, he is. I started dialing 9-1-1."

We all laugh then. Even though it was a crappy thing to do, he pulled it off beautifully, especially on such short notice.

"It sounds like you three had a great time as teens," Julian says.

Enzo and Carly share a fleeting glance that tells me they're both thinking of how their relationship ended, but they push the darkness away and smile just as fast.

"I loved spending my time in the Mancini household," Carly says.

"You were always with us," I say. "I loved that. You weren't mean to me like my siblings."

"You were young and annoying," Enzo says while shoving a chunk of meat into his mouth.

Part of me would like to show him that's still true by taking my hand and ruffling his hair, but I refrain and ignore him. To Carly, I say, "I loved playing with your dolls."

Enzo winces. "How could I forget about your doll collection? They were scary, and you had so many of them."

Carly grins and doesn't seem to be insulted. "You never appreciated them."

"What kind of dolls?" Julian asks and sips the beer Enzo had given him while watching TV.

"Those creepy porcelain ones," Enzo says.

Carly lightly laughs. "I had all kinds. I especially loved my American Girl dolls."

Julian sets down his fork. "Oh, my grandmother had one of those. The doll had long brown hair, and her name was Sam."

Carly's expression glows. "That's Samantha Parkington. She was one of the first three dolls ever released. Your grandmother must've liked the doll or been a collector? The line didn't originate until 1986."

Julian chuckles. "Yes. She didn't grow up with it. She just liked that doll in particular. She had a few other kinds, like a Raggedy Ann and one of those baby dolls that drink their bottle and wet their diapers. I think she had them because they were all originals. Maybe she thought they'd be worth something some day."

I smile. I love stories of his grandmother. She meant a great deal to him and vice versa.

"Did she ever cash them in?" Enzo asks, finally putting his fork down and leaning back in his chair, which signals he's done eating.

Julian shakes his head. "No, I have them in storage."

That I didn't know. Those months I lived with him, I never saw them. They must hold a lot of sentimental value.

"They're probably worth a fortune now," Carly says. "I never kept mine preserved. I loved dressing mine." She puts on a sheepish grin. "I was a teen when I first got mine. The American Girl doll I had came out in 2000. But my father saw it and knew I'd like it, so he picked it up for me. Dad wasn't home a lot. He worked on the road. So it meant a lot. I think he thought the dolls were created after real people, but it was just the historical events that were true."

I don't recall her ever telling me that. I do remember that she spoke highly of her father, but he was never around. "That was sweet of him. So which one do you have? She's blonde, like you, right?"

"Yeah. That's why Dad picked her up. Her name is Margaret Mildred Kittredge, but her nickname is Kit."

CHAPTER TWENTY

I stare at Julian. The lump in my throat takes on massive proportions, and I think I'm going to die from suffocation. Carly's doll is named *Kit*. That's a coincidence, right? I then look to Enzo, who has a grief-stricken look on his face.

He glances to me, quickly, like he's guilty of something and doesn't want me to know. Oh my God, he heard me say Kit to Julian on the phone. This afternoon at the police station, when he asked if I was getting a cat... He knows that Carly is Kit.

No, this doesn't make sense. Zoe is Kit. Carly works as a receptionist at a used-car lot. And Serena works as a server *and* an escort. Having one job doesn't mean she can't have two. My mind flashes to that day Izzie and I were at lunch, and Carly came in wearing a gold skirt. She'd been out all right. Out with a client.

I stand up, grab Enzo's wrist, and twist it until he rises. "Can I talk to you for a sec?"

"Ow, ow," he whispers while I drag him back to his bedroom.

Once inside, I shut the door and turn on him. "You knew she's Kit?"

He runs his fingers through his hair. "I recognized the nickname. She only talked about that stupid doll a trillion times while we were dating, but I don't know if it's the same Kit you were talking about. I don't even know why you were talking about a Kit, other than it being candy."

Okay, so yeah. He has been out of the loop.

"Kit is the name of the escort Frank Mason used to see before he started seeing Serena."

"Escort?"

"Yes, as in call girl, high class hooker."

He shakes his head. "No, that's not Carly. She'd never. Besides, she just broke up with her boyfriend."

I scrunch up my face, unable to understand that logic. "What does that have to do with being an escort? You think a girl can't sleep with men for money, as a job, and not date someone at the same time?" He's a cop for crying out loud. Hasn't he seen all walks of life by now?

"I mean... I don't know what I mean."

I pace in front of his unmade bed and hope she and he haven't been doing the horizontal mambo. Then I realize I'm thinking about sex and my brother and shudder. I refocus my thoughts on Carly.

"She just broke up with her boyfriend. What if she broke up with him by him ending it with her because he was seeing someone else? One of her coworkers. Or..." I make air quotes with my fingers. "*Broke up* really means she meant to blow up the competition but blew up the boyfriend instead."

"Huh?"

I stop pacing and break it down for him, telling him everything Frank and Serena have told me.

When I'm done, he's glowering. "And you've kept all of this from me? I thought we were sharing information to help you help your friends move on to the light and to help me get promoted."

I sigh. "We are. I just didn't want you to arrest Serena and Na...her boss." I don't have to spill every detail, do I?

"Everything okay in there?" Carly calls out.

I freeze, eyes wide. "What are we going to do?"

"We're fine. We'll be out in a sec," Enzo shouts to them and then lowers his voice to me. "We're going to pretend all is fine because we don't know for sure it's not. Then tomorrow I'm going to look into her activity over the past few months, and I'll prove she's innocent."

I bite my lower lip. "And if she's not?"

He sucks in a deep breath. "Then I'll have to arrest her."

"Can you do that?"

He looks off for a moment. "Yeah. If she created a bomb to kill a person, I can definitely arrest her."

I let out a breath. Good. "But how am I going to get through the night?"

He gently grabs my arm and pulls me to the door. "With a smile. You can do this. You talk to ghosts."

Again, he makes no sense, but I let it slide this time. I can do this. I'll just keep my mouth stuffed with food. I'm good at that. And maybe I'll fake illness. Hopefully she won't take offense if I suggest something she cooked has tainted my insides. That's it. I'll put on my goofy hat, make a lot of jokes, and endlessly mock Enzo. That should get me through the rest of the night.

Enzo opens the door, puts a smile on his face, and steps forward. I don't bother telling him he looks like a creepy pod person.

We step into the dining room, and my entire body goes numb.

Julian is still seated in his chair, but he's wearing a deep frown. Carly stands to his side but one step behind. She's crying. I mean, whole face scrunched up, snotty sobbing. Tears stream from her bloodshot eyes, and her cheeks look like she's just bathed them by dunking her face in a sink full of water.

What on earth is going on?

That's when I notice the gun she's holding and pointing at Julian's head.

Feeling doesn't return to my body. I'm still frozen to the spot. But my mind begins to race, and my first, corny thought is, *Well, I guess that answers our question of whether she's innocent or not.*

I don't expect my brother to engage in idle chitchat, but when he says nothing, I glance at him.

His gaze isn't on his lunatic ex and my gorgeous current. He's looking into the living room.

I follow his stare and see his gun box, on the shelf, open. It's not locked? What is it with him and locks lately? I slug him in the arm.

"*So* not the time," he whispers.

Then, as if someone flipped a switch, all of the numbness leaves my body, and I slump against Enzo. Not Julian. No, this can't be happening.

"Carly, what are you doing?" Enzo asks while putting an arm around my back and steadying me. He squeezes my arm, giving me the strength to right myself. This is not the time to fall apart.

"I-I'm so sor-sorry." She chokes out the words between sobs. "I don't want to hurt any of you. I love you all."

Yeah, that shows.

"Then put it down," Enzo says calmly.

She shakes her head. "I can't. You know, don't you?"

I put a stupefied look on my face. That's not hard to do sometimes. "Know what?"

"About Kit. I saw the looks the three of you exchanged. Don't lie to me," she shouts, shaking the gun near Julian's temple.

His jaw is tense, and his expression is dark. I'm sure he's more pissed that she somehow got the gun without his knowledge than he is that he's in danger of having a hole in his skull. I, however, want to cry. How can this be real? Even though Enzo and I just briefly discussed Carly being Kit, it wasn't real.

"We can figure this all out," Enzo says in his calm cop voice. "But you need to put the gun down so no one gets hurt. You don't want to hurt Julian, do you?"

Her eyes widen, which allows more tears to escape at a faster rate. "No. Never."

I take half a breath, 'cause she can say whatever, but as long as that gun is pointed at him there's a chance it can go off by accident.

"Good," Enzo says and takes one step forward. "Then put it down, and we can talk."

I follow his footsteps. On some illogical level, I'm hoping that if she sees us continually side by side, she won't realize we're edging up on her. Her tsunami sobs have to be blurring her view.

"I'm not stupid, Enzo. After what I've done, I'm only going to jail. There's no sense in talking."

From the corner of his mouth, Enzo whispers, "Keep her talking," before taking another step.

I keep up and say, "I want to know what happened though, Carly. I want to understand. You're family."

Enzo lightly nods his approval.

She lets out a shaky breath and quickly wipes her face with the back of her free hand. "What do you want to know?"

"Why'd you set the bomb?" Seems like the big question. "Why'd you kill Frank?"

She lets out a crazy kinda chuckle. "Frank. I thought he was Thomas Sterling, like everyone else."

"Did you find out he wasn't and got angry?" And if that's the case, there are many less deadly ways to express that anger.

She frowns. "No. I didn't know until that night we all went to dinner, when Enzo told us."

It sucks that she found out that way.

"I didn't want him to die." Her voice sounds strangled, and the tears start flowing again. "I loved him. I wanted her out of our way."

She intended to kill Serena. Just like I thought. I realize I'm smirking and push it off my face.

During our conversation, I hadn't realized Enzo took a few steps to his right and widened the gap between us. I take a small step to my right and catch Julian shaking his head. I freeze. He stops shaking it. He wants me to stay put, and I wonder why? I guess my earlier assumption of Enzo and I staying side by side isn't best. Anyway, I don't spend time dwelling on it. I need to keep her talking.

"What did Serena do?" I ask. It's pretty obvious to me, but I'd like to hear her thoughts.

Carly gasps. "She stole Thomas from me."

"How?"

"She knew he and I were dating, and she flirted with him and got him to ask her out."

I'm a bit confused. "She told me she never met Kit. She didn't know you."

She scoffs. "She knew of me. She knew he was dating someone else."

She keeps tossing around the word "dating" as if they were a real couple. "Weren't you paid to be his escort?"

She blinks rapidly. "Yes, at first, but then I fell in love with him. He was so smart and beautiful."

Enzo's closer to her side of the table, and now I get why Julian wanted me to stay still. If she's concentrating on talking to me, she may not see Enzo coming. And if I kept up pace with my brother, she definitely would've noticed.

"Okay, so she flirted with him and stole him, but if he was really in love with you, wouldn't he have stayed?" Maybe it's a bad move to point out her crazy.

She nods and lets out a wail of a sob. "But we didn't have enough time. If she'd stayed away, if we'd had more time, he would've fallen for me the way I did for him. I know it."

I don't bother arguing with her. Maybe she's right.

"Why didn't you just scratch her eyes out or something? Why go to that extreme?"

She widens her eyes. "I tried. I called him, texted him, ran into him. I sent her threatening letters. I did everything I could. They chose to not care about my feelings."

From my peripheral, I spot Enzo move another inch. Julian stares at me and gives an encouraging nod. Okay, where are we?

"So...uh, what about us?" I ask. "Why did you come back into our lives? Was that a coincidence?" I get the sneaking suspicion it's not.

She shakes her head, and the gun shakes too, but it's still aimed at Julian's head. Please don't pull the trigger. "No. I purposely went to the station that day to reconnect with Enzo. I was never mugged. It was just a ruse."

Enzo stops short. He must be surprised by this news. He opens his mouth to say something, but shuts it, probably remembering not to call attention to himself.

So I ask, "Why?"

"I saw an article in the paper about that clown that died on the beach. The woman Izzie was accused of killing. The article said that charges were dropped, Izzie's brother was a cop, and that Izzie's sister had discovered the real killer. I figured getting close to Enzo would be a way for me to know what was going on with Frank's investigation."

How ingenious. How sneaky.

"I didn't count on Izzie's sister running her own investigation. I should've known though. You were always a snoop and talked to imaginary friends as a teen. What was with that?"

If one of my imaginary friends was here they'd...

That's it!

I look to a spot on the wall behind Carly so I can concentrate, and I think of Freezer Dude. He probably won't show up after earlier, but it's worth a shot.

Before I get a real chance to try though, Carly jams the handle of the gun into Julian's skull.

He groans and falls forward. His forehead rests on the table. He doesn't move.

"Oh, my God, Julian." I take two steps toward him, and Carly raises the gun, aiming it at Enzo. "No one move. Do you think I didn't see you inching closer, Enzo? I'm distraught. I'm pissed. But I'm not blind."

He and I glance at one another. The width of the table is between us. What options do we have? If one of us makes a run for her or the door, the other gets shot. Will she actually shoot us though? It's not something I'm willing to risk.

"You planning on killing Gianna?" Enzo asks.

Carly looks from him to me. Despite the hunk of metal in her hand that can put a hole in my head, she looks sweet and kind. She doesn't say anything though.

"And me? You can shoot me? We once loved one another." His voice has a sharp edge to it. Where is calm-cop Enzo?

"I don't want to hurt any of you. I'm sorry for hitting Julian."

"Then what are you doing?"

The gun is still aimed at him. "I need you to give me a minute to think."

"That doesn't sound so bad," I say.

Enzo shoots me an are-you-crazy glance.

She looks around the room, as if she's looking for something. "Do you have rope or duct tape?" she asks.

Great. We're about to be tied up.

"No."

She gives Enzo a look. "Every man owns duct tape." He cocks his head toward the back of the house. "There's some rope in my closet. Top shelf."

She thinks about this for a moment and then looks at me. "Go get it. No funny business. If you take too long or don't come back, I'll put a hole in him. I don't want to, but I will."

I swallow hard and nod.

"Wait. Where's your phone?"

"In the kitchen."

"That's right. You had a text earlier."

On the upside, if I don't show up to Zoe's later, maybe Serena will get suspicious. I doubt it though. We aren't that close.

"What about yours?" Carly asks Enzo.

He pats his left pocket.

"Take it out. Slowly."

He does that and tosses it on the table. It's closer to me than him, but there's no way I can grab it without her seeing.

"Go," she says and waves the gun at me but aims it back at Enzo immediately.

I turn and flee from the room. I yank open his closet door and see not only a rope on the shelf but a roll of duct tape beside it. Rope should be easier to get out of. Smart brother. I grab it and quickly look for a weapon small enough to fit in the palm of my hand. But while my bedroom has tweezers, cuticle clippers, and bobby pins, Enzo's is void of anything small.

"Hurry up," Carly shouts.

I shut the closet door and rejoin them, holding up the rope. Julian is still slumped over, and I pray he's not dead. My stomach churns. I want to cry. And I seriously want to smack Carly.

"Great," she says. "Tie up your boyfriend first."

I stare down at the mess of rope in my hands. "It's too long."

She juts her chin toward the carving knife beside the rest of the roast. "Cut it, and then put it back."

I do as told and, with two rope pieces in hand, I hurry to Julian's side. I kneel beside him and gently lift his head.

He winks at me, and I suck back a breath. Then he looks down, and I see that he has a steak knife in his grip. He inches it toward me. I take it and stick it into my back pocket. Thank goodness I wore jeans tonight and not something inappropriate for weapon hiding like a dress. See, Ma. Dresses aren't all that.

"He'll be fine," Carly says but doesn't look at us. She's too busy staring at Enzo. "Hurry up."

I glance up, and her hand is starting to shake.

Enzo looks at me, and I nod. I doubt he'll understand, but I don't know another sign for *he's alive and awake and winking at me.*

I go to the back of the chair, grab Julian's hands, and pull them to me.

"Make sure it's tight," Carly says.

I do just as told, with grunts to demonstrate how tightly I'm tying it. But what she can't see is that I've tied it into a bow and put one of the rope ends into his palm. All he'll have to do is yank it to free the knot. Now his head lolls to the side, and he's doing a good job of making it look like he's unconscious.

I take the knife from my pocket and stick the blade between Julian's thigh and the chair cushion. The handle sticks out, but Carly's on the other side of him. As long as she stays on that side she won't see it. There is a knife by each setting, so I have three others to grab. Julian may need this one.

Then I shut my eyes and will Freezer Dude here. I don't care how creepy he is or if he's angry. We need help, so I need him. I'd call on Frank if he and I had a connection.

"Now your brother," Carly says and points the gun to where she was seated for dinner.

Enzo sits in the chair and puts his arms behind it.

I walk around, eye the roast-encrusted knives, and then kneel behind my brother.

"I truly am sorry, guys."

"So you keep saying," Enzo says.

Her breath hitches. "I know it's hard to believe. I just need time to get away. I can't go to jail, Enzo. I won't last in there. You'll all be fine. Your mother will come knocking when she hasn't heard from one of you by bedtime. She's very controlling."

Enzo snaps his head up. "Don't speak about Ma. She was so right about you."

Ouch!

I mean, yeah, Carly fooled us all, she's a murderer, and she's holding us hostage. She deserves jail time and to be beat with a wet noodle. But I'm a little surprised at Enzo's tone. He used to love her. I expect him to have some compassion regardless of the circumstances. He was always the empathetic one.

"What's taking you so long?" Carly asks and nudges me with the gun barrel.

I tie this one in a sailor's knot, like Pop showed me, Izzie, and Enzo years ago. She's staring at us. There's no way I'll get away with a bow.

She nudges me again. "Okay, get up, and go over there."

I stand and move a couple of inches to my left. I don't want to leave the table. I haven't gotten my hands on a knife yet. "Come on, Mitchell. I know you're mad, but this isn't a trap. I promise."

Enzo glances at me, and Julian twitches.

Carly doesn't notice Julian though because she's too busy frowning my way. "Who are you talking to? Who is Mitchell?"

I stare into her eyes. "One of my imaginary friends."

"What?"

Right on cue, my finger begins tingling. Yes. Then he appears in front of me, on the other side of the table. His frown is deep and practically hides the blue of his eyes. "What do you want?" His tone is harsh.

I point to him and say to Carly. "See, there he is."

Of course, she's staring at a naked wall. Enzo and Julian look too.

Freezer Dude takes in the tied-up men and Carly's gun and does the only thing a vengeful, angry ghost can do. He starts laughing. Not a little giggle, but a side-busting chuckle so hearty I'm surprised it doesn't rattle the windows. "What did you get yourself into?"

"Whatever. Just help."

"Say please."

I narrow my gaze.

Carly pushes me. "Stop trying to distract me. I'm just going to lock you up, and then I'm out of here. I won't bother any of you again."

It would be easy to just let her go. She can flee and run away and never be seen or heard from again. But then I see Julian move his arms. He's freed himself. And it's possible that during a struggle the gun can go off. I can't lose anyone in this room.

I look to Freezer Dude. "Please. Maybe you'll be able to stay inside."

He stops laughing abruptly. "All right." He flies forward and into Carly.

Her body twitches and then convulses.

"What's happening?" Julian asks and stands up.

"There's a ghost inside her."

Both men raise their brows and look uneasy. Welcome to my world.

Julian rushes over to my brother and cuts through his ropes.

"The ghost won't be able to stay inside her much longer," I say just as Freezer Dude is thrown from her body. Shoot. Even though it would be ironic if he stayed and was sent to prison for another lifetime, I didn't want him to stay forever. I did, however, want him to stay inside her another minute.

Without thinking, I jump at Carly while she's still dizzy and doesn't have her bearings back yet. I grab on to the front of her shirt, and we stumble back into the chair Enzo just rose from. We go down. Carly on her back with me on top of her.

"Get the gun," Julian shouts. Surprisingly, it's still securely in her hand.

Enzo grabs Carly's arm and slams it back onto the floor repeatedly until her fingers open, and she releases it. He snatches it away and steps back.

I look down at Carly.

She's crying again, and for a second, I feel bad for her.

Julian grabs my waist and guides me to my feet. "Are you okay?"

I nod and catch my breath. "You?" I look up to his temple. There's a red mark, but the skin's intact, and there's no blood.

Enzo is on his cell calling it in. He's watching Carly, who's still crying but has curled into the fetal position.

Julian pulls me away and puts an arm around me.

I glance to Freezer Dude. "Thank you."

He shakes his head and snickers. "Yeah, remember that next time you want to capture me." He vanishes.

I hear a loud sigh, look over, and see Enzo is off the phone. The gun in his hand shakes a few times. He's more upset than he's showing.

I look up at Julian. "Will you watch over her until the police show?"

He nods and walks over to my brother. Julian takes the gun from him.

Enzo doesn't object. He takes a few steps back and leans against the wall. I go to him and wrap my arms around his chest and place my cheek on his shoulder. I can't imagine what he's going through.

He wraps his arms around my shoulders and rests his chin on the top of my head.

We hug until we hear sirens.

CHAPTER TWENTY-ONE

I open my mouth, and the lyrics of David Guetta's "Titanium" pour out. I don't see the people in the audience. I don't have to focus on a spot above anyone's head. It's as if the music and words are a part of my soul. In fact, I'm so tuned in to the song that my mind wanders.

After the police arrived at Enzo's, the three of us spent the night at the police station answering questions. I was very happy Detective Sanchez questioned me alone, while his partner spoke with Julian. I couldn't deal with Kevin on top of the evening we had. It was pretty cut and dry, and when we were let go, Ma, Pop, and Izzie were waiting for us.

I spent that night in my childhood bedroom at Ma's insistence. She likes to fuss over us when we're sick or have a gun pointed at us. I slept like a baby and woke the next morning to find covers and a pillow neatly folded on the couch and Enzo and Julian at the kitchen table gobbling down breakfast. As it turned out, Ma insisted that we all stay the night, including my boyfriend. Gosh, Ma loves him. And from the cute grin on his face when Ma gave him a second helping of pancakes, he loves her too.

I helped Frank say a final good-bye to Serena and watched him pass through the new deli freezer. His mother is still at large, and Freezer Dude hasn't been seen since. I'm not complaining. I haven't been ready to deal with him yet. He helped me, so I owe him one, but he can't just stick around. He needs to cross over soon.

I glance over at the bar and spot Serena and Zoe. They both look stunning, even in their uniforms, and both are smiling at me. Serena and I will never be close friends. We travel in different worlds. Hers is champagne and seriously rich men, and mine is prosciutto and seriously dead men. And that's okay. I like my world better. But I decided there was no reason to quit a perfectly good singing gig, so she and I will still be in one another's orbits for the time being.

    Enzo never asked who Carly and Serena's boss is—the madam. He also never told the police that Serena worked as an escort, just Carly. He knows I know it all, but it's okay that he doesn't. He says there's talk about him becoming detective. I hope it's soon. He deserves it.

    The pianist plays the last few chords as I hold my final note. When it ends, there's a round of applause. I smile and zone in on the part of the audience that's standing, clapping, and whistling.

    First, I spot Julian looking all sexy in a steel-gray suit to match his eyes. The look on his face says he can't wait to get me alone later tonight. I wonder—his place or mine?

    To his side are Enzo, Izzie, and Paulie. My niece is spending the night at a friend's house, so Paulie and Izzie are out on their first date since before she got pregnant. She looks relaxed and glowing in a light pink-and-white maternity dress, even though she's not showing yet. At least she's finally embracing it. At the table right behind them are Ma and Pop. I finally broke down and told everyone about this gig last night. Ma said she was thrilled, but I wasn't sure.

    I stare at her.

    She's clapping the fastest, "woo-hooing" the loudest, and the proud grin on her face makes tears well in my eyes.

    Who needs friends when I have such an amazing family?

ABOUT THE AUTHOR

Jennifer Fischetto is the *National Bestselling Author* of the Jamie Bond Mysteries. *Unbreakable Bond*, her adult debut novel, has received a National Reader's Choice award nomination. She writes dead bodies for ages 13 to six-feet-under. When not writing, she enjoys reading, cooking, singing (off-key), and watching an obscene amount of TV. She also adores trees, thunderstorms, and horror movies—the scarier the better. She lives in Western Mass with her family and is currently working on her next project.

To learn more about Jennifer Fischetto, visit her online at www.jenniferfischetto.com

Enjoyed this book? Check out these other reads available in print now from Gemma Halliday Publishing:

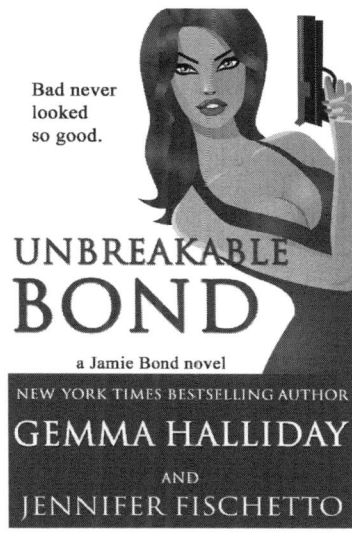

www.GemmaHallidayPublishing.com

Printed in Great Britain
by Amazon